# ALL OF US

*and*

# EVERYTHING

*bridget asher*

**CORVUS**

# ALL OF US
## *and*
# EVERYTHING

Bridget Asher is the author of *My Husband's Sweethearts*, *The Pretend Wife*, *The Provence Cure for the Brokenhearted* and *All of Us and Everything*. She has also published award-winning novels for younger readers under the pen name N. E. Bode as well as books under Julianna Baggott, most notably, The Pure Trilogy.

She is an associate professor at Florida State University's College of Motion Picture Arts, and holds the William H. P. Jenks Chair in Contemporary American Letters at the College of the Holy Cross.

BridgetAsher.com

BY BRIDGET ASHER

*My Husband's Sweethearts*
*The Pretend Wife*
*The Provence Cure for the Brokenhearted*

First published in the United States in 2015 by Bantam Books,
an imprint of Random House, a division of Penguin Random House LLC,
New York.

Published in e-book in Great Britain in 2015 by Corvus,
an imprint of Atlantic Books Ltd.

Published in trade paperback in Great Britain in 2016 by Corvus.

10 9 8 7 6 5 4 3 2 1

A CIP catalogue record for this book is available from the British Library.

Trade paperback ISBN: 978 1 78239 942 1
E-book ISBN: 978 1 78239 943 8

Printed in Great Britain by CPI Group (UK) Ltd, Croydon, CR0 4YY

Corvus
An imprint of Atlantic Books Ltd
Ormond House
26–27 Boswell Street
London
WC1N 3JZ

www.corvus-books.co.uk

*For my sisters – those from birth and
those I've picked up along the way.
I love you all.*

# The Prologue

*In which Augusta Rockwell attempts to teach
her three daughters how to conduct
a storm set to classical music.*

SUMMER 1985

*O*ne evening in June 1985, Augusta Rockwell lined up her daughters—Esme, Liv, and Ru—in front of the rippling, leaded window on the third floor of the old Victorian on Asbury Avenue. She handed them small white conductor's batons made of birch with pear cork handles, and, as dark clouds clotted the eastern sky over Ocean City, New Jersey, she informed them that she was going to teach them how to be conductors—not of music, but of storms.

"Storms are one way to define people," Augusta told her daughters, squaring their shoulders in front of their glass reflections. "There are those who love storms, those who fear them, and those who love them because they fear them."

The home on Asbury Avenue had been in the Rockwell family for generations. No relation to famed Norman Rockwell, painter of quaint Americana, these Rockwells had made great profit in the fishing industry, and later, after too many of them had died at sea, munitions, and after too many had died at war, banking. Augusta had informed her daughters that they were, by association and hand-me-down, sea-profiteers, war-profiteers, and finally greed-profiteers.

The third floor comprised one large room with a hall that led to the staircase. Here the girls enjoyed doing loud things that echoed well— singing along to Duran Duran, tap dancing, clogging. A long old mahogany table ran the width of the room at one end. It was surrounded by mismatched chairs from different eras of past Rockwell generations. A record table and organized collection of albums sat in its middle, along with a stack of the girls' favorite Nancy Drews, which had floated up from their library—consisting of three bookshelves running the length of one wall in the living room on the first floor.

*It's important to mention that Esme, the oldest, had read all of the Nancy Drews in order, noting on the inside cover how long it took her to finish and initialing the data. Liv, purely because of her competitive nature, also marked her times and initialed them, but eventually gave up reading except for assignments. Ru, the youngest, read leisurely and for pleasure, and occasionally, out of spite, she changed her sisters' times, slowing them down.*

*This room on the third floor had also been headquarters to Augusta's monthly meetings of The Personal Honesty Movement, a fledgling group she'd founded that winter. It had ended a few weeks earlier—a fiery argument that echoed cacophonously in the large room. Her followers—at the height of the movement there were only four, plus her daughters—wrote her an angry letter about her stubborn withholding, and disbanded. Augusta preferred vague Statements of Personal Honesty, which disappointed members who'd expected a kind of full-blooded confessional movement.*

*The abrupt end to her movement had shaken her, and it wasn't a coincidence that she was teaching her daughters how to conduct storms. It was, after all, an attempt to seize control of the uncontrollable.*

*And her decision to teach the girls to storm-conduct was also tied to the fact that they'd never known their father. He and Augusta had never married. This made the family seem unmoored in a way Augusta couldn't have predicted.*

*But she wasn't clear enough on the links among any of these things to make a Statement of Personal Honesty about it.*

*Augusta picked through the stack of albums, glancing at the dark clouds and waves beyond the windows, trying to decide what kind of storm this might be and how that would best be expressed in a classical arrangement. Thunder rumbled distantly.*

*Liv was staring down at the tourists—a teen in a neon bikini, thumbing a wedgy from her bum, a boy in plaid surfer shorts, shoving a cooler and two orange plastic beach chairs into the backseat of a convertible. Liv didn't want to conduct a storm. She wanted to conduct other human beings. She thought,* Take me with you.

*Esme was tapping her baton on the window. "Which type of storm people are we?" She'd been thinking of starting her own movement but something completely different from her mother's.*

*"We aren't a type," Augusta told them. "It's how to define other people. We aren't other people."*

*Esme's sophomore year of high school had challenged her mother's strongly held conviction. It seemed as if Esme was other people's other person. She'd written in her journal, "I feel otherly." It was a negative self-assessment.*

*"We're not other people because we're us," Ru said. Her mother and sisters were never quite sure whether Ru was being simpleminded—she was the baby after all—or profound, so she often went ignored.*

*Liv rested her forehead on the glass window, staring out blankly. She wondered what type of person she would be if she could choose from every type in the world. She was restless to be someone else. Maybe many different people.*

*Augusta slid an album from its paper sleeve and put it on the record player.*

*The needle made a soft crackling noise.*

*"Batons up!" Augusta said.*

*The girls lifted their batons in unison, as if they'd done this many times before. Hector Berlioz's* Symphonie Fantastique *filled the air, quietly at first, and almost innately the girls started moving their single batons to the music.*

*"Eyes on the sky, the waves," Augusta said, taking her place at the fourth window.*

*The girls didn't need any coaxing. They understood they were taking control of the uncontrollable, and it set right with each of them.*

*And Augusta saw that she was giving them a coping mechanism. Life is as unruly as storms. Even the appearance of control can make one feel real control.*

*She'd been a quiet, nervous girl with a sparrow's quickness—small sharp movements, a skittishness as if she were about to startle and* take flight. The first time she decided to conduct the ocean, she was twelve and had come down with rheumatic fever, which would take a toll on her heart. She misheard it too—she thought she had a romantic fever. She thought of love as a disease, and, in her dreamy fevered state, her parents' fighting made her believe the house was filled with vicious gulls. She cranked the Victrola, moved to the window, and had just enough energy to orchestrate a squall.

A few measures into the music, Ru recognized the piece. Only nine, she already had a keen memory for things she heard. Later she was diagnosed with a superb memory overall and a nearly perfect eidetic memory by a therapist her mother forced her to visit in her teens after Ru ran away from home. At this moment, the notes bobbing in the air, she shouted, "The Boston Symphony with Munch conducting, 1962!"

"Correct, Ru," her mother said.

"But how would we know if we're like other people?" Liv asked, unable to let it go. "We don't know what other people are like."

The girls weren't encouraged to have friends. If anyone asked about their father at school, Augusta had instructed them to tear up, say he was dead, and refuse to talk about it. The closest Augusta had come to friends in recent years was the followers of The Personal Honesty Movement. She told the girls they were too mature to waste time with children who were only going to grow up to be automatons. She treated her daughters as small adults. "Better to be an individual than to find yourself in the heart of the herd," she said, a summarizing sentence to a much longer speech.

Esme had started to desire the hearts of herds. She was pretty sure that her rebellious movement would be against the individuality her mother forced upon her.

The music quickened. The girls bounced their batons. The rain started up, fat drops splattering the sidewalk, slapping the window, the roof overhead. The waves kept heaving themselves onto the beach.

"But we do know Jessamine!" Ru said, smiling. She loved their *housekeeper. She was their link to the outside world. She bought all of their food, clothes, and school supplies. She drove their large green station wagon around town and taught the girls how to do banking, how to order in restaurants, how to buy yards of fabric to make curtains.*

*"Don't be an idiot, Ru. We pay Jessamine," Esme said. "It's not like she's going to let us know who she really is. That's the thing with money."*

*Jessamine, standing on the other side of the door, could hear everything, but the Rockwells' opinions of her had no effect. She saw them as an intensely neurotic family, barely kept together by their mother's thin swaddling of self-deception. She kept her personal life private and never told anyone about the Rockwell household, as per the contract Augusta had made her sign.*

*"Yes, but I have lived a life—before you three were born," Augusta said. "I have known many people so you'll have to take my word for it. Other people are generally disappointing."*

*"They can't all be disappointing!" Esme said. Her arms were burning. She let them drop but found herself hoping—despite her rational mind—that her sisters' conducting would be enough to keep the storm moving.*

*"Trying to find one who doesn't disappoint you would take a lot of time and energy and that's not necessary. We are enough. None of us would turn on the other." Each of the girls had already turned on one another in small ways and felt a pang of guilt. Esme knew bigger betrayals were looming, and that her mother was really talking about men and love.*

*"What if only one person is worth it?" Liv said, and her mother feared that, at this young age, Liv was already a romantic. "Then isn't all the time and energy worth it? For just one?"*

*Augusta didn't answer. Her heart suddenly clenched in her chest. She told herself it was the remnants of the old rheumatic fever flaring. She pressed her hand to the cold glass.*

"I'm going to Smith College one day!" Esme said, as if to warn them of her future betrayal. "I'm getting out of here and moving into the real world."

"Smith College is hardly the real world!" The pain passed. Augusta shoved her hands into the pockets of her housedress.

"But I can go, right?" Esme faced her mother.

"We'll see."

Liv was conducting vigorously, her thick blond bob swaying as if her ears were onstage and someone kept opening and shutting the curtains. "I'd like to at least try to be like other people and see if it's any good."

Ru's conducting was jerky but on-beat. "I'd like to meet Dad one day." She was young enough to still say these kinds of things.

"Shut up, Ru. He's a spy. He can't meet you," Liv said, echoing what her mother had said many times. "It would be too dangerous."

Talk of their father was so rare that Ru ached to keep going. "Maybe one day when he retires, we can meet him!"

"He can't just retire! He has enemies," Liv said.

"I've explained the Cold War," Augusta added.

This muted the conversation. The music turned inward with the plaintive call of oboes. Augusta hoped this would end the conversation, but she sensed the idea of their father as absentee spy was suddenly delicate—a soap bubble in a storm like this. It couldn't really endure, could it?

As the music turned and swelled, Augusta watched her daughters lift their batons higher—even Esme returned to the work at hand—coaxing the ocean to rise with the violins. And as if the ocean could hear it, the waves rose and pounded, rose and pounded.

"I'd prefer you all stay close to home," Augusta said. "Nothing can take the place of family."

With this comment, Esme realized that her mother would never let her go willingly. She'd already given up on the idea of her father as a spy; her suspicions were affirmed during the painful meetings of

*The Personal Honesty Movement with her mother's refusal to actually reveal much by way of personal honesty.* Esme wheeled away from the window. "You can't keep me from going to Smith!" She spiked her baton. "I'm applying my senior year, early decision."

"We haven't made a decision about Smith yet. I'll talk to your father and . . ."

"How do you talk to him?" Ru cried out, orchestrating as hard as she could. "Why can't we talk to him?"

"She doesn't talk to him!" Esme said. "There is no him at all!"

*Liv's arms fell to her sides. She felt a sudden pooling of despair, a pain she'd eventually learn to medicate (and sometimes self-medicate abundantly).* Liv breathed, "She made him up."

*Alone, Ru felt grave responsibility to keep the storm going. Lightning fluttered against the horizon.*

*Augusta was afraid that Esme was poisoning Liv and Ru. She had to contain this.* "Are you calling me a liar, Esme?" *In light of the Movement, however failed it was, the word* liar *was still the worst thing you could call someone in this house.*

"Yes. In fact, I'm calling you a bad liar!" Esme said. "No one has a father who's just a spy, who can never be met or talked to. You probably had sex with strangers!"

*Ru predicted lightning. She felt it in her chest. She straightened her arms and a bolt stroked the sky. The thunder followed quickly.*

"Why would I do that?" Augusta asked her daughter.

"Because you have intimacy and trust issues," Esme said quickly, "but you wanted a family."

"Stop," Liv said to her sister. "Don't."

"Who told you that?" Augusta asked Esme.

*The music was teeming with strings.*

"No one."

*Ru was memorizing each word of the conversation, each note, the roars of thunder and beating rain. She would remember it all—as if it were one piece of music in and of itself—forever.*

"I know you didn't make this up yourself. It's what some college-educated, slightly jealous woman would say about me! It's the babble of an armchair psychologist! Do you have a friend you haven't told us about? And does this friend have a mother—a conventional one who's possibly threatened by my choices?"

Augusta was right. Esme had overheard two moms at a Teacher Appreciation Potluck gossiping about Augusta in the bathroom.

The lightning and the thunder were simultaneous. The shadowed room was flooded with a bright flare. The solitary tall tree across the street—a rarity in this coastal town, having withstood punishing storms for so long—lit up as the bolt touched down, searing a limb that cracked and fell onto the electrical wires where it balanced, bobbing in the wind and rain.

They crowded Ru's window.

Ru tried to keep the limb balanced there with her baton, but it was no use. The winds were too strong, the wires too flimsy, the branch too thick—a barrel-chested thing that made her think it was a manly branch—it made her think of the word father because they were talking about her own father, his existence.

She couldn't save the manly branch.

She sighed, dropped her arms, and the limb exhausted its support; the wires broke, snapping with electricity. The tree limb fell hard, denting the hood of their own wide green station wagon, which had been parked beneath it.

"Damn it," Augusta said.

The electricity clipped off, and the whole world dimmed, darkness bleeding out over the ocean where heat lightning strobed. The music whined into minor chords as the needle ground to a stop.

Esme, Liv, and Ru looked at their mother in the dim light.

She stared out at the shore. She said all she was able to say on the matter of their father—three Statements of Personal Honesty that were also facts: "Your father is a spy. He can't be known. I love him, despite myself."

*Ru circled back to the beginning of the lesson. "There's a fourth kind of person. The kind who tries to control a storm, right?"*

*"Correct, Ru. More or less," Augusta said. She patted Ru on the head. "You did the best you could." She held her fist to her compromised heart.*

# Part One

*In which we learn about the lives of
Augusta Rockwell and her three daughters
before and during the hurricane that unearths
the package destined to change
their lives forever.*

SUNDAY, OCTOBER 28, 2012

"I didn't know you were supposed to shave collies," the headmaster said while he patted the dog's long thin snout and took a seat in Esme's living room. "I mean, I've just never seen it."

"I don't think it's recommended but imagine living with him! It's like having a Russian in your living room who refuses to take off his fur coat and hat in the middle of the summer. Like Dostoevsky himself, brooding away." Littering a conversation with literary and pop-culture references had become an anxious habit for Esme, maybe the result of the stiflingly crowded overeducated population that made up faculty housing at a boarding school. On campus, all of the dogs and cats—and many of the faculty children themselves—were named with some clever allusion in mind. Atty, Esme's daughter now fifteen and sitting beside her on the sofa, was named after Atticus Finch, a man's name, yes, but Esme didn't want to saddle Atty with the name Scout and she was set on which book she wanted to allude to. Ingmar, the collie, was often mistaken for a Bergman reference but actually it was a more obscure reference to the lead character in a Swedish film that Esme and her husband, Doug, saw when they were dating.

"But it's October," the headmaster said. "Shouldn't he be bulking up his winter coat?"

"Still, the metaphor stands even if it's cold out. *I mean, hey, take off your coat, fella, and stay awhile!* Am I right?" Esme said, trying to lighten the mood. She'd actually shaved the dog specifically for this meeting. Ingmar's coat had become matted from muddy romps out by the pond, and dogs weren't supposed to be off their leashes. She looked at her daughter for a little help.

Atty—a budding social media guru—looked up from her iPhone, leaned forward, and said, "This dog's no Dostoevsky. Don't you worry." As if the burden of being in the same room with a dog capable of literary genius would be too much for the headmaster to bear. "A corgi on human growth hormones, maybe, but that's about it. He couldn't get a kid out of a well if his doggy life depended on it." She then tweeted both sentences with the hashtag *#lifewithcollie*.

"There are no wells on campus," the headmaster said, defensively.

Atty looked at Esme in a challenging way. Neither of them was a great fan of the headmaster. Behind his back, they both referred to him as Big-Head Todd. He had a very big head and the history teacher, also a Todd, had a very little head so they called him Little-Head Todd. Atty's look was meant as a reminder to her mother that she'd promised to call the headmaster Big-Head Todd to his face, one fine day, before she graduated.

Esme understood the look immediately and shot her a look that meant, *Not now.* Then she smiled at Todd. "Listen. What do you need to tell us? You're here, making a house call on a Sunday with a huge storm moving up the coast."

"A *Frankenstorm*," Atty added. She'd been following video clips on weather.com, the growing buzz of online hysteria, mandatory evacuations on the coast—even in Ocean City, New Jersey, where her grandmother lived. Did her mother really care about this storm? Was she too busy bracing for this meeting, which was clearly going to be about Atty's shit midterm grades and her diminishing prospects for a good college education? Atty could almost hear the headmaster saying, *We're talking fourth tier at best, now. Fourth tier.*

"And you didn't cancel because of the storm, which would have been fine." Esme knew this visit might have something to do with Doug. He had led a group of sophomores on a study abroad program in Europe. Atty was a sophomore but her grades had been too low to make the cut, which meant that Esme had to stay behind with her. Esme had asked if Doug was dead as soon as Mrs. Prinknell had called to make the appointment. "No, no," Mrs. Prinknell had assured her, "for deaths, he calls people in pronto."

But that was Friday evening and this was Sunday morning, and Doug had missed their Skype session, which had made Esme anxious. He was the type to prioritize one of the student's emergency issues over his own life and so she'd decided this was an issue with one of the kids on the trip.

The headmaster was still balking. "It's just, maybe Atty has some studying to do and we can talk privately."

"I believe in honesty," Esme said. "Not just, you know, expressing one's feelings, and listing your grievances and airing out emotions, but the *truth*, the *facts*. I have nothing to hide from Atty." The dog looked at her sharply with his very small eyes. It was a genetic problem; his eyes were literally too small for his head, but these looks—little admonishments—always reminded Esme of her mother. The collie looked like pictures of her mother from the late 1950s—skinny arms and legs and a boxy middle, wearing woolen skirts with formfitting pleats tight through her ample hips. Why had she gotten a dog who reminded her of her mother? Maybe she'd done it subconsciously.

"Okay, okay." Todd pulled back his suit jacket and looked at a walkie-talkie clipped to his belt. "If the squawk box goes off, I'll have to take it. Sorry about that."

"That's okay. I've got a call in to my mother, who's being evacuated on the Jersey shore." Her mother was the stubborn type who refused to leave during storms. Esme was prepared to try to talk her into leaving, knowing she'd fail.

"Yep, yep. Hurricane Sandy has us on a twenty-four-seven alert. All-in, you know."

"All-in," Esme said, "of course." She had no idea what *all-in* meant, and she hadn't been paying attention to the storm. If storms defined people—those who love storms, those who fear them, and those who love them *because* they fear them—Esme was the type to try to ignore them because you can't control them. She preferred limiting her life to things she could more easily control. It's why she'd fallen for Doug. He was so practical, so tractable and reliable. And Esme had thought motherhood would be an experience of ultimate control—shaping a child, molding and nurturing them into adulthood. Raising Atty had proven her wrong.

Todd smiled sadly, and then he actually swept his hand over the wisps of hair on his big head and bent forward, leaning his elbows on his knees. It was the least robotic thing Esme had ever seen him do. In fact, it was so deeply human, she was worried. The news was bound to be very, very bad. "Doug's left the study abroad program."

"Left?" Esme said.

"It seems he's run off with his dentist."

"My dad's gay?" Atty said. This wasn't about her shit grades? She didn't have to give her speech on the psychological effects of being a faculty brat? She immediately thought: My father has always kept a very tidy closet, but really gay?

Todd shook his head. "His *female* dentist."

For a second, Atty felt guilty for assuming that the dentist was male. "Sorry," she said, apologizing for her sexism.

"It's not your fault!" Esme said quickly. She knew kids would blame themselves for marital issues. She herself had wondered if she'd been to blame for her absentee father. For years, she'd wondered if there'd been some good fatherly type that she'd driven away—so early in her life she couldn't remember him.

Atty assumed her mother was taking blame for having raised Atty in a sexist culture, but didn't dwell on it. She pulled out her iPhone and tweeted, *I feel weirdly abandoned.* Her tweets were usually so sarcastic that her followers weren't sure what to make of the vague emotional baldness. If Atty's grandmother were a follower—she didn't have a Twitter account—she would have recognized it as a Statement of Personal Honesty, the factless variety, which she preferred.

It was a true Statement. Atty *did* feel unmoored—that disorienting moment in childhood when you realize that you've reached up and grabbed the wrong father's hand and a stranger looks down at you and says, "Are you lost?" When this happened to Atty once at a Memorial Day parade, she'd gotten so embarrassed she turned it on the man. "I'm not lost! Let go of me, creeper!" And then she'd walked off and started crying. Doug found her in seconds.

Esme barely registered her daughter typing away with her thumbs. She irrationally assumed that Atty was going to look up the headmaster's story on the Internet—as if she could find out if it was a hoax or an overseas scam—*I'm stuck in Paris. A female dentist stole all of my credit cards and identification. Can you please wire money?*

Part of Esme knew the story was possibly true. One of Doug's molars had been killing him. She'd encouraged him to get it checked out. They were in Paris. Socialized medicine and all . . .

Esme stood up. Her arms hung at her sides. They felt loose, almost unattached from her body. She felt armless. She walked to the bay window. It was dark and rainy. The storm was coming.

"He's no longer an employee of the school," Todd went on.

"You fired him?" Esme asked.

"He quit."

This was a very bad sign. "He quit? But he doesn't have another job . . ." She shook her head. "He's not the kind to run off. He has a really strong TIAA-CREF account. He's not like this."

"He told me that he has a plan."

"You talked to him?"

"Well, yes. It's how I knew he quit."

Somehow she thought it had been handled by rumors and hearsay, as so many things were handled on campus. But, no. Doug had called the headmaster. And with this small detail, she knew that her marriage was over. She quickly blamed her mother-in-law. That side of the family was so uppity and elitist that there had been marriages between first cousins that had resulted in poor teeth, which meant Doug had to go to a dentist in Paris in the first place.

And then she thought, irrationally, that maybe her marriage was ending to make room for Ru's. Augusta had told Esme the news one week ago today. What if there was a kind of curse—the family of three daughters and one mother could only contain one real marriage at a time. Esme's brain used the caveat *real* because Liv's marriages—all three of them—had always felt fragile and dubious—mainly because Liv so loudly insisted that these loves were great, sweeping epic loves that none of the other women in the family could really grasp. What was there to grasp? Liv married for money and did it well.

Once Esme had flitted through all the blame she could muster, she wanted to feel something. A deep splitting ache in her chest. But she wasn't sure she loved Doug. Countless times, she'd imagined him leaving her, her leaving him, his sudden death. Awful things, but in truth she was not sure she'd ever loved him. She knew she'd never loved him the way she did her first love, Darwin Webber, who disappeared from college, not even leaving her a note. (And he was still nowhere to be found. She'd Googled him a bunch of times and he had no Internet footprint—not even a death notice.) She'd met Doug a year later, and having given up on the idea that she could love anyone again, she opted instead for what felt like a good partnership. (Was she just in the earliest stage of grief?)

"Do the kids on the trip know?" Atty asked.

Esme turned and looked at her.

"I mean, Maeve Brown is on that trip, and Piper Weir and

George and Kate and Stew," Atty rattled off. "What about the other chaperones? Jesus!" She rotated the small stud earring on one of her earlobes the way she'd been taught to do in the months that followed getting her ears pierced—when she was eight years old. Esme wondered if she was regressing before her eyes. "Do you know how big this is?" she said to her mother, wide-eyed, cradling her iPhone.

Her daughter had no idea how big this would be—personally. "This isn't a public phenomenon, Atty. It's a private matter."

"What world do you live in? *Everything* here is public. We aren't an actual family. We live on campus and *represent* an actual family so the boarding students can see how they function on a daily basis. We're like those American towns set up in Russia so Russian kids can grow up to learn to be American spies."

"No, we're one big family," Todd said, but he seemed shaken by the comment, like Atty had just laid something bare. "We're a real community. We care for one another."

"*Sure. Right,*" Atty said. "This is about to blow *up.*" She wanted to add that this would blow up atomically, and they would end up like the statues of human char she'd read about in oral histories of the bombings on Hiroshima and Nagasaki assigned by Little-Head Todd.

Esme turned back to the window. She tapped her fingernails against the glass, hoping to remind her body that she wasn't armless. She wanted to run away. Ru had run away from home when she was a teenager for a total of twenty-one days. For three full days, none of them had noticed, not even Jessamine who assumed that Augusta knew what was what. Ru was so upset by that fact that she refused to tell any of them where she'd gone or what she'd done.

Atty was right. This was about to blow *up.* What kind of home, if any, would be left after the detonation?

Todd sighed. He knew Atty was right too. "I've been in situations like this—well, not quite this exotic—but yes, like this, and it's not pretty, the deterioration is bad . . . people take sides—and when one partner is absent, sometimes it's easier to blame the one who's here. And some of the students come from divorce themselves. They act out various hostilities. It's not pretty."

"It's not pretty," Esme repeated.

"It's actually a time bomb," the headmaster said. "I mean, Atty's right. That's the metaphor I use."

"A ticking time bomb." Esme looked at the trees, the pumpkin-lined street. Atty's bike and helmet were in the yard and she'd told her a million times to put them in the shed. When would she see Doug again?

Would they be divorcing via Skype—all disjointed, their voices not quite synced to the movement of their mouths? Would she divorce her husband of seventeen years like a badly dubbed Asian monster movie?

And then Esme spun around. She finally heard what Todd was trying to tell her. "Oh, we should leave. Move. You want us to move."

"No, no, no," Todd said. He leaned back, propped one ankle on one knee, and tapped his duck boot. "We have a contract as well. Your husband's in breach. We'll deal with that. But you can stay— through the end of the year."

Doug had been the real hire. She'd been placed in the library as an unnecessary assistant. She was expendable. She hated Big-Head Todd right now. It was strange how she should be furious at her husband for running off with a French female dentist, but maybe being angry at Todd was helping her at least locate her anger.

She heard clicking. She turned and looked at Atty, who was texting madly. "Are you tweeting this?"

"Shiz is going down," Atty explained.

"Are you on the record with that? Your father's having an affair and you're writing *Shiz is going down*? That's how you're going to tell this story one day. *And then I tweeted all my followers that shiz was going down*?"

It hadn't dawned on Atty that this was a story she'd be telling for the rest of her life. She was telling it now. "I'm live-tweeting commentary."

Todd sighed and stood up. He took Esme by the arm. "You've got to get a handle on her, Esme. You don't want this to be a soap opera with a Greek chorus. I know these kids. Their Greek chorus work is dark."

He walked to the door. It wasn't their door. It belonged to the school. The house was appointed to them by the headmaster. Everything was a gift, even Atty's education. It was part of their benefits package. She thought she'd only leave at retirement. But now she saw they were just passing through.

Todd opened the front door, popped open an umbrella decorated with the school's crest, and looked at the groundskeeper, in a bright-green slicker also emblazoned with the school's crest, who'd been waiting for him in a truck parked in front of the house. "We've really got to get this under control," he said. "This is going to be one hell of a storm."

For a second, she wasn't sure if he was talking about the collapse of her marriage or Hurricane Sandy. She quickly realized that now outside he was talking about the literal storm.

"You can't control a storm," she said frankly. She thought of her sisters. She missed them deeply. She hadn't had a real conversation with either of them in years. "Some people think they can. It's not possible."

He looked at her, cocked his head, as if he weren't sure if she was speaking of the collapse of her marriage or the literal storm, but he didn't ask. He turned and walked out onto the wet lawn.

Esme thought about her mother and she didn't want to tell her about Doug's disappearance. Her mother hadn't ever been sure that Doug was the right one for her. Plus, her mother didn't seem to care for the institution of marriage, and Esme feared a too-soon I-told-you-so.

Atty watched at the window, blurred by rain. She wondered where her father was this very moment. She imagined hastily packed foreign valises, and all the bitchy snots on the trip gossiping about her father. She hoped the dentist was pretty. If she wasn't, it would be really embarrassing. Atty briefly wished the dentist had been a man. It would be really awful to make fun of a girl whose father was suddenly gay. I mean, she'd be further protected by political correctness, and she'd get to become an activist with a personal stake in it all. The LGBTQ kids would welcome her in, and she'd finally have something to write about for her college entrance essay.

Atty felt a surgical sting in her chest, and it was as if the attachment she had to her father were something physical. She could feel sutures being tugged.

*No,* she told the stinging. *Don't.*

The stinging seemed to answer her, *It's not just your dad you're losing. You're getting kicked out too. You'll lose everyone except your mother and the dog.*

Ingmar stood beside Atty at the window. He could have been a fur model. He used to look like the collie version of Fabio, and now he was just a crew cut. She tweeted this quickly and then thought, This is my last year. And alongside the pain, she felt a twinge of freedom. She decided to lean away from the pain and into the freedom.

Atty ran to the front door, past her mother under the eave, out into the driving rain, and waved to the headmaster who was sitting in the passenger's seat of the truck's cab. "Thank you, Big-Head Todd! Thanks so much for the four-one-one! Talk to you soon! Good luck in the storm!"

Her mother didn't flinch. Atty had done it. She'd called the headmaster Big-Head Todd to his face.

Esme couldn't tell if he'd heard her. The windshield wipers beating across the glass, the blur and noise of the rain, his brow knitted, he gave a small salute.

The truck barreled out of the driveway and on down the road, leaving Atty standing in the yard, Esme behind her, the rain ticking all around them like thousands of time bombs.

CHAPTER *2*

Liv Rockwell was living in an apartment on the nineteenth floor of the Caledonia in West Chelsea.

Actually, she was a squatter.

She'd once shared the place, now almost completely empty, with her ex-husband—her third and most recent husband, Owen— before his second wife got pregnant and they moved to Chappaqua.

The Caledonia offered bamboo trees in the common open-air garden, a Boffi stainless-steel chef's kitchen with a Wolf stove, and a view of the High Line park. These things were important to her because she wasn't going out much. She ordered delivery from Bombay Talkie and Bottino—except for flan, which she made herself. She found the egginess a comfort. Her mother never cooked but flan was the specialty of their long-standing housekeeper, Jessamine.

She'd only replaced one of her favorite items—a Gaggia espresso maker that ran her almost two thousand dollars. She had money— that wasn't the problem. She was simply losing faith in it.

She could have easily bought fluffy linens, even a luxury bed, but she refused to indulge herself. She slept on spare pillows topped with down outerwear she'd found in a box in a spare closet, plumping them in the middle of the floor in her old bedroom. She took down a white sheer from the living room and used it as a sheet, and her full-length fur coat—inherited from an elderly Rockwell auntie (her sisters had refused to wear it on moral grounds)—as a blanket.

She was well aware that any day now a real estate agent was going to show up with movers delivering high-end rental furniture to stage the place for sale. She had other places to go, of course, including rehab, but she was feeling weirdly homesick—maybe because she was between husbands—and so she went to the place that felt at least a little like home, albeit a broken one.

(And she had to believe that the head doorman had alerted Owen that she was back, and Owen had been kind enough not to make a stink about it. He didn't like stinks. The real estate agent would be stinky enough. If Owen didn't want her to still have access to the place, he should have changed the locks.)

The storm had started to rattle windows, and the toilet had stopped flushing though the electricity was working. (It had crossed her mind that her toilet issue was a problem with her specific toilet, not the building, but she couldn't call maintenance. It would draw attention.)

Liv sat in an Adirondack chair in the living room. She had a flashlight nearby, bottled water and salami in the fridge. That was the extent of her preparation.

She was drinking a Scotch and water, surrounded by newspapers—the London *Observer, The New York Times,* the L.A. *Times, The Washington Post,* the *International Herald Tribune.* This was her work. She was researching a potential fourth husband.

In childhood, her mother had told her many times that she and her sisters were profiteers of various kinds. She didn't understand what this meant because, honestly, she'd learned to tune out her mother early on. But then one of the more subversive teachers at her boarding school explained the seedier side of the school's wealth — munitions. (Liv was the only daughter in the family sent to boarding school. It was during a particularly defiant stage.) She'd squirmed in her seat during the mini lecture — it rang a bell — and found herself awash in shame. Her mother didn't believe in shame — in addition to The Personal Honesty Movement, Augusta had founded many short-lived movements, one of which was The Anti-Shame Movement; Augusta had taught them to recognize shame and to mentally wash it off. So she replaced her shame quickly with a sense of fiery pride. *I'm a profiteer who hails from a long line of profiteers, and there's nothing wrong with profit.* It was the foundational idea for her college entrance essay, which she'd later blamed for her rejections from her top-choice colleges.

And she clung to the pride. In fact, she embraced it as one of her defining traits, and she picked up profiteering as an art form. For the past twelve years, she'd been a marriage profiteer.

Her strategy was cherry-picking engagement pages. Her first husband was Icho Hi, an international businessman. He died of heart failure. Her second husband was a patent holder, Sven Golbin. They'd divorced amicably. Owen was an art dealer who came from Old World family money. He wanted children. Liv didn't. (A marriage profiteer should be smart enough to know that this would only divide profits.) He left her for a younger woman.

Sometimes, though — like tonight — she wondered if she should have had a child, not to appease Owen, but to have someone to impart knowledge to and raise with a philosophy of Liv's own design. This didn't strike her as a good reason to have a baby, however.

That afternoon she clipped certain engagement announcements from the newspaper with nail scissors, and, with duct tape found in a kitchen drawer, she lined them up on the living room wall.

On her second Scotch and water, she popped an Adderall to balance things out. She found a Sharpie in the drawer of a small built-in and started writing notes under each clipping directly onto the wall. The key for the notes only existed in Liv's head. It went like this:

A. *Estimated Assets and Income.*
B. *Family Money, a ten-point scale.*
C. *Apparent Attraction in Type of Woman.*
D. *Accessibility Rating.*
E. *Desperation Quotient.*
F. *Intangibles.*

On her third Scotch, her sister Esme called. Usually she'd let it go to voice mail, but she wanted the company.

"Have you heard from Mom?" Esme asked.

"No, why?"

"They've evacuated Ocean City."

"She won't leave."

"I know, but I wish she'd tell us she's not leaving." Esme gave this little *tsk* noise at the end of her statement, a habit she'd had as a teenager, one that Liv hated.

"Why should she tell us?" Liv said flatly.

"So we'd know she's okay. That's why."

"You know our mother," Liv said. "She won't tell you anything that she thinks you already know. She's not redundant."

"Are you calling *me* redundant?"

"No, but you seek reassurance, and by nature those kinds of people are usually redundant."

"Fine," Esme said, taking the criticism. She'd told herself long ago that she no longer cared what her sisters—especially Liv—thought of her. (Ru was the baby. No one ever really cares much what a baby thinks of you.) "I don't even know if Jessamine is with her. I just wish she had friends who'd look in on her."

"She's never wanted friends, only followers. And she's never been successful at getting either."

This was true. None of Augusta's movements had gathered steam. Mothers United for Peace ended in petty squabbles over the logo. Raise Your Voices and The Movement's Movement were two groups dedicated to empowering people to start movements; both died for lack of momentum. The Self-Actualization Cause, The Individuality Movement, The Deeper Self-Reflection Cause, and The Anti-Shame Movement all failed in less than a year.

"This is serious," Esme said. "There's a reason why the governor has asked people to evacuate!"

"He's just covering his ass," Liv said.

"Aren't you watching the news?"

"No."

"Well, DC got hit hard. There's a full moon. It's going to hit New Jersey at high tide and New York too. You should be prepared."

"New York City is a fortress built of fortresses." Then Liv thought, *I'm a fortress built of fortresses.*

"I don't think you're taking this seriously."

"New Yorkers are immune to natural disasters. We're too callused from shoving into the subway at rush hour." It had been many many years since Liv took the subway, but the memories were vivid.

Esme sighed. "Are you going to ask how I'm doing?"

"Yes," Liv said. "How are you doing?"

"I'm doing very badly."

"I'm doing very badly too," Liv said.

"You're so competitive."

"Yes," Liv said. "In fact, I'm more competitive than you are."

Esme hung up.

Evening settled in and things became a blur of rain, wind, lightning, then a buzz from the doorman punctuated the air. Despite the inclemency, Mrs. Kwok, Liv's acupuncturist, had shown up in the lobby, waiting to be let up. "Sure! Of course!" Liv told the doorman. Liv had forgotten she'd called Mrs. Kwok.

When Mrs. Kwok arrived, she said, "I am here for your session, right?"

"My liver is going to hell, Mrs. Kwok. Why wouldn't I call you?"

Mrs. Kwok shuffled in with her collapsible massage table and her box of equipment—needles, glass cupping jars, some with the rubber bulbs to create a seal, and smokeless moxa sticks. She was wearing a flower-printed smock dress like a pediatric nurse, but her short haircut and jewelry were high-end boutique. Mrs. Kwok owned the business and had exquisite taste. She might have even had some work done, a little Botox, perhaps? Liv herself had recently turned forty, but she passed for thirty-two. "What happened to this place?" Mrs. Kwok asked.

Liv looked around at the walls covered with clippings and Sharpie and realized that it must look like the plans of an ambitious serial killer. She managed to say, "What happened? Well, the toilets. They stopped working." And she wanted to add: *How long can we go without toilets before we turn into savages, Mrs. Kwok? How long?* But she stopped herself.

"No, what happened to the stuff in the *apartment*, Mrs. P. It's almost empty."

"I'm Ex Mrs. P. now, Mrs. Kwok. *Ex.*"

"He took all of your pretty things?"

"He bum-rushed me." Liv meant on an emotional level and she wanted to cry. She felt suddenly drunk in a heavy way, as if gravity were pulling her down more than normal.

Mrs. Kwok looked at Liv. "You drink too much tonight?"

"I drink too much."

Then Mrs. Kwok got worried. "This is a *hurricane*. I came here in a *hurricane*. You are going to pay me, right? You still have money, right?"

Liv had always taken Mrs. Kwok's verbal tic of ending sentences with a questioning "right?" as a lack of self-confidence. Now, suddenly, it seemed that Mrs. Kwok didn't lack confidence in herself but in Liv. Granted, Liv wasn't terribly trustworthy. She didn't answer the question. "What do you think of marriage?" she asked instead then quickly added, "But without, you know, the communist lens, the husband-as-hardworking-Chinese-industrious thing—no offense—and more about the soul. I mean, do you believe that two souls can be one? Are you a romantic, deep down?" Liv wondered momentarily if this sounded racist, but she quickly decided it was okay. She'd said "no offense," and her excellent liberal education had to earn her some political capital, right? The question echoed in her head, but not for very long.

"Two souls as one? No." Mrs. Kwok scratched her forehead, the bit hidden up under her bangs.

No, no. Mrs. Kwok was practical about all things, including marriage. This was what the two women had in common. Liv loved Mrs. Kwok in that moment, a big sweeping love. All of her friends bought into the idea of soul mates. But not Liv and Mrs. Kwok. Not them. Feeling suddenly close to Mrs. Kwok, Liv reached out and hugged her. Liv was aware enough to know that hugging Mrs. Kwok was a very drunken thing to do, but she couldn't help herself. Scotch sometimes made her especially sentimental. "I'm going to tell you something," she whispered. "Something I've only told one other person in the whole world and that other person was unconscious at the time, due to a bad batch of Ecstasy."

Liv walked Mrs. Kwok to the row of clippings. "These are the men who have publicly acknowledged that they are (A) capable of asking a woman to marry them. It's how they've gotten into the engagement pages. So the commitment-avoidant man-child types have been screened automatically."

Mrs. Kwok examined the photographs, bewildered but not exactly *awed*, as Liv thought she should be.

"This is genius, Mrs. Kwok. Do you understand how many years a woman can waste trying to wade through all the commitment-avoidant mama's boys of New York City—while sitting down week after week, flipping through the engagement announcements and never really seeing them for what they are? Gold!" Liv gestured like she was panning for gold. "See?"

Mrs. Kwok stared at Liv. "What?"

Liv felt the Adderall propelling her forward, her mind whirring decisively now, flitting above the Scotch like a clipper ship. "This is a directory of men who are capable of asking a woman to marry them. Period. A directory, Mrs. Kwok."

"But they are getting married to someone already, right?"

Liv shook her heard. "This brings me to (B)." She walked Mrs. Kwok down the row. "These men are in a vulnerable position—dibs have been called but they aren't yet off the market."

"Dibs?"

"Don't ask questions right now. Okay?" Liv paused and stared at one couple, the man's arms wrapped protectively around his fiancée's shoulders. "And (C). Look closely."

Mrs. Kwok squinted at the photograph.

Liv pointed to the man's bright and yet terrified smile. "These are the faces of men under the most stress of their lives. They want out. Look at them."

"He looks happy to me," Mrs. Kwok said, pointing to the man's teeth.

"He isn't. None of them are. Their fiancées have changed on them almost overnight. Before the engagement, they were happy and content. These men are being forced to make decisions and no one cares about their opinions. They're being railroaded into buying things they don't want to buy, arrange people's seating in ways they don't want to arrange, pick from samples of food they don't want to eat, list their friends in a hierarchy, cut cousins off lists. They're spending more time with their in-laws. Look, Mrs. Kwok. They're dying inside. These are photographs of desperation."

Mrs. Kwok shook her head.

"What? You don't believe in the quiet desperation of weddings?" Liv picked up *The New York Times*. It usually contained the best contenders, and she'd been saving it for last. She spread one of the pages open on the floor. "Do you see all of those eyes staring up at you? Might as well be looking at dogs in the animal shelter. They want to be saved, Mrs. Kwok. We all just want to be saved." She thought of the conversation with Esme and felt guilty. Esme wanted to be saved too. From what? Who knew? She had a perfectly good life, constructed in a very purposeful way.

Liv stared down at the faces. She was dizzy—drunker than she'd thought. The faces swam around like fish trapped in an indoor pond. She put her bare toes on the edge of the newspaper, hoping to pin it down.

And there she saw a face she recognized—a woman with wide eyes, curly hair, a crooked smile.

Liv knelt down, spread her hands on the floor, and read the names aloud: "Clifford Wells and Ruby Rockwell." She hadn't thought about her sister Ru in a long time. She was a novelist who also adapted her own work into screenplays, a hit cult-fave whimsical romantic comedy—and totally ripped from Liv's own life. Liv had never forgiven Ru for using Liv's life as material—thievery— a point Ru seemed oblivious about.

Liv and Ru hadn't seen each other in years. Ru had surrounded herself with creatives, and Liv didn't care for artsy types. They didn't appreciate the things that Liv appreciated. The last time she'd been at a party with Ru's friends, a German woman had gotten naked and let people write on her body—for free. Liv didn't understand it. Why not at least charge a nominal fee? That didn't make it stripping. And even stripping could be deemed art. Moreover Ru ignored the whole scene and was talking about an old children's book about a duck named Ping or some shit.

"You okay?" Mrs. Kwok asked.

Baby Ru was getting married? How was that possible?

The notice referred to her as *the acclaimed novelist and screenwriter whose hit film*—Trust Teddy Wilmer—*garnered comparisons to Charlie Kaufman and Nora Ephron.*

"Fuck her," Liv whispered. "*Trust Teddy Wilmer* was based on my life," she said loudly. "Not Ru's!" The comparisons to Kaufman and Ephron were partially *Liv's* comparisons. But did anyone ever point that out? No.

Liv didn't read novels on the grounds that they weren't true. She made no exception for her sister's novel, even the thievery of Liv's own teen romance. Teddy Wilmer was an obvious knockoff of Teddy Whistler, Liv's first love—the rebellious (and possibly crazy) young man who ended up in a juvenile detention center and, later, a private mental institution, and a relationship that led directly to Liv's own stint in boarding school, a sentence of its own.

After she'd read the review of the novel in *The New York Times Book Review* three years earlier, Liv had left a message on Ru's voice mail. "Why don't you write about your own life, Ru? Or is that you've never really lived one? You've never grown up, Ru. You never will."

Ru never responded. They never spoke of it.

Liv had watched *Trust Teddy Wilmer* while drunk, on the grounds that she didn't want to see something indecently private about herself while vulnerably sober.

She once confided to Esme that it was an awful thing to have a writer for a sister.

Esme said, "Oh, no. I wish she were a memoirist! Rip away the bullshit of fiction and really tell it. Memoirists are the only writers with any real guts." Liv was relieved. At least Ru wasn't a *memoirist*! That was something to be happy about.

Liv quickly scanned Ru's fiancé's short biography. She sifted through her mental list. Check, check, check . . . She looked Clifford Wells in the eyes, and for a split second she thought, *He's ripe for the picking.*

She stiffened. She was a monster. She'd actually considered stealing her sister's fiancé.

And then, worse, she rationalized it. Again, the processing was so fast she had no control over it. *If the marriage is going to work, he won't be so easily lured away. If he is, I'm doing Ru a favor. Some marriages are defunct on the molecular level.*

And then she rationalized it personally. *Ru stole from me to turn a profit. I can steal from her.*

"I don't know," Liv said, in response to no specific question.

"You're worrying me, Ex Mrs. P."

"I just don't know," Liv said again.

She stood up and walked to the bank of windows. It was pouring outside. She thought for a second of the windows in her childhood home on Asbury Avenue, the third floor. Esme and Ru probably ignored what their mother had taught them during that one weird summer storm, but not Liv. In moments when she was completely alone, she'd spent hours at those windows, classical music in the background, conducting spinning seagulls, cars trolling for parking spaces, dogs bouncing on leashes, quick clouds against blue sky.

And when she got the chance to run her own life? She could make choices, set goals, and attain them. And now? What about now?

She opened one of the windows and stuck her upper body into the wind and rain. She then lifted one hand, as if holding one of the conductor's batons her mother had given them.

"Don't do this!" Mrs. Kwok shouted.

"What's the name of a Chinese monster?" she shouted over the storm, waving her imaginary baton. "Tell me the Chinese monster that scared the crap out of you as a child!" Liv was screaming. She could hear the shrill noise of her own voice in her ears but it seemed disconnected. It belonged to someone else who was screaming the things that Liv wanted her to scream.

Mrs. Kwok pulled on her arm. "Come back in!"

"A Chinese monster!" Liv shouted again, still trying to conduct. "Which one really scared you, Mrs. Kwok?"

Lightning streaked across the sky. Liv froze, and then her body shuddered.

"Don't jump!" Mrs. Kwok shouted.

Liv hadn't been planning on jumping, but then she looked down. A person would hit hard, die instantaneously. They'd likely feel the cold air rippling, mouth forcibly filled with wind, and then nothing. Not fear, not regret. No Owen, living with some woman he loved more than Liv, a woman whose belly was swelling with a baby who'd be born pink and fat and happy and grow up in Chappaqua where the public schools are fantastic and the children aren't afraid of monsters at all.

Nothing.

Mrs. Kwok didn't know what Liv knew. She wasn't the dying type. She was lucky. She'd once choked on a menthol drop on a subway platform and an old man, perfectly practiced in Heimlich — like he was on his way home from a CPR certification course — walked up, grabbed her around the ribs, and with a sharp tug saved her life. But her life had already been so charmed that she'd half expected the old man. She remembered that he asked if she was okay. She nodded and he left before she even thought to thank him. "I'm not going to die! Just tell me! Okay? Is that so hard?"

"I will tell you a Chinese monster if you come inside!" Mrs. Kwok said.

"Tell me first!" Liv said, gripping the window ledge.

Mrs. Kwok spoke quickly, like the confession was being ripped from her. "As a young child, I was afraid of Gong Gong!"

"What did Gong Gong do?"

Mrs. Kwok lowered her voice. "Gong Gong was a monster of the sea. I grew up along the Yangzte River."

For one split second, Liv felt like she was a maiden carved onto the prow of an old ship, but then the image flipped and she was the Gong Gong looking up at the maiden carved into the ship, wanting to destroy her. "I'm a monster," she whispered, her lips wet with rain. She blinked up at the sky. "I am Gong Gong."

"You promised to come inside!" Mrs. Kwok shouted, and then she pulled on Liv's shirt so hard that it ripped.

Liv fell back into the room and looked at the rip and then at Mrs. Kwok.

"Remember," Mrs. Kwok said. "I came here in a hurricane for your session! In a *hurricane!*"

"I'm sorry I scared you," Liv said, and she sat down on the floor.

Mrs. Kwok walked to her collapsible massage table and started to put her supplies back in her satchel. Liv watched as she folded the table and walked to the front door. "You need help, Ex Mrs. P. Your liver and your spleen. We can try next week, right?"

"Right, right," Liv said. How long before she got kicked out? Would she be here next week? What would become of her? "But we could all be savages in a week's time. Savages and monsters."

Mrs. Kwok left.

The lights flickered and died.

"Right," Liv said.

# CHAPTER 3

The third floor of the house on Asbury Avenue was lit by flashlights propped up on duct-taped boxes marked ESME, LIV, RU, or the initials of Augusta's various defunct movements. In addition to all the boxes, there were dollhouses, bicycles, oversized lamp shades, an aged fake Christmas tree, stacks of books and record albums, eight-track and cassette tapes, an air hockey table, a full-sized loom, a pottery wheel and kiln, banjos, violins, saxophones, hatboxes, crutches, and deep down, in the bottom of a steamer trunk in a long white box sealed in plastic — a wedding dress from 1974. Pearly with a long row of buttons down the back and on its sleeves, it was a dress that Augusta had worn once and then had professionally packaged so that it wouldn't yellow with age.

Still, she was no one's wife.

The torrents of rain and wind made the house shiver. The thunder was so loud it shook the panes.

Augusta and Jessamine were sitting in old beach chairs, side by side. Each wore a cheap headlamp secured by an elastic band around her head, vaguely reminiscent of coal miners.

"They wanted us to leave!" Augusta shouted over the storm.

"You know we don't like to be ordered around, Jessamine!" By *we*, Jessamine knew she wasn't talking about the two of them. She was talking about the Rockwell family—dating back generations.

"We'll have to tough it out!" Jessamine said.

Jessamine's aged face was brightly lit by a bolt of lightning. Augusta barely noticed her own white hair, sagging neck, and puckered dimples, but she knew time was wearing on because of Jessamine, her lids droopy and creased, her face sagging to a handful of draped skin tucked under her jaw, and arms and legs dotted with liver spots and white spots and pink spots. What were all of these spots? And Jessamine had gotten shorter and more frail—so much so that, instead of dying, Augusta sometimes worried that Jessamine might disappear. Everything seemed to have changed incrementally while Augusta wasn't paying attention.

"I wonder where my girls are!" Earlier, Augusta had pulled out a stack of records, filmy with dust, in the hope of doing a little conducting. She'd even found an old Hector Berlioz record that had stood out to her for reasons she couldn't name.

"Esme has called many times," Jessamine said.

"No, no," Augusta muttered. She didn't mean where her grown daughters were at this moment in time. She'd meant it figuratively. Where were the little girls who'd once been her daughters, the girls who—once upon a time—had taken so naturally to conducting storms? She missed her girls, and her daughters would never be able to fulfill *that* longing. The thought scared her, as did the lightning. A bolt cracked so loudly that she felt it in her ribs. This was dangerous. They could die. The governor might be right after all. "Jessamine," she said, "maybe you should go home to your husband."

Jessamine shook her head. "He's dead."

"What?" Augusta said. "When did he pass?" She almost wondered if he'd died in the storm, just now, as if Augusta had missed an urgent call.

"It's been six months."

Augusta was startled by the news. "Jessamine, I'm so sorry. Why didn't you—" She was going to ask her why she didn't share the news but, of course, she knew why. They had boundaries. It was how they'd lasted so long together.

Jessamine answered the question anyway, letting Augusta off the hook. "There wasn't a good moment. Plus, this became the place where I didn't have to deal with it."

"He was a good man," Augusta said, but then realized she had no idea if this was true. She'd never met Jessamine's husband. "Wasn't he?"

Jessamine nodded. "He was a very good man."

"I'm so sorry," Augusta said, and then she felt a twinge of jealousy. Jessamine's loss in love could be public, could be addressed. Augusta's own losses had to be kept quiet all these years. Maybe this was why she hadn't known that Jessamine's husband was dead; Jessamine couldn't be honest with Augusta because Augusta could never really share anything with her. It's strange how the decision to be private affects things you'd never expect.

And now Augusta felt disoriented. Once upon a time, this room had been nearly empty. Time had filled it up. The accumulation of life and its stuff, but sometimes she wondered if she'd ever really lived.

"This storm could take us," Augusta said.

Jessamine nodded. "Yes, it could. The waves have crested the houses just there," she said, pointing across the street. "These waves will reach us too, most likely."

The two women had no idea how bad things were—that escalators would start pooling, subways flooding, that taxis would soon bob and knock together in newly formed rivers in Lower Manhattan. Block after block had already gone dark. Ground Zero would turn into a series of waterfalls. Ambulances were lining up for evacuations. Oxygen supplies were going dead, knocked out with the power. Sudden tidal pools would soon blast people into glass-front stores.

A seven-hundred-ton tanker, unmoored, unstaffed, floated toward Staten Island.

Waves from the East River crashed against the acrylic walls that encased Jane's Carousel, which from afar looked like a dimly glowing box of hand-painted wooden horses. Finally the lights flickered and dimmed. It was swallowed by darkness.

People were being washed out to sea, drowning in basements, killed by fallen trees.

And the fires of Breezy Point were about to spark and catch and burn.

Houses were being battered and splintered. A roller coaster was being shoved out into the ocean itself, its rickety body thrusted by waves, which were heaving sand onto the shore—eventually into people's living rooms, including their own.

Homeless, lost, searching, stricken . . . and temperatures primed to drop . . .

Augusta thought of someone she'd loved and lost and wondered if he would get word of her death. She assumed she would get word if he'd died—how exactly, she wasn't sure. She was very scared but she didn't feel it the way she should. "I'm not as scared as I ought to be."

"We can't leave now." This was a practical consideration. It would be more dangerous to wade out than to stay put, on higher ground.

"Do you mind if I hum something?" Music for Hurricanes, she thought.

"I don't mind, Ms. Rockwell. Not at all."

"You can call me Augusta."

"After all these years," Jessamine said, "I don't think I can."

"Fair enough."

But then a strange thing happened. Augusta lifted her hand to conduct the storm, and the hand was shaking. Her body was betraying her will; she was more afraid than she realized. "Will you look at this?" she said, holding the hand in the air.

Jessamine saw the trembling and immediately she took Augusta's hand and held it tight.

Augusta didn't hum any music. She didn't try to conduct this hurricane. The two women sat together, holding hands as the storm lashed and raged.

Change, Augusta thought. Storms churn things up and they set things in disarray and one is forced to right them. What change would come? Would she be here to see it?

Maybe she was no longer interested in keeping things as they were.

Change, she thought to herself. So be it.

CHAPTER *4*

Ru Rockwell was the only one in the family who knew nothing about the storm. She was living in a longhouse in a M'nong village in the Highlands of Vietnam. She shared the longhouse—just one room—with seventeen people, one family spanning three generations. The fourth generation was in utero.

When the storm reached its crescendo on the East Coast of the United States on Monday night, it was already Tuesday morning in the village. The children had been capturing crickets, and after the appropriate daylong wait they were cooking them over a fire in the center of the room, which didn't have a chimney. The lack of chimney was supposed to help the house-on-stilts keep its structure—she wasn't sure how—while also deterring unwanted insects. It made it hard to see and breathe.

When the matriarch offered some smoked crickets to Ru, she ate them, of course. She was trying to assimilate, which was why she was wearing a long striped skirt down to her ankles, even though the children were in Hello Kitty and Elmo shirts.

She noted that the crickets weren't as seasoned as the stir-fried ones she'd picked off the appetizer section of the menu at Typhoon in Santa Monica, not as nutty, but not bad.

*I miss doughy foods,* she said softly into her handheld battery-operated recording device. *Some people equate doughy fullness with a kind of maternal love. Augusta outsourced that maternal task.*

She didn't record her thoughts in order to remember them. She had an eidetic memory. She wrote them down in case she died here.

The thought crossed her mind many times a day. The idea that she was here to experience something visceral now seemed so manufactured that she was sure that an ironic death would be more fitting, that her death seemed inevitable—if only from a writer's perspective.

She wasn't really a novelist or even a screenwriter so much as a collector of one-liners that went viral. She'd won a Win-Back Award for her leading man's famous speech to win back the woman he loved. Her cult following had inched over into a short-term mainstream popularity. For a short time, it became a kind of flash-mob thing—to videotape someone in a mall, for example, start to give the Teddy Wilmer win-back speech to a clerk, only to be joined by all of these other people previously arranged to join in. There were thousands of Teddy Wilmer win-back variations on YouTube; one performed by a four-year-old in Teddy's famous baby-blue tracksuit had over seven million views.

But what she'd really mastered in her career was the art of taking meetings in offices, fiddling with water bottle caps while pitching story lines, and sucking on pot lollipops—Jolly-Lollies kept her calm, an eccentricity she'd become known for.

Why in the hell had she decided to chuck it all—including the Jolly-Lollies—for something *more serious?*

Desperation, that's why. Her second novel was three years overdue. They'd amended the contract so many times to push back the due date that Ru had lost count. Her editor, Hanby Popper, had acquired Ru's first novel when she was a very new assistant editor for a low six-figure bid. Hanby had quickly scaled the ranks. The movie-tie-in editions sold gangbusters. The second book was likely to grow a bigger audience still. Ru's book played mysteriously well in ex-communist countries.

But Ru had no more whimsy, romance, or comedy in her tank. She'd decided to turn her sights on nonfiction—in particular the inner workings of this matriarchal society. Maybe she could borrow authenticity. Wasn't that what nonfiction was? Borrowed authenticity?

Now she was here waiting out the rainy season, constant drumming on the thatched roof. With her eidetic memory, Ru would have learned the language the way she had many others—with tapes and subtitled films. But that wasn't possible with M'nong. They'd only created a M'nong alphabet for the first time in 2008, along with a twenty-five-thousand-word dictionary that translated to Vietnamese.

She'd learned Vietnamese before she came so she could use the damn dictionary.

That morning—while Ru's oldest sister Esme kept calling her errant husband on his Skype account, to no avail, and Liv was scaring her acupuncturist by sticking her upper body out of a window in a hurricane, and her mother watched waves reach across Asbury Avenue and splash into the downstairs of the old family home—Ru dictated her notes into a mini tape recorder in the far corner of the longhouse, eating crickets.

*Light peeks in through the woven walls.*

*The matriarch says she wants the new baby to be a girl. This is a typical desire of the M'nong's matriarchal bias. Daughters are preferred to sons.*

She thought of the matriarchal household of her own childhood. It felt imbalanced by a weighty invisible presence, the old absent spy. A girl among girls, she was the only daughter who still harbored him. At sixteen, she started researching Vietnam because a spy her father's age would have surely been involved in the war somehow, right? Her father was a secret secondary reason why she'd picked this place to write about.

Fathers were hard, she'd heard from all of the men she'd dated. Even Cliff. Sometimes, lying in bed, she'd put her head on his chest and listen to him talk about his father's heavy expectations—a drum of a voice talking about his father drum.

Hadn't her fatherless childhood been a good thing?

One of her main female characters once said, "Marriage is billed as an end to loneliness, but each of us is alone in this world. The only unit is the self." Of course a quirky young man—handsome, damaged, and tinged with some intangible lovability quotient—would change her mind.

In some ways that character, Marta Prine, was based on Ru's mother, Augusta Rockwell, and sometimes Marta was Ru herself, and sometimes Marta was Liv and occasionally Esme. Ru only knew what she knew.

Did Ru believe in love and marriage? She was engaged to Clifford Wells. That was proof of something.

After *Trust Teddy Wilmer* was a hit and Clifford Wells proposed to her and she accepted—a knee-jerk reaction—she realized that she'd actually never lived in a family bound by marriage. She had no idea what she was committing to.

The elephants were lowing in the distance. She read into her recorder, *The domesticated elephants are having conversations. They have inner lives. They understand love more than human beings do. I'm sure of it.*

Maybe the elephants would be the key to her book. She was getting used to their different kinds of calls.

She said: *Note to self: More elephants?*

Just then, a man in a government uniform walked up the steps to the longhouse and pointed at her. He spoke to the matriarch, who looked at Ru. The man was asking permission. The matriarch was giving it.

The man pointed again and said in Vietnamese, not M'nong, "Letters for you." He held out a bundle bound by a rubber band.

Ru walked around the family members huddled by the fire and took the bundle. "Thank you," she said, but he held on to the bundle.

"You are still not a missionary?" he asked Ru in Vietnamese. The region suffered human rights violations due to religious persecution. She hadn't really researched this enough.

"I'm still not a missionary. I'm here to research love."

"Love?"

"Like marriage."

The man laughed, showing his blunt dark teeth, and let go of the package. "Like marriage!" he said and walked out of the longhouse back the way he'd come.

She returned to her corner spot, squatting as the other women often did, flat-footed, knees to her chest. The children gathered around her, and one petted her hair. Ru was getting used to this.

The letters were all from Cliff. She opened the sealed envelopes and sorted them by date.

And as she read, she responded in a letter—in the order of the questions asked.

Cliff had written, *How long are you planning to stay?*

She wrote, *I haven't seen a ritualistic teeth filing.*

She already realized that she probably wouldn't see this. Only the M'nong elderly had filed teeth and elongated earlobes. The tradition had waned. It made her think of a future time when piercings, gauges, and certain tattoos would be a sign of having outlived a tradition.

She went on . . . *or the crying for the bull ceremony.* If he looked this up—and he would—he'd know that this was tied to New Year's, two months away.

*No one's died yet so I haven't seen them banging the drums beside the coffin.* She added this hesitantly, not wanting to sound like she wished this on anyone in order to fulfill her mission.

*And most of all, I haven't seen anyone get married, which is key. I'll have to stay on a good while longer.*

He'd written in the next letter, *I'm worried that you left so quickly and right after we got engaged. Are you happy about the engagement? Do you feel pressured? I didn't mean to pressure you. I'm so sorry but my mother insisted on sending the news into the* NY Times *engagement announcements and they're running a notice.*

She wrote: *No need to apologize. It's a public fact. It's a ritual that is recognized. It's the truth.* A Statement of Personal Honesty, she thought.

Reading the mounting anxiety in Cliff's letters, she wondered if she was just running away.

She'd run away many times before. The first time was when she was just sixteen.

She ran away from college twice to live off the land. That was where she'd started indulging in pot for its calming effects. She was otherwise too high-strung and her memory was too sharp—always sending her backward into the past instead of forward.

She ran away from a graduate program in archaeology to become a novelist, and ran away from writing her second novel to be a screenwriter, albeit one who only adapted her own work.

She'd run away from three previous serious relationships—an Olympic fencer, a pot farmer (long before pot was legal anywhere and eventually where she'd get her pot lollipops), and a producer of indie horror films.

*I have to stick this out,* she wrote to Clifford. *I can't leave. Not until I know something true.*

At some point, we all want the truth even if we aren't particularly suited to accept it.

What truth was she after?

She said into her recorder, *If I am running away, I can't run away from running away.*

This was the moment when she froze and her mind recalled *Symphonie Fantastique,* each of the girls standing at the windows on the third floor of the house on Asbury Avenue. She could feel the lightness of the small baton in her hand. She heard the notes as they started to dance. She remembered everything that was said, but mostly the exact ring of their voices set against the hard rain. Her mother's declaration, *Yes, but I have lived a life—before you three were born.* And young Liv, hopeful and defensive at the same time, saying, *What if only one person is worth it? Then isn't all the time and energy worth it? For just one?* It was strange to think that Liv was once a believer in love. The lightning, thunder, and then Esme leveling her accusation at Augusta, *I'm calling you a bad liar. No one has a father who's just a spy, who can never be met or talked to. You probably had sex with strangers!* There was the snap of the limb, the dented hood of the car. And then Ru's own voice piped up, so small and high-pitched: *There's a fourth kind of person. The kind who tries to control a storm, right? We're that kind.*

No one is that kind.

Ru didn't know about Hurricane Sandy, and yet she was sure something was coming, a vibration in the air.

Suddenly anxious, she moved to a slit in the weave of the long-house's wall. A tiny window, a view of fat green leaves.

Meanwhile, Esme stood at the bay window of the home she was getting kicked out of in eight months' time, her daughter curled under the sofa comforting the nervous collie.

Liv, wrapped in a fur coat, sat in the Adirondack chair in the empty apartment where she used to live, facing the wide-open windows, the wood floors wet and curtains gusting.

Augusta was on the third floor of the house on Asbury Avenue, her face so close to the dark glass that her breath misted the window and she couldn't see anything but fog. She backed away and still saw fog—the dusty white bloom of cataracts. Below her, the ocean rushed in over the polished wood floor of the living room, rising up the thin ankles of the piano.

Each of them was looking for something.

Maybe one another—in some form of memory, nostalgia, ghosts of who they once were tucked away inside the others' collective memory and what they once meant to one another. Isn't that sisterhood and motherhood—a way to find versions of yourself locked away in others?

*I'd prefer you all stay close to home,* Augusta had said.

Home.

In three days' time, Ru would write Cliff a letter, telling him she was sorry but that she was calling off the engagement. She would suggest that she wait to return the diamond ring in person, instead of trusting international mail.

But right now there was some scurrying in the middle of the longhouse near the fire.

The matriarch, with a pipe clenched in her teeth, made a clicking noise at Ru, indicating that she should gather near. Ru stared at the broad bare globe of the young woman's stomach. "The baby?" Ru asked. "It's coming?"

The matriarch waved Ru closer.

"I wasn't expecting that," Ru said to herself. "And that's the one thing I should have seen coming."

The fourth generation in the longhouse was about to be born.

# Part Two

*In which we meet the man who arrives with the package unearthed by the hurricane and the family is rejoined—piece by piece.*

EIGHT MONTHS LATER . . .

CHAPTER *5*

Esme and Atty had been living with Augusta in the house on Asbury Avenue for a week, their long-snouted collie in tow. It had proven to be a turbulent school year. After news of Atty's father's affair swept the boarding school—Doug stayed in France—Atty chunked the rest of the year in a downward spiral that ended, spectacularly, in a "behavioral prank" involving the history teacher's Civil War–era musket. Esme and Atty didn't offer more details to anyone than necessary. After a disciplinary hearing, she was NIB'ed—a polite way to say that she'd received a letter stating that she was "Not Invited Back" for the following year. The letter was overkill; they weren't coming back anyway, so why be so official about it? Atty hadn't yet been placed in another boarding school because Esme hadn't found another job on the boarding school circuit, which she blamed on a prejudice against the non-Ivy-League-educated; inexplicably, she hadn't gotten into Smith or any of the Ivys and her guidance counselor had thought she'd be a shoo-in. Meanwhile Doug, Esme's soon-to-be ex-husband, was quite happily glomming off his French girlfriend, the dentist.

While Esme and Atty tried to recover from their personal hurricane, many others were still reeling from the *actual* hurricane.

Hurricane Sandy had killed over 125 people. It destroyed over seventy-two thousand homes and businesses in New Jersey alone, causing over sixty-two billion dollars in damage.

It broke people down.

But it seemed to have broken Augusta open.

Esme sensed that her mother was altered by the storm on what seemed a molecular level. Augusta told Esme that the storm meant that life was precious—including her own—and she felt herself, for the first time in a long, long time, pushing outward. "How else to explain it?" she'd told her daughter. "I'm pushing—*outward*."

The house on Asbury Avenue got off light compared with many others. The hurricane destroyed the family furniture on the first floor—the piano, sofas, armchairs, books. The entire set of Nancy Drew mysteries—fifty-six books in total—taking up a low shelf were either damaged or swept out to sea; even the bottom halves of a few paintings had been damaged. The faces of old, now dead Rockwells seemed to be bobbing heads, the paint beneath their shoulders forever chipped and blurred. Augusta kept the paintings on the walls. However, her great-grandfather's whimsical taxidermy of various rodents in elaborate dress having tea had to be thrown out. All other furniture had been cleared away and temporarily replaced by beach chairs and a small circular glass-topped garden table.

Augusta wanted the house exactly as it had been before the storm—which was the same as it had been for decades.

And so she sent Esme and Atty around to antiques shops, secondhand shops, garage sales, and Goodwills with pictures of the living room and dining room in hand, trying to match the furniture as closely as possible. So far, they'd only been able to replace the dining room table and chairs. Some items would prove much harder—an antique secretary's desk, a specific grandfather clock, and, impossibly, the glass-encased display of two taxidermied squirrels sipping tea in a parlor.

The day that the man with the package appeared at the house on Asbury Avenue, Esme and Atty were at an estate sale on Sea Spray.

"This can't be psychologically healthy," Atty told her mother as they walked through the pallid living room. "You get cheated on, kicked out of your house, fired, your daughter—once a golden girl—has a breakdown, and then you're forced to re-create your childhood home like a twisted museum?"

Esme noted that her list of failures was too quickly rattled off not to have been previously cultivated, perhaps even tweeted.

"Were you really once a *golden* girl? Isn't that a little revisionist history?" Esme said. They had developed a frank camaraderie over the course of the troubling year.

"Next to that girl with the musket at parents' weekend, I'd say, Yes, I was once a golden girl." She tweeted this, adding *#sarcastic-yolo.*

After the musket incident, while the school year wrapped up, Atty had taken a leave of absence and worked intensely with a therapist. This would supposedly help repair her badly dinged high school record. Those fourth-tier schools she'd once feared were now aspirational. There was some talk of trying to address some of this positively in her college entrance essay. Atty couldn't figure out a way to package the musket incident, though—an interest in historical firearms? Esme's colleagues would ask how Atty was doing with such saccharine sympathy that Esme wanted to slap them. It was a humiliating time for both of them.

Esme had told Augusta that Atty wasn't crazy. That weird, uptight, self-reverential school was! Heap on top of that a father who skips the preset Skype calls with his daughter and, well, Atty was deservedly pissed off. To be honest, Esme had been jealous of her daughter in that moment on the field hockey field, giving an oration on life and the living, musket in hand—armed with a piece of history.

Rockwellian teen years were sometimes difficult. Liv had dated a local bad boy while Esme was already off at college. (Obviously the whole thing made a great impression on the impressionable Ru, who'd written a book and film loosely based on it all.) Liv was shipped off to a prestigious boarding school as some lavish form of punishment that Esme had always envied. Things always weirdly worked out for Liv. Even her recent arrest for illegally vandalizing her ex's apartment had landed her in a rehab center that was more like an upscale spa.

And Ru had been a troubled teen. She ran away at one point—Esme couldn't remember the details—but she'd come back and had to go to counseling too. She was probably a writer because of some therapeutic necessity, a better kind of coping mechanism than Liv's drug use and boozing, but not too different in root cause, probably. It wasn't their fault anyway. They'd been raised by some-one who remained pathologically delusional. Esme loved her mother, but she was troubled.

Still, Esme worried. Atty had lost it, plain and simple, and al-though the therapist felt she was taking great strides, Esme was sure there was something Atty wasn't telling anyone.

At this very moment, her sisters were on their way home. Would they be positive or negative influences on Atty? Esme wasn't sure. She only knew that she alone seemed to be the Rockwell woman who had managed to keep her shit together.

She was looking at embroidered pillows, none of which looked like items from her childhood, but was distracted by Atty's voice echoing in the distance. "Hey! Excuse me! Do you have any taxi-dermied squirrels? High-class ones, sipping tea like they're British?"

And she knew that Atty was only asking so that she could tell the story in a tweet to her followers. Atty's most recent update was that she had 3,465 followers—who on earth wanted to hear what her daughter had to say?

The bigger question, though, wasn't how many followers she had, but if she had any friends—the living, breathing kind. And Esme was fairly sure she didn't.

# CHAPTER 6

The collie lay down and Augusta slipped off a shoe and rubbed his freshly buzzed back. He let out a contented moan, a moan so human that it reminded her of having a man in the house, something she didn't really know anything about.

Augusta had spent a good bit of the last few months looking up charitable organizations and writing checks and shipping them off to help others get back on their feet. She'd never been the type to give to others all that much. As the Rockwell money had been made by people now dead, Augusta's notion of money was that it was tied to independence and forever dwindling. She'd worked hard to protect her inheritance, which she never saw as selfish because she was a single mother with three children to support and then she was the aged mother who didn't want to be a financial burden. But now, suddenly, with a tragedy hitting home, those sentiments felt like flimsy rationalizations. She was giving and it felt good.

And amid all of the grief and loss, weirdly she felt—for the first time in a long time—hopeful. Yes, she had sent Esme and Atty out to find replicas of their old life, but that was mainly to keep them busy. Change was coming and it would be bigger than the trappings of interior decor.

Augusta couldn't tell what was next, but she knew that it was going to be swift and absolute. Maybe she was preparing for death, but it didn't feel like it. Instead she was pretty sure she was going to take one more swing at living. She simply didn't know how.

Right now, she was thinking about what to say to Atty. She felt like she had to rehearse things because she didn't know how to approach the girl. She was an edgy person, that Atty. And not edgy as in cutting edge. No. She was edgy in that she had edges—sharp ones. She'd even been an edgy baby. Her cry sometimes sounded more like a caustic criticism than a baby crying. Augusta wanted to reach out. How much longer did she have to make a connection with her granddaughter?

The hurricane certainly made her aware of the very fine scrim between life and death. It reminded her of the play *Our Town*. Liv had once had the role of Emily in a high school production. Her daughter was onstage—a dead girl, wandering around the edges of her life. It had been disconcerting to watch, but worse because Liv had been so convincing. This was right after Liv had broken things off with a very bad young man—that Teddy Whistler—who'd upended their lives and finally ended up in a detention center. Maybe Liv had felt dead a little. Later—months or even a few years— Augusta would find herself in some small ordinary act and imagine that some ghost was watching her, envying her this simple domesticity. And now she envied her own life, because she and Jessamine could surely have died in that storm. Her life felt so newly frail.

And her daughters were set to converge on the old homestead? She was quietly overjoyed. Maybe the newness of living her life would be getting the chance to raise the girls again—this time as grown women. Surely, she'd do a better job this time around.

That was when she heard the knock at the front door.

She wasn't expecting her daughters quite yet. Ingmar started barking. Augusta was surprised by this sudden display of typically masculine protectiveness; Ingmar's fluffiness and dainty snout had feminized him in some way. Augusta shushed him and moved to a window and saw a young man holding a box. He stood there for a few moments and then backed up and stood in the small front yard, looking at the house itself, searching it.

Actually, he wasn't a *young* man, really. He was probably middle-aged or nearly so. But she realized that she was old enough now to think of anyone middle-aged as young. He didn't appear to be evangelical. The God peddlers, as her mother used to call them, usually traveled in pairs and avoided the wealthier neighborhoods, where God was already assuredly in place.

The box was large and square enough to contain a cake or a hat. Was he bearing a gift?

She decided he was probably bringing a gift *to someone else.* Maybe an old boyfriend of Esme's had heard she was getting divorced and back in town.

Or maybe he was at this door by mistake.

In any case, he seemed harmless.

She walked to the door, vaguely self-conscious that the house might smell like Indian food. Esme had recently cooked one of those dishes that smelled like body odor.

By the time she opened the door, the man was heading back to the sidewalk.

"Hello!" she called. "Can I help you?"

He turned around and looked at her as if he expected to recognize her but didn't.

"Who are you looking for?" she asked.

"Augusta Rockwell," the man said and then he walked toward her, extending his hand. "I'm Bill Huckley."

She took his hand and shook it.

"I think you knew my father, Herc," Bill said. "Hercule Huckley the Third. My mother refused to keep the tradition going. I got lucky."

Augusta drew in a sharp breath, prepared to say something—but what? She felt a little light-headed. There was too much sun, too much glare bouncing off the cars. The grass looked glassy. Herc Huckley.

"Are you okay?" Bill asked.

"Yes, yes," she said, smiling.

"So are you Augusta Rockwell?"

"Ah . . ." She turned around for a moment, looking over her shoulder at the house. She felt like it was a boat that had lifted anchor and was now slowly floating away from her—so slowly that it was almost imperceptible. Or was she the one moving?

Herc Huckley. She remembered him clearly. A pale young man back then, sandy-haired, a little doughy. She could see him clearly sitting at the thick-legged table in the rental he'd shared with Nick Flemming—she'd met Nick on a bus in a snowstorm. The night before John F. Kennedy's inauguration. She could see Nick's face clearly in her mind too; she could smell the wet wool of his coat.

She felt exposed suddenly. Her cheeks flushed. She wasn't allowed to know Nick Flemming, not at all. Ru, as a teenager, had read sci-fi novels—dank, brittle things picked up at the used-book store—that talked about different universes, and that was where Nick Flemming and Herc Huckley belonged. None of her daughters had ever heard these names.

She looked at Herc's son and saw little resemblance, but it was there when he smiled at her. A crinkle around his eyes, one errant dimple.

"It is you. Isn't it?" he said, boyish with hope.

She nodded, clamped her hands together. "It's been so long!" She laughed nervously. "Your father was a law student at George Washington when I met him." She didn't add the rest: *He was friends with someone I knew well.*

Ingmar was sniffing through the screen, trying to get the stranger's scent.

"And Flemming?" Bill said softly. "Nick Flemming?" His expression was hard to read.

Was he coming to tell her that Nick was dead? Was this the way she would find out, once and for all, that it was truly over? She felt unsteady, glanced up and down the street. "Do you want to come in?" She didn't want him lingering in the yard. She wasn't supposed to say Nick Flemming's name—not ever.

Bill looked down at the box in his hands. It wasn't for Esme or someone else on this street. It was for Augusta. The realization shook her.

"Sure," Bill said. "You know it wasn't easy tracking you down!"

The house was dark compared with the bright day, almost tomb-like. "I apologize if it smells like Indian food and mildew, and for the lack of furniture. Storm damage. We haven't quite . . ." She trailed off, looking for a specific word.

"Rebounded?" Bill offered.

"No, but it does start with an *r*," she said. "I won't be able to think of the word until I stop searching for it directly." The mind is a bear trap, she thought to herself, yawning open and then suddenly snapping shut.

"Memories work that way too," Bill said, and for the first time he looked older to her, truly middle-aged. The harder edges and contours of his face had been wiped clean when they were outside, bleached by the sun. But now, in the cool dark of the house, his face was shadowed. He looked heavier—or maybe more weighed down.

Ingmar nosed him impolitely, but backed off when Augusta told him to go lie down. He wandered a few yards away and plopped on the hardwood.

They sat in the beach chairs, and he balanced the box on one knee, his hand spread flat on its lid.

"I forgot to ask," she said. She wanted him to tell her if Nick was dead or alive, but she didn't want to appear anxious. "Do you want something to drink?"

He shook his head then glanced back toward the front door, as if he was having second thoughts about being here at all. "I'm fine. I don't want to take up too much of your time." He lifted the box then and put it on the glass-topped garden table between them. "I found some papers going through my father's things. He kept this footlocker in the basement office of the bar he inherited from his father."

"How is your father?" she asked. Grown children only went through their parents' old things when they had to.

"Physically, he's very healthy, but he has Alzheimer's. It's fairly advanced."

"I'm so sorry." Augusta deeply feared the disease. She didn't want to be the husk of someone long gone. There but not. A demanding physical reminder that our frail memories are what make us who we are. "And Flemming?"

Bill shrugged. "I don't know," he said. Augusta was immediately relieved. She'd have preferred the news he was robustly alive, but this was hopeful. "Hurricane Sandy leveled the bar," Bill explained. "It's just a footprint now, and when I helped clear what was left, I found the footlocker and these papers."

Papers. The box was filled with papers. Augusta nodded. "I see."

He then slapped his knees and rubbed them like he'd once been an athlete and the knees pained him. "Maybe I shouldn't be here."

"What papers?" Augusta said.

"Your name shows up. And I think, I don't know, I think maybe some of what's written might make a difference to you." Ingmar was back, wedging up close to Bill, indicating that he wanted to be petted. Bill obliged, distractedly. "Or maybe it's filled with things you already know. Maybe it's stuff you've made peace with. But, well, I don't know if I'm here because I want to help you or because I'm hoping you can help me."

She looked down at the box, reached out to touch it, but then pulled her hand back to her lap. "Help you? How?"

"Help me understand my father, who he once was, what kind of person he was. I just feel like . . ." He crossed his arms on his meaty chest. "I need to know him or I can't really know myself somehow."

"Well, I don't know that I'm going to be much help," she said. "I didn't know your father all that well. We met a few times. Briefly."

He leaned in then, elbows on his knees. He lowered his voice and said, "But you've heard of The Amateur Assassins Club, haven't you?"

Her heart started beating so quickly she wanted to put her hand over it, as if saying the Pledge of Allegiance. Instead she locked her hands in her lap. Her face must have revealed some recognition because he scooted forward to the very edge of the chair. Ingmar lifted his snout and sniffed the air as if he sensed change as a scent.

"The Amateur Assassins Club," Bill said again. "Those words mean something to you. Don't they?"

CHAPTER 7

When Ru settled into Noi Bai International Airport, she dutifully plugged in her cell phone, dreading the inevitable messages from the life she'd temporarily abandoned.

She'd told Cliff her plans to come home so that they could settle the matter of the engagement ring. Cliff only left one message. "Hey, call when you can. We can set a time to . . ." His voice trailed off. "Just let me know."

Ru wondered what she should feel—guilt, relief, nostalgia, regret? For someone with such a gifted memory, she had trouble sometimes attaching appropriate emotions to events, moments. This was one of those times.

Ru's agent, Maska Gravitz, had left many messages. The woman was legendary, decades of handling drunken literary elites and writers who became franchises. She once said to Ru, "I've talked some of the greatest literary geniuses of our time out of jumping off bridges."

Her messages were stern and candid. She hadn't told Maska she was going to Vietnam so the first message was a little fiery.

"Cliff called me and told me you're in Vietnam. For shit's sake, tell me where exactly and I'll come over there and kick your ass in."

Her second message was about Ru's editor. "I can't tell Hanby that you've fled the country. The veins in her head will explode. You know she's afraid to call you about your effing engagement announcement." Ru hadn't told anyone she'd called it off. "The poor kid has made a demigod out of you because she thinks her career depends on this next book. Jesus H. Christ, I hope you're working on it."

Her third message was a little drunk, and played out like the lyrics of a country song. "You got to do what you got to do even if your heart's sore." Why Maska thought Ru was heartsore, Ru didn't know. She should have assumed Ru was in love. She decided it was projection. Heartsore was after all the human condition, and why country music endured, against all odds.

In her final message, Maska confessed to wrangling Ru's arrival dates out of Cliff and she said she'd given "brittle little Hanby Popper the go-ahead to set up a bookstore event in Ocean City. It'll be the blogger set, for the most part. Tumblr, tweeterers, all that shite. She thinks that engaging your fans might light a fire under your tushy."

The idea of a bookstore event made Ru feel as brittle as Hanby Popper, who was brittle indeed. Ru hated the questions, especially anything to do with inspiration, a term she found both weirdly religious and also deeply destructive to American culture. Inspiration can't be sustained. "You can be inspired to write a first paragraph, but not a whole book. That requires work," she told interviewers. "That's why there's a career called novelist but not first-paragraphist. As a culture, can we please stop asking that stupid question?"

It was largely believed that an author's interaction with fans increased the fan base. In Ru's case, she was sure that each time she met with fans, she lost more than she gained.

Ru erased the messages one by one and didn't call anyone back.

Wearing the traditional ankle-length skirt with a tank top and a shawl, she boarded the plane, and although it was a long calm flight—with an empty seat next to her, which she accepted as a gift from the universe—she had trouble sleeping.

The second flight out of Chicago was packed. She was wedged between an ancient lady reading a bodice ripper that didn't keep her awake and a large salesman from Kansas. They sat on the tarmac for so long that the delay allowed one very late traveler to rush down the aisle—untucked blue shirt, jeans, breathless from jogging to the gate, no doubt. He was tall with bulky shoulders and while taking his place, just one row up from Ru, he was apologetic. He said to his seat mate, "If this flight weren't delayed, I'd have never made it. Sorry to take up the spare room. Really. I'm so sorry." And then he turned and gave a general apology to the people around him.

Ru assumed he was Catholic, what with his need for generalized atonement, and that maybe he'd played lacrosse but surely not football. She mostly saw him from behind. His hair was a little long and when he sat down it swung forward slightly and he pushed it back in a way that she felt was egotistical or overly stylized or precious, maybe even a little British.

She turned away from him, and shortly after takeoff she fell asleep.

A little while later, Ru woke up, and was disoriented by all the Caucasians in their jeans and haircuts, sipping their complimentary drinks in plastic cups. They were all slightly blurry; she hadn't worn her glasses since she left the States. Slightly blurry wasn't a bad way to experience life, she'd decided. She said, aloud, "We believe what we're told."

She was startled when she realized that the overweight businessman from Kansas had been replaced by the possibly Catholic former lacrosse player. He was grinning like he knew something she didn't. "Hi."

Ru rubbed her eyes, disoriented. "Hi."

"You've been sleeping on my shoulder."

She remembered, suddenly, the smell of him in her sleep. She'd read once that people smell one another's DNA, in fact, and were drawn to DNA scents that would work well with their own. "Sorry. I didn't mean to sleep on you." And then Ru blushed because it sounded more intimate than she'd meant it. She hadn't blushed in months because the M'nong people didn't make her feel embarrassed.

"You actually curled your hands around my arm. You slept pretty hard," he said and then he added, under his breath, "on me."

"Where'd the other guy go?"

"I switched with him. I hope that's okay. When I got up to go the bathroom, I recognized you."

"Oh," Ru said, "right." She straightened up, expecting to be asked about her writing secrets or for a signature or to read a manuscript written by the man's cousin.

"You don't recognize me, do you?"

She knew this wasn't professional. This was personal. And then in a flash of recognition—beyond the blur of her less-than-perfect eyesight—she knew who this was: Teddy Whistler. The buzz of the plane roared in her ears, and her chest felt like it was filled with small wires, suddenly charged with electricity.

"Maybe you'll remember that you wrote a book and made a film about me? Thanks for changing the last name from Whistler to Wilmer, by the way."

She kept staring, speechless. She saw how his face had become tough-jawed and lean. He'd grown into his blocky nose. He still had the same sad eyebrows and dark hair, but he no longer wore glasses, so his eyes were crisp and proportioned to his face. Bright-blue eyes with dark lashes. "Jesus H. Christ," she whispered.

The novel and subsequent adaptation of *Trust Teddy Wilmer* was based on a portion of Teddy Whistler's life—this man sitting next to her. When he was a teenager, the press named him a local hero three times during the summer of 1988 when he saved a woman from drowning, then a dog from a burning car, and survived a near-mauling by a neighbor's kinkajou—a vicious member of the raccoon family—only for it to later be revealed that he staged all of the events in order to be thought of as a hero and win the girl he loved—who later turned him in.

Ru's sister Liv was that girl.

"I'm sorry," Ru said quickly.

"About what? Your sister turning me in? Or the book? Or the adaptation? Or having me played by that hyper-good-looking actor I could never live up to? Or not calling to give me a heads-up that you were turning a deeply personal part of my life into something for public consumption."

"I wasn't in charge of casting."

"That's all you have to say?"

She shook her head. "No, no. I mean, I thought of trying to look you up and tell you about the book but then I decided that I'd changed it so much that it was no longer about you and so telling you that it was about you would have been confusing because it really wasn't."

"Really wasn't? I mean, the man who played my father has my father's exact lisp and tattoo and wore the same lifts in his shoes. Should I go on here?"

"I'm sorry. It's art, you know? I mean, I thought I was making art. I thought, if you saw it, you'd think it was a form of admiration."

He pinched his nose. "That never dawned on me. It was just so . . . weird. It was just so intimate and me but not me. Plus, you got some stuff wrong."

"That's because it wasn't really about you."

"Oh, I see. That's how you're going to play this."

"No, I mean. What did I get wrong?"

"Nothing. It's personal. Have you ever had someone write a book and make a movie of the most messed-up time in your life? No? Then I guess you wouldn't understand." He squeezed his eyes shut. "God, I loved your sister."

"She was in love with you too."

"I loved her first."

"Does that matter?"

"No, I think it only matters who loves who last, but that also would have been me."

He rubbed the cuffs of his shirt and without looking at Ru, he asked, "How is she?"

Ru was pretty sure that her sister's life was a disastrous mess and that she was miserable. "Good, I think. You know, we all have our things."

"I see," Teddy said. "She was kind of my Daisy. I guess I'm just lucky I'm not floating facedown in a pool at the end of your story of my life, right?"

"That's a little overblown, don't you think?"

"Can I tell you that I didn't really see my life as a chick flick that made hipsters cry into their monogrammed hankies?"

"*Chick flick* is kind of a pejorative term."

"Really?"

"Yes, really." Was he doubting her?

"I think if you've profited from a genre, you can't really bad-mouth it much."

Ru said to herself, "I was just getting on a plane and minding my own business."

"Funny. I always imagined I'd one day run into you and how it might go."

"Is this how it goes?"

"Not really. You're usually more contrite. But maybe that's not really who you are. You know, I remember this time when I met you. You were twelve or so and you were wearing pajamas, leaning out one of the bedroom windows. Your mom and Liv were having a screaming match about me, to be honest. I was out of sorts. I could see them through the windows. And I asked you what your name was. You said Ru Rockwell and you added that you weren't related to the painter."

"We're not."

"I knew that already. I was dating Liv, but then you asked me my name and I told you my full name, Teddy Whistler, and you asked me if I was related to the painter who painted his mother. You were just a kid. How did you know that?"

"I have an excellent memory. In fact, I remember what you said back to me."

"What was that?"

"You said, *Whistler painted a lot of things.*"

"Well, that's true. He did."

"And then my mother called the cops, if I've got that right."

"And they were prompt and hauled me off in cuffs."

They sat there for a while. Ru wasn't sure what to say. Teddy Whistler was such a huge part of her childhood. He was a myth, a legend, a hero and a villain, a saint and a lover—the undoing of her sister. Ru had exploited all of that. She didn't want to apologize again but she clearly owed him.

"What did you mean by what you said when you first woke up?" Teddy asked.

And for the first time in her life, Ru didn't remember. She stared at Teddy. His hair was groomed like he was going somewhere that entailed grooming. "What did I say?"

"*We believe what we're told.*"

"Oh," Ru said. "Right. I know what I meant by that." She smoothed her bangs, aware now—suddenly—that she had a weird lopsided haircut—the child who'd taken up the habit of petting her had cut Ru's hair one morning while she slept. She hadn't worn makeup or shaved her legs or worn perfume or deodorant since she landed in Vietnam. She thought of her eyebrows. They had no arches. She looked past the sleeping old lady out through the small window. Ru was still wearing the engagement ring, but only so she wouldn't lose it.

"And what did you mean by it?"

"I meant that if someone tells us that something like quitting or, say, running away is bad, we buy into it—personally and collectively as a culture. But that's not true."

"So, what are you quitting or running away from?" he asked.

"I'm just heading home." She glanced at him. "Catching up with family."

"I'm running toward," he said.

"Toward what?"

And without any sarcasm or hint of insincerity, he said, "I'm going to see Amanda."

The name charged a distant memory. Amanda. "The girlfriend you broke up with before Liv?"

He nodded. "You cut her from the movie."

"I thought it was simpler with just one girl."

"The one who turned me in."

"Really, I made it about your father because it *was* about your father."

"More or less. Movies can be redactive."

"Or expansive."

"I wrote Liv letters in juvie. She never wrote back."

"Maybe she did, but she just never sent them. Liv was sent off to boarding school after . . ."

"Amanda was there before Liv and Amanda was there to get me through the aftermath. She stuck it out with me for a long time." He took a deep breath and held it. "I'm going to win her back."

"What?" Ru hadn't heard the term *win back* for nine full months. Of course, he wasn't referencing the name of a Hollywood insiders' screenwriting award that she'd won, but still her previous life flooded back to her—L.A.'s dry air, the interior of her BMW, and Cliff—handsome, with his windswept hair, a little sunburn on his nose, naked in a pool in Beverly Hills at night. She felt stricken with panic. She'd called it off? Jesus. It had made sense while living in a longhouse in Vietnam, but here, now, hurtling through the skies over the United States of America? She swallowed drily. "To win her back? Why does she need winning back?"

"It's a long story." He shrugged off his passion, but not very convincingly.

"We've got another hour and a half," Ru said.

"Are you going to rip it off for another book?"

"I'm writing about elephant calls now—guttural breathing, growling deep in the ribs, sharp blasts, circular whirring, deep purring, and this noise like European mopeds."

"Okay then."

And so then Teddy Whistler told Ru about Amanda.

They grew up in Ocean City together, same street, and went to each other's birthday parties. "After I got out of juvie and a little time somewhere private, we finally dated through high school, college." When he was in law school, his uncle died and left him a booming international real estate company, headquartered in Seattle, but with satellite offices all over the world. "It's the kind of thing that you don't say no to," Teddy said. "I had to give it a shot." He expected Amanda to follow.

She didn't. They broke up, but only to give each other a little space to grow up, be independent, and then—or so he thought—they'd get back together once he'd built up the business and opened an office wherever she wanted to live.

When he heard she was engaged, he was in Chicago. "I bought a ticket and I'm flying home to Ocean City to tell her I love her, to win her back."

There were those words again. "Okay," Ru said, as if he'd asked her a favor.

"Okay . . . what?"

"I owe you, don't I? And I specialize in win-backs."

"Win-backs?" he asks.

"Yeah, classic scenes. I've written a bunch of them. It's, you know, a set piece."

"A set piece? Well, I'm actually talking about my life right now. Not a classic scene. Not a set piece."

"I pull from the truth to try to reveal a deeper universal truth." This was something she'd learned to say early on.

He seemed to be considering it and then he smiled a little. "I liked it when my character said, 'The dog dragged me in.' And when he put his fist through the window. And 'Even Teddy Wilmer isn't really Teddy Wilmer.' Those were good lines."

"What about 'I'm not a hero. I'm just here. I'm the one who stays.' That's the line most people point out."

He shook his head. "Ah, well, that's where you might have gone wrong. I'm still trying to be a hero." He fiddled with the latch on the tray table. "But I liked what she said after that."

"'Then stay, and keep staying,'" Ru said softly. She hadn't had a conversation about these lines in a long time.

"Yeah," he said. "That."

Ru had failed in Vietnam. Though she understood the different calls of elephants and the situations that aroused each of them, she'd made no progress in communicating with them. And she'd long since given up on trying to understand the inner workings and/or implications of a matriarchal culture as well as trying to feel what it might have been like for her father if he had, in fact, served in Vietnam. She'd never even learned how to make sour rice soup or how to dry a gourd to hold the soup. She sucked at weaving cotton. The only thing she'd been good at was swaddling the baby to her chest and taking her for long walks—the fourth generation in the longhouse was, as the matriarch had wished, a girl—and Ru missed the smell of that baby's head.

So, after being of little use in the M'nong village for the last eight months, she suddenly felt like a doctor on a cruise ship volunteering to deliver a baby on the lido deck or, more appropriately, as she put it to Teddy, "It's like you've had a heart attack while trapped on a plane—but it's okay because you're seated next to one of the best heart specialists in the nation."

"Are you making me an offer?"

"I'm an award-winning win-back writer and you need a win-back."

He rubbed the back of his neck. "But it has to be from me. It has to represent how I really feel."

"Yep. I can do that."

He nodded slowly, saying yes while still thinking it through. "Okay, okay. It's like the universe is speaking pretty clearly. Not even a lisp or a stutter. I'm sitting next to an award-winning win-back writer who owes me. Okay." His head snapped up. "Let's give it a shot."

For the next half hour, Ru raked him for details, moments. And he ran through everything he could, sometimes closing his eyes tight and leaning his head back against the headrest, trying to remember it all, just right.

At a certain point, Teddy said, "God, I miss the way she looked at me. That look—it just could knock everything down. That look—it could strip everything away. And then it was just me and her. I've been missing that look ever since I left. I can't spend my whole life missing it."

Ru stopped writing. She looked out the small window again, the clouds sailing past the old lady's elegant profile. Ru felt breathless. She thought of Cliff, somewhere down there. Had he looked at her and felt everything stripped away? Had she felt that way when she looked at him? Had she *ever* felt that way? Maybe it just wasn't part of her genetic makeup.

"Can we put that in?" Teddy asked.

She tapped her eraser on the tray table. "It might be a little too earnest and borderline cloying," she told him. "But not bad. You could go with that. Or . . ." She raised her hand and told him. "I've got this."

And then for another hour or so, she wrote Amanda—this stranger, engaged to someone who was not the love of her life (according to Teddy Whistler)—a love letter.

When she was done, she handed the letter to him.

He read it slowly, sat back in his seat. "You're good at what you do." He folded it and put it in his shirt pocket.

They settled into quiet for the rest of the flight, but Ru still felt jittery and, well, very, very alive. The most alive she'd felt in a very long time—even more alive than she'd been watching a live birth. She was rocketing back to her childhood home, her family, the past. It was like Teddy knew it and had shown up to confirm that her life wasn't just characters and plots and ideas for books she couldn't write. It was real—undeniably real—and by extension, Ru was real too.

She'd run away and escaped her own life for a while, but Teddy Whistler—of all people!—had made her remember she was supposed to be living her life.

After landing, Teddy said, "Norman Rockwell. He painted sentimentally, right? Whistler was against sentimentality. He loved art for art's sake."

"Actually Rockwell's first wife wanted an open marriage and divorced him to marry a war hero. She killed herself and his second wife had a lot of mental issues, addictions. They went to the famous therapist Erik Erikson. Stages of psychosocial development? Did you take Intro to Pysch?"

"I did."

"Well, they didn't have a perfect little picket-fence life. No one does."

"I guess not."

Ru unclipped her seat belt.

"Do you want me to let you know how it goes?" Teddy handed her his business card. "You could call me or I could call you."

She shook her head, refusing to take it.

"You don't want to know? Wouldn't it be nice to hear that it was a success? I could call you only if it's good news, if you want."

"Success is overrated."

CHAPTER *8*

After Herc Huckley's son asked her about The Amateur Assassins Club, she'd told him that she wanted to know what was in the box. "Is it mine? Are you giving it to me or not?" Her tone had become chilly, a voice usually reserved for moments when she had to stick up for herself around pushy salesclerks or know-it-all hairdressers.

He told her he'd made copies, but these were the originals. "All yours."

"I'd like to look at them in private. That's fair enough, isn't it?"

"Of course," Bill said. "No problem. But . . ." He reached out and touched the box in a way that declared he still had some ownership. "I'd really love to talk to you about it all, after you're done. My mother doesn't know anything about what's in this box. She met my father years later and now my father's gone, in a way," he said, his voice cracking. He coughed and then went on. "This is all I have left of him."

She'd told him that maybe the contents of the box would jar loose some memories. He jotted his cell phone number on his business card—his work was related to green technology, whatever the hell that was—and gave it to her. She ushered him to the door.

And within moments he was gone. Augusta and Ingmar were alone again in the cool, dark house.

Augusta walked upstairs, leaving Ingmar—who was mistrustful of stairs—behind. He nose-whined his lonesomeness.

Using a small step stool, Augusta shoved the box onto the top shelf of her bedroom closet, behind a stack of quilts. She shut the closet door so tightly she imagined she was sealing up the past. The contents of the box would surely jar loose some memories; the question was, could she bear it?

The Amateur Assassins Club? Yes. Those words meant something to her. They shot through her like fissures across the surface of a frozen lake.

Nick Flemming abandoned her. Herc Huckley and the other members of the Assassins Club were the unwitting witnesses.

And then Flemming came back and her life, for a long while, wasn't hers.

She sat on the edge of her bed then lay down on it with her shoes still on, and she remembered snow swirling on the other side of the window on the fifth floor of the Commerce Building where she'd once worked, the life she'd lived before her daughters existed. The secretaries gathered by the window, pulling their cardigans in close. They didn't like Augusta. Women didn't, in general. Men did. She was odd and yet comfortable with being odd—or, perhaps, unaware—which men sometimes mistook for mysteriousness.

It was the eve of John F. Kennedy's inauguration and someone said, "How are dignitaries going to get to all of their parties?"

"Who cares?" Augusta said. "How are *all of us* going to get home?" She'd left her combative parents in the house on Asbury Avenue as soon as possible—in fact, while still just eighteen and having only completed a short secretarial program. She was living in a small apartment in Arlington that she shared with an older woman who'd never married and who seemed to need no one. Augusta admired her.

The snow had been drifting down since midday, but now it was

really starting to accumulate. As it was, she only had a pair of galoshes that fit tightly over her high heels. They would be of little
use. The snow was already ankle-deep where it hadn't been shov-
eled from the sidewalks, and the galoshes were bound to become
pockets for snow.

"Do you think they're going to have sense enough to let us go?"
Augusta asked, rhetorically. At eighteen, she was already a committed career woman. Her co-workers thought she'd prematurely ad-
opted the jaded tone of some of the older higher-level secretaries,
for effect, but Augusta had been a jaded toddler. She found an early
Christmas present in her father's closet—a tricycle. She pulled it
out, took it to the third floor, and pedaled it around.

When her father found her, he said, "That was supposed to be a
gift from Santa."

"It was in your closet."

"It's a special Christmas gift. You should wait until Christmas
morning for it."

"Why?" She sat on the red leather seat and stared at him blankly.
"That makes no sense." She meant it seemed arbitrary, but she
hadn't yet learned the word.

At quarter to four, Mr. Shapiro walked out of his office, coughed
loudly, and then clapped his hands over the clatter of their typewrit-
ers. "I have an announcement!" he shouted. "Can I have your attention?" He was exasperated even though they all quieted
immediately; he was often preemptively exasperated. "All government employees are getting out an hour early! You can pack up and
head home at four P.M."

Augusta finished her final report, tidied her desk, and was leaning over to put on her mother's galoshes when Lloyd Bartel, a
young patent attorney, walked up. "You need a ride?" He spread his
hands on her desk, leaned in, and smiled.

"I'm okay," she told him. "I've got a ride." She didn't have a ride.
She was going to take the bus.

"Full tank of gas, working heater. You sure?"

She nodded. "Thanks." It was just a car ride but, still, she was suspicious of men, in general, and was dating a young dental student named Max Stern in part because it took her off the market. She hadn't yet broken it to him that she didn't believe in marriage. Her parents assumed he was going to propose, and she'd been practicing a speech for that moment. Sometimes the speech was meant to let Max down easy, but often it was a treatise on the pointlessness of marriage: *People who get married seem either encased in blocks of ice, so stiff they can't even blink, or rabid with anger, setting out to kill each other over the course of a lifetime.* Those were her parents' only two modes and what she assumed all couples reverted to in private.

He rapped on the desk with his knuckles. "Keep warm!" he said. "Bundle up!"

She bustled out with the other workers, packed into the elevator amid the cheery nervous chatter—"About time!" "It's a blizzard out there!" "Call in the reindeer!"—and then through the lobby, the wind-gusted revolving doors, and onto the street.

The snow was coming down so quickly that Augusta stopped for a moment and stared up into it, like a child might. She clutched the collar of her mannish camel-hair coat—identical to so many of the women's coats that season—and let the snow light on her face, daintily. She smiled. She couldn't help it. She was out of the stuffy office and in the world. And although she'd been an adultlike child, she could also be a childlike adult. It was as if age didn't apply to her chronologically, but instead it was mood-based, experiential, like matching an age to an experience rather than experiencing things through the lens of age.

The snow felt like a reminder that nature still existed, that the world wasn't simply made of boardrooms and buildings and streets and bridges. It could still be overtaken. The city and all of its important bustle could be blotted out—just like that. All white, covered in a blanket, as if what they did here was unimportant, antlike, as if they'd never existed at all.

She was shoved by the crowd. Some had thought to bring umbrellas; popped open, they surrounded her with their silver spokes.
She only had a long thin scarf, which she wound over her head
and around her neck. She wedged her way into the herds, slipping
now and then. The traffic had already slowed, barely inching
along. The city was home to many southerners who had no experience driving in snow. She knew it was bad and only going to get
worse.

Her nylons were wet and freezing cold. As she approached the
crowd huddled at her bus stop on the corner of Fifteenth and Con-
stitution, she realized that there was no way she'd be able to board
the next bus or the next.

A man in a tuxedo and a woman in a fur coat stepped out of a
limousine and into a small restaurant. The woman was crying.
"What a waste. A horrible waste. Are you listening?"

Augusta turned then and headed east toward Twelfth Street.
She'd have to reverse the route to its origins at the depot if she
wanted a warm and dry seat for the next few hours. She passed a
garbage truck, outfitted with a plow.

At the depot, she found a bus from her line just about to head
out. It was idling. She tapped on the door. The driver opened it.

"Can I board here?" she asked.

"You're in for a long night." He was bundled and flushed, his
eyes puffed and bleary, like he'd been making rounds for a long
time already.

"I figured that much." She opened her change purse and paid.
All of the seats were empty. She took one in the middle of the bus,
slid all the way to the window. She thought of Kennedy. She'd
voted for him, proudly, and it seemed that all this snow was nature's
confetti. She loved Kennedy in such a deeply personal way that she
wasn't sure it was healthy. When she heard his voice, she sometimes welled with such hope that her eyes teared up. She breathed
on the glass and then made a print of her hand.

At the next stop, men and women shuffled down the aisle, doubling up. Augusta kept her eyes out the window so that no one would try to catch her attention and ask to sit next to her. She knew she'd have to share eventually; this was a habit more than anything else. An only child, she usually preferred solitude.

As the bus lurched from the curb, she sensed someone's presence on the sidewalk. Maybe it was a flutter of motion that she saw out of her peripheral vision, maybe it was something more inexplicable—sometimes we sense things beyond our senses. She turned and saw a young man running along, his overcoat flapping open. He had dark hair that, if not cut so close, would have been curly, and shining eyes. He raised his hand and called out. He looked at Augusta and opened his arms wide, slowing his pace, as if to say, *I'm at your mercy.*

Augusta was about to call to the driver but someone beat her to it. "One more!" a voice shouted.

The driver nosed forward but there was nowhere to go. He opened the bi-fold doors and the young man jumped up the steps. He made a quiet joke that made the driver laugh loudly.

As he headed down the aisle, he looked directly at Augusta. His gaze was so intense that she immediately looked down at her lap, fiddling with the metal snap of her purse. The bus lurched again and she heard the swish of his jacket and then felt his weight as he took the seat beside her. "Hope it's okay," he said.

She slid toward the window immediately, glanced up, and smiled. "Oh, yes. Of course."

"My name is Nick," he said, and he held out his hand. "Nick Flemming."

"Right," she said, shaking his hand. She realized now how hard her heart was beating. She tugged at her scarf. "I'm Augusta Rockwell." She wanted to keep this formal.

"Rockwell?"

"No relation," she said, "to the artist. Norman, that is."

"*The Saturday Evening Post,* right? Baseball games and fishing holes and Santa. I don't know if I ever really bought it."

"Bought the newspaper?" Augusta said, but she knew that wasn't what he meant. He was talking about authenticity.

"The whole ideal. If there's a place in America that's perfect like that, quaint and tidy and all tucked into bed at night, I wouldn't want to live there."

"Why not?" Her own childhood was a strange lopsided triangle. Her mother and father fought, but all the while her mother took care of her father, who drank too much and took pills for his nerves. With what energy she had in reserve, her mother took care of Augusta. As soon as Augusta was old enough to take on some element of her own rearing, she relieved her mother of the duty. It was as if she fired her mother, task by task, as Augusta grew up, and her mother wanted to be fired.

Nick ran a hand through his hair, wet with snow. He leaned back and smiled—a bright, slightly lopsided smile. "Because it's not the truth, is it? I like the truth even if it's ugly. Don't *you*, Augusta Rockwell?"

She looked out the window, now densely fogged with the heat of the crowded bodies. She felt almost breathless. Yes. She didn't know it until this moment, but yes—she preferred the truth even if it was ugly. Marriage, for example, felt like an enormous lie—joy, happiness, twin souls. She would work this into her treatise against the institution, but she didn't know this stranger well enough to explain what was going through her mind so she said, "What plans are you missing out on because of the snow? You were going somewhere, right?"

"All these big shots in town? Where do you think I was headed?"

"I don't know," she said. He was gazing at her—not staring, *gazing*. "Maybe you're the type to crash galas and parties. Am I right?"

"So you're saying I'm not the type to get an invitation?"

She shrugged. "Are you?"

He shook his head and then whispered, "I was on my way to an assassination, but I've been delayed."

"I didn't know assassins took the bus."

"What can I say? I'm not highly paid."

"Why are you making up stories? I thought you preferred the truth."

"Do you think I'm lying?" he'd said, sheepishly.

"I think you're horsing around."

"I couldn't lie," he told her. "Not to you."

The night went on, attenuated by snow. Hours passed on the bus. Dark gathered all around them as the bus inched forward. He told her that he was a law student at George Washington, that he was the youngest of five boys, that he liked jazz and had voted for Kennedy, of course. She confessed things too, but nothing about Max Stern, the dental student.

At one point, Nick took liquor orders for people on the bus. He hopped off to bang on the window of a shuttered liquor store. The owner was inside, socked in by the snow. Nick talked him into selling a few bottles. The man appeared at the plate-glass storefront. He was sleepy, bleary-eyed. Some of the passengers waved, including Augusta. He waved back, stuffing bottles in brown bags.

The bus got rowdy after that. They sang Christmas carols, though the season was over, and a few pop tunes—"Mack the Knife" and, fittingly, "I Want to Walk You Home."

"We should get out of here and hit one of the galas," Nick said. "They'll have food and booze and bands, but not many people showing up to dance."

A little tipsy, she said, "Yes, let's!"

They got off the bus, doubled back the direction they'd come, and hustled up E Street. Eventually they started passing restaurants and large hotels.

"Just up ahead," Nick said, "another block." Finally, he stopped and said, "This was where I was headed. This one, right here. Should we crash it?"

"I'm not dressed for it," Augusta said.

"I don't think they're being picky."

There was no need to crash. Two anxious men in top hats ushered them in off the street into a large nearly empty dance hall. There were pyramids of fresh shrimp, a full open bar, servers carrying trays of small hot hors d'oeuvres. The band was fantastic; the drafty dance hall echoed. Every time the door opened, the entranceway fluttered with snow as if a ticker-tape parade were passing by on the street. They danced to everything, warming up enough to take off their coats. As a girl, after the rheumatic fever, she'd been stricken with Sydenham's chorea, also called Saint Vitus' dance, her face and hands and feet taken over by occasional spasms. Her handwriting became broken and blocky, her face sometimes went rigid while her body squirmed restlessly. The romantic fever wouldn't let her go, and she became shy, always scared her body would betray her somehow. But with Nick all of that old self-consciousness disappeared. She could remember, even now, the heat of Nick's skin when he pulled her in for a slow song, the feel of his hand cupping the small of her back, the breadth of his collarbones. Sometimes falling in love is immediate, headlong, and permanent. She knew that he wasn't like anyone she'd ever met before or would likely ever meet again. She didn't believe in marriage, so could she believe in love? None of that mattered. The night wasn't of this earth. All of the landmarks were blotted out by snow. This wasn't Washington, DC. This wasn't even America.

And she knew that even though she was falling in love, she could never keep him. He was too urgent about living. She could never hope to contain him. She knew it from the beginning.

Sitting at a round skirted table, he said, "Jesus, it's him."

Augusta followed his gaze to a man in a red blazer. In his midsixties, the man had a waxed mustache, a bulbed stomach, and short arms. He walked, chest-puffed, to the men's room.

"Excuse me a minute," Nick said, standing up so quickly that his chair nearly kicked backward.

Augusta grabbed his sleeve. They were both a good bit drunk by this point. She laughed and then regained her composure and said very seriously, "You're not going to assassinate him, are you?"

"It's just a game," he said. "I've got to get within five feet of my mark."

"A game?"

"A club." He leaned down, putting his cheek to hers, and whispered, "I've told you too much already." Then he pulled away, winked, and followed his mark into the bathroom.

Later, Augusta would come to understand the club. It was simple—overachieving law students challenged one another to mock assassinations. This was before Americans became so deeply and personally scarred by the word *assassination*—before the deaths of Martin Luther King Jr., John F. Kennedy, and Bobby. They had no idea what was looming, how, one day, the club would feel Old World, cast over in darkness.

A few minutes later, the old man walked out, as chest-puffed as ever, his short arms swinging at his sides, and Nick appeared next.

He jogged over to her and grabbed her hand. "Let's dance."

The band eventually played the last song. They walked back out into the snow. After four blocks, they found the very same bus. The passengers were quiet now. Many dozed against the windowpanes.

After they boarded, they approached the Ellipse and saw, through the front windshield, a motorcade rocketing through the park, headlights cutting the darkness, spinning red lights churning the air.

Augusta imagined trying to explain this night to her daughters— and the months that followed, so passionate she felt devoured. Esme wouldn't understand. She'd never accept that her mother was once—even briefly—a different kind of person. Liv might accept it. She lived a nonconventional life. And Ru? Ru would nod as if she already knew the truth. Ru was prescient this way.

This was the night that changed Augusta's life, and for a short time the world was a completely different place. It was impossible to explain, too close to something sexual, but it was more than sexual. It was a kind of desire that, once stirred, never left her.

It was a costly desire, and her love for Nick Flemming would eventually exact great sacrifice.

Was it time to tell her daughters the truth? Would they even believe her? There was a time—after the dissolution of The Personal Honesty Movement—when the girls had questioned whether she was lying about their father. Esme accused her of having sex with strangers—she'd never forget it.

The box probably contained some proof. If Herc Huckley's son knew about The Amateur Assassins Club, what else did he know?

She sat up and planted her shoes squarely on the floor.

Ingmar had given up on his nose-whining and was likely dozing. The house was completely quiet.

She stared at the closet.

This was what had come to her. This was what had bobbed to the surface of the storm—*for her*. This was what she could no longer ignore.

She walked to the closet door and put her hand on the knob.

She would open the box, spread its contents on her bedspread, and allow what was to come.

# CHAPTER 9

Liv knew that Ru would know where to find her, if not consciously then instinctively. Liv had picked Ru up at this airport twenty years earlier—when Ru was sixteen and had disappeared for twenty-one days. Just like last time, Liv parked her mother's wood-paneled Wagoneer in a handicap spot in the short-term lot and smoked a cigarette out the open window.

Liv was nervous because she was always nervous. She missed the quiet routine of the spa-like rehab center—the persistent smell of tea tree oil, the quiet watercolor painting lessons, the soothing blink of the EMDR lights, and the long, winding conversations about her childhood—the one she invented bit by bit, loosely based on her own past. Ru wasn't the family's only storyteller! Liv didn't tell her therapists her main secret, that she was lucky—weirdly, perversely, and oddly lucky. Yes, she worked for things here and there, but overall the world extended offers she couldn't explain, and she took them. She simply had learned to accept it.

Frankly, she didn't trust therapists, and she'd hated the rehab center's trust-based activities—trusting addicts is counterintuitive. She didn't really fully trust anyone, and certainly not herself.

She was taking an antidepressant, and the occasional Xanax for

spikes of anxiety. She'd scored a few Valiums—her favorite antiques, as she called them—from a friend whom she visited briefly
after rehab for the express purpose of possibly scoring her favorite
antiques. She took a Xanax now—not wanting to waste a Valium—
and lit another cigarette. She was well aware that Ru had taken her
place as the youngest in the family, the baby, and hadn't even had
the courtesy to be the opposite gender, which would have allowed
Liv to be the baby *daughter,* if not the actual baby. On top of that
thievery, Ru had also been a bit of a genius though airheaded and
impractical in that way geniuses are allowed to be. It was Liv's life-
long job to take Ru down a few pegs, to keep her humble, to make
sure that she had firm footing in the real world.

It was exhausting and didn't make Liv feel like a good person,
deep down. But that was her role and so she stuck with it. Changing roles at this stage would only disrupt all of the familial patterns,
causing great upset to everyone involved, and wouldn't actually
last. The old roles were like ruts in a well-traveled dirt road. Eventually they would be drawn back to them.

With the motor running and the air-conditioning on full blast,
Liv put out her cigarette and thought of her mother's house, her
childhood home. Did she secretly wish it had been washed away by
the hurricane? She wasn't able to decide. She knew it was time to
go back, but mainly because she had nowhere else to go.

The end of her stint at the Caledonia had been a bad scene. It
was the real estate agent who did the dirty work. The agent, middle-
aged with a recent face-lift, was terrified that Liv would attack her
so she called the cops. Liv had only left the apartment once in sixteen days—to eat her favorite meal at her favorite restaurant—but
mainly during this stretch of time she'd remained drunk and high,
plotting cherry-picked marriages on the walls in Sharpie. (One of
the cops was a single woman and had actually asked some earnest
follow-up questions about Liv's method on the ride to the station,
which was slightly vindicating.)

It didn't help that she'd found one of her ex's dismantled hunting guns — he came from pheasant-hunting types — and had tried to put it together in case the post-Sandy fallout turned to civil unrest. She was trying to explain this, slurringly, to the cops and real estate agent, whose face was propped with gauze, but only made things worse by picking up the parts of the weapon and swinging them around.

But it was all okay. The world would forgive her. It always did and it would show it by offering her something soon.

In fact, her oversized Louis Vuitton bag was filled with engagement pages pulled from her mother's *New York Times* and *Washington Posts*. She fiddled with the leather drawstring but resisted opening her bag. She'd taken them just to feel close to one of her old addictions, not to fall back into it.

"The universe loves me and will provide," she whispered. It felt like a comforting little dinner bell jingling in her chest, and then she lay down on the front seat, curled up, and fell asleep.

She was woken up by a knock on the window.

There was Ru's face. She wore no makeup. Her brown hair was unkempt, not dyed. She was wearing a long cotton wraparound skirt, a tank top, and some kind of weird shawl. "Christ," Liv muttered.

She sat up and rolled down the window.

"What the hell?" Ru said. "Why didn't you meet me in baggage claim?"

"I thought we'd meet in our usual spot."

Ru cocked her head.

"This isn't my first time picking you up at an airport after you've run away."

"I was doing research," Ru said, too quickly not to have touched on a sore spot.

Liv shrugged.

"You fell asleep," Ru said.

"I'm taking a lot of antidepressants."

"Why?" Ru gripped the door where the window had been rolled

down, and Liv noticed her engagement ring. If Liv had to guess—
and she knew diamond rings—it looked like it weighed in at around
thirty thousand dollars, and she also knew that Ru probably had no
idea what it cost and therefore didn't seem to deserve it. And why
wasn't the fiancé picking her up?

"I'm depressed," Liv said.

"Why?" Ru asked again.

"Don't ask *why* like a toddler. People are always going to think of
you as a baby if you act like a three-year-old."

"You're the only person who thinks of me as a baby."

"I'm not the only one."

"What if you aren't depressed and you're just sad?"

"Sadness is an appropriate response when things are going badly.
Depression is feeling bad even when things are going very well."

"Are things going very well?"

Liv squinted through the windshield. "In fact, no." Then she
looked at Ru through the open window. "You're wearing a blanket."

"Unlock the fucking doors, please."

"Oh, look!" Liv said. "And now you're going to throw a temper
tantrum?"

"I'm speaking in a very normal voice," Ru said slowly and calmly,
but not in a normal voice at all. She was thinking of elephants—the
way they roared to intimidate one another and sometimes when
they were joyfully reuniting with another elephant, returning. She
couldn't ever really differentiate between the two roars. "I'm thirty-
six years old," she said to her sister. "Can you please unlock the
fucking doors?"

Liv had forgotten that she was in the car and Ru was locked out
of it and that they were actually heading home.

# CHAPTER 10

Her daughters would be home soon.

Augusta stared at the box delivered by Herc Huckley's son. It sat on the middle of her bed. Its lid still in place.

She couldn't keep it in the closet behind the quilts. It seemed to be pounding like the heart hidden under the floorboards in that Poe story.

But she couldn't quite open it either. She remembered all the things she'd given up, and all the things she'd gotten because of her chance encounter with Nick Flemming.

After the night of the snowstorm, Augusta broke things off with Max Stern, sitting side by side on a sofa in his mother's living room. She opted for the version of her speech that was less treatise and more a gentle letting-down. He didn't seem to mind being let down. In fact, she thought that Max might have even admired her a little. He said, "Well, that's okay. I think a girl like you's got bigger fish to fry."

She assured him that she simply wasn't ready to settle down. Max surely was. Within three months, Augusta read his engagement announcement in the newspaper.

Later, on the phone, her mother said, "One day you'll be tired of that office and you'll wish you were home in a house paid for by a dentist."

Her father, on the other hand, liked the idea of an old maid. "You'll take care of us when we're old."

She had no intention of doing this. In fact, after the breakup she felt relief that she wasn't going to have to take care of Max Stern, as her mother had done for her father.

She didn't want to tell her parents that she was dating a law student. She knew the relationship wouldn't last. Why get her parents' hopes up?

One night walking home from seeing *West Side Story* for the third time, she told Nick what she thought of marriage.

"Interesting on a philosophical level," Nick said. "But I still don't know what you think about marrying *me*."

She loved him. He made her ache. She wanted to spend her life with him. But still, hadn't her parents been in love once? She said, "Are you proposing?"

"Should I?"

After that, he did propose a number of times, but never very seriously. Once she had whipped cream on her nose and as he wiped it off with his finger, he said, "I want to marry you, Augusta Rockwell."

Another time, he curled to her back and whispered into her hair, "I want to take you for my wife," as he was falling asleep. It reminded her of the old nursery rhyme "The Farmer in the Dell," where the farmer takes a wife, the farmer takes a wife, hi-ho the darrio the farmer takes a wife.

Was he serious? No, she couldn't let herself believe that he was. They didn't have sex, but it was all so passionate that she had to assume this wasn't a confession as much as just getting caught up in the lustfulness of it all. Although she feared sex might burden her heart—rheumatically and romantically, she'd wanted to give in. It was Nick who said they should stop. In retrospect, she realized that he might have already been recruited.

In fact, when he talked her out of having sex with him that summer, it was an ending, though she wouldn't see that for a long time.

He was living in a large rooming house that he and his friends had rented out together. It had a shabby clay tennis court and leafy pool that they didn't know how to take care of. It had been a near-mansion at some point and now it was a rental—cheap, when split among them.

She remembered it all vividly. Herc had been the one to answer the door when she knocked. He told her to come in and get out of the heat. The old house was airy, shadowed, and cool with a wealthy dampness.

The drunken meetings of The Amateur Assassins Club were held in the dining room and weren't secret at all. In fact, the club was a point of pride. People who walked into the old house were often asked to add a target name to the list. There were great late-night drunken arguments about the best means to get in close. For patriotic reasons, there were a lot of communists on the list, but overall it wasn't personal.

As Herc took her through the dining room to the backyard where he'd last seen Nick, she passed the corkboard with magazine clippings of a few famous foreign dignitaries stuck to it. Augusta noticed that someone had added a clipping of a downtown bank.

"What's this?" she said.

"Nick's gotten bored. He wants to include fake bank robberies," Herc told her. "He wants to make two teams. Each would case the banks, work out the details of the perfect heist, present them to the group as a whole. The one with the best chance of success would win. We'd get a panel of judges. Do you want in? You seem practical and, I don't know, more like one of us or something, not like some of the other girls."

It was supposed to be a compliment. She knew what he meant;

Augusta had never really hit it off with women. She usually just didn't know what stories to tell and when. She'd say something and the other women would stare at her. She wasn't sure if it was her timing or her content, but she was always slightly off. "You'd have to change your name—The Amateur Assassins and Bank Robbers Club."

"Pisky's saying no to the whole thing so I don't know if it'll happen." Joel Abbington was nicknamed Pisky because his father was an Episcopalian minister who came from family money and was the one who bankrolled their parties. "He thinks bank robberies are classless. He wants to go into high art theft, if anything."

"I see."

"Anyway, some of us have to study." Herc wasn't as smart as the others—or at least didn't seem to think he was. He took everything more seriously.

He opened the back door. Nick was bent over a hose, untangling it to water the courts. "Nick!" Herc called out.

Nick looked up, saw Augusta, and waved.

Augusta's stomach flitted. She tried to smile. She'd shown up, having made the decision to give herself to him wholly.

Herc ducked back into the house. Nick was wearing shorts and tennis shoes. She'd worried over whether to wear Bermuda shorts or a dress. She'd opted for the dress and now it felt too formal. He said, "Tennis later?" They'd never played together before. "I bet you have a vicious serve."

She walked to him quickly. "Let's go to your room."

He straightened up. "What was that?"

She smiled.

They scuttled up the butler's stairs to his room. But as he started to kiss her and then fumble with the buttons on her dress, he stopped abruptly, like a voice had shouted at him in his own head.

Already a little breathless, they lay together in the bed, still dressed. He said all the right things. "We'll get married first. I'll finish up as fast as I can here. We'll get a little place. A walk-up. Maybe out in Alexandria. I'll meet your parents. You'll meet mine—a little uptight but they'll be relieved to see me settle down. We'll have a wedding, something small . . . We'll start a family."

And she said, "This is what marriage is about, really. Not love, but family."

"It's about love," he said. "I love you."

She wasn't her mother. He wasn't her father. They would become a family. They could get married and still be who they were, still love each other.

But a few days later, they were supposed to meet at a little restaurant near her office just after work. And he never showed up.

As she was paying the bill at the counter, Herc Huckley appeared. He was pink from having hurried there. He wiped his forehead with a hankie that he tucked into his back pocket.

"Herc," she said quickly, "is Nick okay?" She was afraid he'd come to deliver some tragic news.

"He's gone."

She spread her hand on the glass countertop. "Dead?"

Herc reached out and touched her elbow. "No, no. He left."

"What do you mean?" She started to feel a very new kind of anger.

"He packed up. Nothing's left."

"Why are you here then?" The anger made her feel incredibly powerful.

"He left me a note. He told me to come here and tell you."

"Tell me what?"

Herc looked around the small lunchroom—bustling waiters, people talking, eating, the clinking of silverware and glasses, all of it doubled by a bank of mirrors on one side. "He wanted me to . . ."

"Look, Herc. Forget it." She folded her receipt and tucked it in her change purse, snapping it shut. "You're not his errand boy." She walked out of the restaurant then. Her eyes stung from the sidewalk's bright glare. She was furious. She worried she might throw up. She smoothed the tight fit of her dress against her ribs.

Herc was there at her side again. "But maybe you shouldn't take it too personally. I mean, he abandoned everything important to him."

"This is more personal than you can imagine."

"He got a call."

"From whom?"

"One of the biggies. CIA or FBI or NSA. I don't know which one. He made an application. He's been up for the most elite corps, I think. He told me he couldn't ever be a good husband. He fell in love with you that night, but he also fell in love with assassinating some prime minister of some country in the Western Hemisphere in the men's lavatory."

"And he's choosing *that* over me?"

He squinted up at the sky. "You can stop him if you want."

"What do you mean?"

"There's a series of interviews. They've called me up. I'm on the list. Only you and I know about, well, his relationship with you. His promise."

So Nick told Herc that he'd proposed. "What promise?" She scavenged her purse for a mint.

"You can get him bounced out or maybe rerouted to something safer, I think."

She looked at the restaurant's plate-glass window. Normal people, doing normal things. "No," she said. "He's right. He'd be a lousy husband."

"I want to help." Herc pressed his lips together and nodded quickly. "Let me know if there's anything I can do," he said. "Now or in the future. I'm here for you. I mean it. Anything." He looked at her gravely. He was saying he'd step in, wasn't he? Was she so fragile that he thought she'd die without a husband? It was so chivalrous, she couldn't bear it.

"I have to go."

"I hope I see you again." He looked at her with great hope in his eyes.

"I don't know how we'd ever cross paths again," she said. "I don't even want to know if he comes back. Okay? If you see him again, tell him that I want nothing from him. Nothing at all."

He stepped back. "Okay."

And with that, she started walking down the street—in the wrong direction, but she kept going, her reflection flashing beside her in a series of plate-glass storefronts. She didn't believe in marriage but still found herself thinking that she couldn't go back and renegotiate with Max Stern. He was already taken. Lloyd Bartel was dating someone in the secretarial pool. Herc wouldn't work because it felt like Nick was manipulating her life. Had he sent Herc as some kind of backup?

Her parents had been delighted when she'd told them she was getting married, so deeply relieved. She realized that she'd actually wanted to make them happy. But now she'd return to her life. Even though she came from a family of the sea-profiteers, war-profiteers, greed-profiteers and she didn't really have to work—she wanted to.

In a few blocks, she stopped at an ice cream truck, ordered an elaborate triple-scoop cone. She took two small bites then threw it in a trash can.

She would never give in to a man again. That was it. This wouldn't just be the end of Nick Flemming. It would be the end of all men in her life. She decided to close up shop, emotionally.

Of course that wasn't the end of Nick Flemming.

Not at all.


Four months later, he showed up at her apartment while she was packing to head back to New Jersey. Her father had died—an aneurysm that took him immediately. Her mother was ill.

She refused to let him in.

He knocked on the door, insistently, and finally her roommate answered. "What could you possibly want?"

He gave the roommate cash, asked her if she wouldn't mind

going out to the nicest restaurant in town and out to a show—on him. "I'd like to bring a friend." He gave her more money, and she put on her coat and hat and left.

Over the course of the next five hours, Nick tried to talk Augusta into a life with him—an unconventional one, yes, in which she could remain independent but not have to work, if she didn't want to, and have children or not. "I can't have something that I love so much that I would sell out my country if it were in danger. A family with you, Augusta? I'd give up every American secret in history for you. I want to have a life with you, but to protect you too."

"Marriage is an overrated institution."

"Then let's do it our own way."

She said no.

He didn't reappear until the summer of 1969. There at the end of the wreckage of the 1960s, after assassination upon assassination, war, rising death tolls, there had been a glimmer of hope. Human beings had landed on the moon. They'd been thinking of each other all those years, but now stronger than ever.

And when he showed up this time, knocking on the door of a different apartment, one she lived in alone, he didn't say a word. He stood there, gaunt and wrung out. And she didn't say a word either. A moment of recognition flashed between them. They loved each other. They could make each other whole. They had to make it work or they wouldn't survive.

He reached for her and they held on to each other. It was a proposal, an acceptance, a beginning.

Later that night, in bed, she said, "I want a family."

"I do too," he said. "We won't do it the normal way. We can do it our way. But don't leave me. Stick this out even though . . ."

The finest of capillaries in her heart burned. "I'm not going anywhere," she said, but maybe they both knew they were doomed.

Over the course of the next few decades, he would become a high-level CIA operative, a spy, just as she'd always told her daughters. And she and Nick would have a marriage of sorts—one that remained illicit, charged, covert, and full of longing, a love that would render Augusta isolated and lonesome most of her days, but also it was a marriage that sustained her in small portions. Finally, when it became too much to bear, that winter of 1984, she would tell him that it was over. Her heart simply sighed, and she decided *nothing* was better than a *portion*.

Though they were never officially married, she divorced him — through a dead-drop letter. She would get full custody of the girls because Nick Flemming had never had any custody at all.

She cut him off and founded a Personal Honesty Movement that failed. Her oldest daughter accused her of sleeping with strangers, and, as a result, on the subject of their father, Nick Flemming, she went silent.

The last time she saw Nick, he was walking away from her, backward, gliding into a crowd of tourists, a dot of blood still fresh on the pocket of his white shirt.

Esme and Atty would be home at any moment, not to mention Ru and Liv. Ru's flight had already landed, hadn't it? She wondered if Ru and Liv had connected. She worried about Liv's sobriety. Fresh out of rehab, her daughter looked washed out and, at turns, jittery or glazed over. Augusta had tried to send Jessamine to pick up Ru but Liv had insisted. She hoped Ru would drive home though even Ru could be absentminded — the dazed artistic type — from time to time.

The box seemed to be filled with coiled springs. It couldn't be kept shut any longer. It was a tall box, square, heavily lidded, the kind you'd put a bow on and fit under a Christmas tree for a department store display.

Augusta put her hand over one corner then popped the lid.

There were letters — some small, others in business-sized envelopes, folded in half.

Nothing was written on the envelopes themselves — no addresses, stamps, post office markings.

Augusta opened one on top. The seal of the envelope had

hitched back together in two spots that easily loosened. She pulled out the letter and lifted it toward the window.

*H.,*

*    I haven't heard from you in a while. I know you're not dead, easy enough to look up. At our age, your silence could be worse than death.*

Augusta knew what Nick meant—senility.

*I've been thinking about you a lot and the old days. It's what people like me do.*

She wasn't sure what he meant by *people like me*. Was he like any other people?

*Should I update you on A. and the girls still?*

This too made no sense, but it made Augusta scratch her neck.

*One more time?*

The box was full of letters. Were these updates about her and the girls' lives?

*Not sure you'll even get this. But here goes.*

She didn't care for his chipper tone.

*They're doing well. A. keeps starting her movements. An activist at heart. She's still radiant.*

Augusta flushed. Her movements began only after she cut Nick off from the family. She was blushing because she felt watched, spied on by a spy—and she'd expressly told him to leave them all alone—but also, she couldn't help it: He'd called her radiant. She closed her eyes, took a cleansing breath, and read on.

> *And E. is still working at the boarding school. They still live on the pond. Her husband is chair. That worked out well enough. And young A. is a sass box, like I was at that age. I believe she gets her distaste for injustice from me. Remember how I used to find it so damn awful? Who knew I'd wind up an accomplice to it? All in all, I don't know that this boarding school is the best place for them. I thought it would be a safe nest. But it might be too stifling. And you know how I dislike the Ivies. They worship the Ivies there. Luckily, I think young A.'s grades are mediocre enough to keep her out of them. Unlike E., who could have gone anywhere she damn well pleased.*

She was gulping the information now. Great swaths. Packed with meaning. She couldn't dissect it all. She said aloud, "He's wrong there. Esme didn't get into any of the Ivies."

> *L. is married again. I admire the girl's incredible ability to acquire a life. I don't know what to do with the sadness—except send on gifts, here and there.*

Was Liv in touch with Nick? What gifts? Anonymous ones?

> *R. is making a go of it. Though you know with that one, I stand down, as requested.*

Augusta had requested that he leave all of his daughters alone. How had he misinterpreted this as only applying to Ru?

> *But I worry, you know. I worry a lot.*

For an assassin, as that's what he eventually became, he was an exceptional worrier.

*As for retirement, I hate it and it hates me. Mutual disgust. I can't shut down the sense anyway so I'll always be on duty.*

She knew that he would always be aware of eyes on him, scanning each room as he entered, knowing who was around him— forever monitoring his threat level.

*Hope you're well, old buddy.*
  *NF*

Nick Flemming was still out there, keeping tabs on all of them.

She walked quickly to her bedroom window, pulled back the curtain, and looked at the street half expecting to find him as she'd last seen him, the splotch of blood like an embroidered rose on his shirt pocket.

Augusta could hear her flooding pulse deep in her ears. She dropped the letter, took the box, and flipped it over, inverting the stack. The letters now on top weren't in envelopes. They were brittle and written on legal-pad paper. She picked up the first one.

*Herc,*

  *I got a call—the one I've been waiting for. And I'm taking it.*

  *I'd make a bad husband, and a worse father. I want to be out there. But, Herc, you wouldn't. Meet A. at the diner, tomorrow at noon. Tell her I love her. Tell her I'm gone. I know you love her, Herc. How many times did you say I don't deserve her? You meant that you deserve her. So do something about it.*

  *Nick*

*P.S. You thought I took the club too seriously. Now I'll live it.*

Well, Jesus H. Christ. She sat on the edge of the bed. She remembered Herc in the diner. Had Herc been in love with her? He'd once said she was different from other girls, sure, but it hadn't been a gushing compliment. He'd been asking if she wanted to be a judge on some bank-robbing panel. He had said he'd do anything for her. She'd assumed he was being chivalrous. Augusta hadn't appreciated the offer. At the time she hadn't labeled it as sexist, but eventually that's how she'd revisited it. Perhaps she'd been wrong all these years. Maybe he'd wanted her to take him up on it because he'd had a thing for her but was too shy to proclaim it and then the moment passed.

She pawed through the stack, ripping open one envelope, scanning the script—skimming—and then the next.

*I followed her downtown last Saturday. She tried on wedding gowns. But you said she's not with you. So who's the guy?*

There was no guy. She just wanted to see what she would have looked like in bridal white. Had he seen her trying it on through the plate-glass window? She was glad she might have made him feel a charge of jealousy.

In another letter, he wrote,

*We're back together, A. and me. I'm setting up a way that we can keep the relationship under the radar and still communicate. It's crazy but it might work. You're the only friend, H., the only one who knows.*

Augusta thought of the tattered family flag with its old Rockwell crest of arms that she would pass up the flagpole when she wanted to arrange a dead-drop letter under the boardwalk at their agreed-upon spot.

He explained their years of clandestine visits, babies being born, and growing up.

*My God, if I'd known what it would feel like to hold a baby of my own—a brand-new baby—I might have given it all up before I started and got in too deep.*

She hadn't been enough but the babies were?

And then she got to the breakup.

*I'm gone, gone, gone,* he wrote. *I have nothing.*

But his nothingness didn't last. What followed was a detailed accounting of years of spying—not on the enemy, but on his own family.

He'd been to Esme's senior year winter choral program, some of her orchestra performances—*only third-chair clarinet, H., but she's damn good*—an art exhibit where she'd showcased ceramic vases. *I would have bought one but it wasn't allowed.*

He'd seen Liv in a geography bee. *She knew Tristan de Cunha. That kid is whip-smart.* He saw her play Emily in her high school production of *Our Town. Choked me up. I could barely stand it. It's how I've lived my life, H. I'm their ghost. Though they don't even know I'm here with them.*

He knew about Liv's relationship with that punk Teddy Whistler. Augusta had thrown herself into saving her daughter from that young criminal, and to shield Ru from all the ugliness, but there was no shielding either of the girls. Augusta was sure that something about Liv's relationship with Teddy turned her heart cold somehow, turned her against love. And then Ru had to go and make it all public! Augusta hated airing family issues in public.

And then, here, at the moment when Nick could have done some good, he wrote to Herc that he didn't worry about this kid. *No threat. My Liv has better sense. She's just trying to piss her mother off. Her method is effective.*

He was blaming Augusta? Good Lord.

Then she got to a letter he wrote about Esme's college applications—those Ivies he hated so much. *I took care of it. Nothing good comes of the heavy mantle of overachievers and that brand of elitism . . . I think she'll take the offer to go to UVA. It's really the best place for her.*

Did he interfere with Esme's college admissions? Did he have no boundaries?

She found a letter discussing Esme's college boyfriend, Darwin Webber. *He'd make a lousy husband. She's better off without . . . I think he'll be easy to convince . . .* Esme had been heartbroken for months, if not years.

He talked about vetting Esme's husband, Doug, and all three of Liv's husbands. Full background checks.

How dare he?

He attended Ru's graduation from eighth grade, giving a valedictorian speech on the space–time continuum and her first-round field hockey game in states, starting as a freshman, but little else.

She found a letter that simply said, *I've been found out. When I see you in person, I'll tell you the whole story, Herc. R. is just like her old man.*

Nick was found out by Ru? How? When? The letters weren't dated. Did she actually contact him?

She found a few mentions of Liv.

*I try to make her life sweeter. Small things. I don't know why she suffers.*

*I've given her an inheritance through a recently deceased neighbor she barely ever spoke to—surprising how little she questions the details of good things happening to her.*

And in a more recent letter from the last five years, he wrote of all the girls, *Sometimes I imagine showing up at their doors, but I'd never actually do it. Nothing good would come of it—not after all these years. They're no strangers to me. But I'm a stranger to them. That imbalance alone . . .*

She let the letter drift to the floor. She spread her hands wide on the bedspread and then gripped it tightly in two fists. She imagined him on her front stoop, young and tan from the summer of tennis on the clay courts, holding the box himself, his hands wide and sure.

And it was as if he'd been standing there all these years, waiting for her on the stoop.

He'd never gotten over her, never been able to let go of her or the girls.

*The girls.*

Should she tell them?

*Your lives,* she imagined saying to them, *have not been completely your own.*

"No," she said aloud. "He should do it himself. In person. The old bastard."

She walked to the little secretary's desk in the corner of her bedroom and scratched out a letter.

*Nick,*

*You need to come to the house. The girls are arriving. Get here soon. We need to settle things once and for all.*

*No one could really be that invested in kidnapping your children now! They're grown women, and certainly most of your enemies are dead or senile.*

She wasn't sure how to sign off. *Love?* That seemed overstated. *All my best?* That would be dishonest. She simply went with a basic *Sincerely.* She was certainly being sincere.

She folded the letter angrily, using her thumbnail to crease it, slipped it into an envelope with no outward markings, and wondered, momentarily, if she'd remember where to drop it. Then she worried if the drop location still existed. It could have been washed out by the hurricane.

Of course, the letters had stopped and Bill Huckley didn't know whether Nick was dead or alive. She could be trying to communicate with a ghost, but that had always been a fear. It was one she was used to.

She put the envelope in her pocketbook and walked downstairs and out the front door. She didn't lock it. The girls didn't have keys.

She marched to the boardwalk, and at the familiar spot, she walked down the wooden steps to the beach, took off her shoes, and set foot on sand for the first time in decades. She dipped under the boardwalk's slats. People clomped overhead, pulling their rolling coolers and dragging their rafts, clipping the light with their shadows.

She found the little cove in the back of the boardwalk—its red paint had faded to pink and some young punk had written SHERRI B. HAS LICE PANTIES over part of the mark, but it was enough to direct her to the familiar crevice.

She slipped the letter in and let her fingers grip the wood for a moment, as she used to long ago, and she remembered—quickly and viscerally—what it was like to miss Nick with her entire body, to feel dizzy and wrung out with longing. As awful as it was then, she missed the feeling now.

They never did have a wedding, but when Esme and Liv were still little and left behind in Jessamine's care for a weekend, she bought a wedding dress, changing on the bench seat of a rented car, and they drove out into West Virginia and rented horses at an old farm.

"We're newlyweds," Nick told the farmer.

"I can tell," the old man said. He looked at Augusta. "She shouldn't ride sidesaddle. It's not safe."

"I won't," Augusta said.

Augusta did ride with her veil on, though. It floated behind her. Out in the middle of a field of wildflowers, they exchanged vows they made up on the spot, ones she couldn't remember.

After that, they stopped at a bed-and-breakfast somewhere in

North Carolina, and for the first time in their lives Nick signed the registry as Mr. and Mrs. Nolan—a stolen name?

Later, after they had sex, Augusta took a drag from his cigarette and said, "Who are Mr. and Mrs. Nolan?" She expected it to be neighbors from his childhood or someone he'd always admired from politics.

"We are," he said, and then he whispered into her ear.

And now she pushed off the boardwalk's underpinnings and walked back into the full sun, which made her eyes flutter.

Nick Flemming. Did he think of her still? Miss her? Had he finally settled down with another woman? Could he be dead or senile—as Augusta had depicted his enemies?

What if the go-between was the dead one? Their dead-drop letter relied on a go-between.

She walked home, muttering things as she went. "Won't be long now . . . One way or another . . . I'll know by not hearing anything . . ."

When she got home, the house was still empty. She marched up the stairs and into her room.

Once there, for the first time in twenty-nine years, Augusta Rockwell went to her family's cedar chest that sat at the foot of her bed, lifted the lid, and unfolded the old, frayed Rockwell family flag.

She opened her bedroom window, thrust her upper body into the salty air, and, with great exertion, attached the flag to its rusty latches and let it snap in the wind.

Down below, two cars pulled up and parked in the narrow driveway, single file. Esme and Atty got out of the first car, a cane rocking chair strapped to the roof. Atty was holding a stack of ten Nancy Drew mysteries and wearing a fanny pack, which Augusta was sure that only old people and heavyset tourists wore these days.

They looked up at Augusta, who nodded to them.

Liv and Ru got out of the second car. Liv wore enormous sunglasses blocking out most of her face. Ru pulled her bag out of the backseat but then, as she looked up at the house, she dropped it on the lawn.

"Good God!" she said.

All of the women looked at her and said, "What?"

"Holy shit," Ru said. "The old spy. You're calling him in."

Esme, Liv, and Atty didn't understand what she meant, but Augusta did, of course. "Yes," she said. "How'd you know?" She also meant—*What* do you know? How long have you known it? And how did you find out?

But Ru took the question literally. "The flag," she said, pointing at it. "Obviously."

# Part Three

*In which Augusta arranges for the reemergence of the truth.*

# CHAPTER 11

As the oldest Rockwell daughter, Esme felt a livid spasm in her chest that made her blush; she was angry at Ru for knowing something she didn't. *The flag, obviously.* What was obvious about the tattered relic of the Rockwells' glory days in commercial fishing, munitions, and banking, and what could it possibly have to do with their fabled father? Being the oldest came with responsibility, overwrought scrutiny, and pressure; the only upside was that eventually you could know things the younger siblings couldn't, things you were supposed to protect them from. Ru was always screwing that up. Even as a little kid, she walked around with her ears popped out like satellite dishes, gathering data that clearly didn't belong to her, as if pretending to be part spy herself.

Their father wasn't a spy.

They had no real father.

Their mother was a woman who'd wanted kids but was too off-kilter to handle marriage.

The old spy was an ancient invention, one that proved Augusta's limited imagination, to be honest.

Ingmar barked from the screen door — again, Augusta didn't appreciate what she perceived as an outburst of the dog's masculinity.

Augusta told her daughters to get inside. "For God's sake," she added, "let's not air this on the front lawn!"

The three sisters and Atty took their seats around the kitchen table with Augusta standing in front of the sink, all thick shoulders and long imperious neck. And Ingmar padded around them, nervously, the way he often did before a thunderstorm.

Augusta faced them, prepared to explain something—something that Ru already knew. Was their mother going to trot out the old lies and was Ru going to support her?

"Jesus," Esme said, "just spit it out." Her anger now felt inextricably stitched to some old instinctive fear—about lying mothers or unknowable fathers?

"I kind of like the overt drama," Liv said.

"You would," Esme said. It wasn't a nice thing to say but Esme wasn't feeling nice. She felt like she was about to be attacked, and the year had offered enough unpredictability—on the boarding school's playing fields, in the mahogany halls, at dinner parties, endlessly. Plus, Liv had been living such an overtly dramatic life that it seemed like she was purposefully trying to live in opposition to Esme's decisions, which, until recently, had seemed safe and responsible. Liv's dramatic lifestyle had felt like a judgment on Esme's practical one.

Liv was annoyed by Esme's impatience. Liv had always been prettier than Esme, and Liv was sure Esme couldn't ever really get over a slight genetic injustice like that. And so Liv had spent much of her life giving Esme a wide emotional berth because of it. She was sick of it now. Her mother deserved a little attention. The girls hadn't been doting daughters. Case in point, Liv wasn't sure what her mother was going to say, but she also didn't really care. Fairly well medicated at the moment, she looked at her mother as if she were made of soap bubbles. Sweet smelling, but ultimately fragile. She thought, *My mother is poppable.* "Just let her have her moment," Liv told Esme.

Ru was silent and wide-eyed. She'd given up on the idea that this moment would ever come, so she was surprised that it had arrived with such little fanfare.

"I'm not going to have a moment," Augusta said. "*You* are."

"Me?" Atty said. Augusta's eyes had been scanning but had accidentally fallen on Atty right at the end of her sentence. Atty was still holding the Nancy Drew books in her lap. She was confused and a little gleeful. Atty's mother had told her stories of her unconventional childhood and Atty knew she was about to see some kind of performative event. She'd gone to an experimental play in New York City with her drama class a few months earlier, where they were allowed to walk from room to room, scene to scene, and interact with the actors. She'd kissed a man's shoulder in a dark hallway. He hadn't been an actor after all, but he kissed her back on the mouth, and it was a strange moment of groping that Atty had never been privy to before. She'd tweeted, *Immersive theater just got handsy. #Idontkissandtell.* Before her father's affair, she hadn't been the type to get invited to the orgies that took place on campus, but after, imbued with a collateral air of illicit sexiness, she had what turned out to be an audition, one that had gone incredibly badly, and which she'd recently decided was the origin point for her downward spiral.

"Not *you*, Atty," Esme said. "You're not going to have a moment. She meant *us*. The girls." She and her sisters would always be *the girls*. Esme said this in an attempt to relieve her daughter but Atty looked a little disappointed. Esme just wanted this to all be over with. "Go on, Mom. Please." She sounded whiny and childish, and hated how these family get-togethers always seemed to make her regress.

Augusta clapped her hands together. "Fine. Yes. Your father. I know I've stopped talking about him altogether. I thought that might be best. But a man came to the door today. Something's been churned up by the hurricane. A box of letters. His father was a friend of your father's and so this up-churning happened in a basement." It was oddly formal but disconnected, as if she'd practiced some version of a speech and was telling it out of order.

"The hurricane," Ru said with quiet astonishment. This is what it had taken—a brutal act of nature—to get to the truth.

"Correct, Ru. The hurricane," Augusta said. "And your father had been writing this friend all these years. Your father and I were never married and so we never really divorced, but we stopped seeing each other in 1984."

"Wait," Liv said. "You're a divorcée?"

Augusta nodded. "In a way, yes. We have that in common."

Esme shook her head. "That's the thing that's most impressed you so far with this story? That she's a divorcée who was never actually married?"

"Oh, I like all of it," Liv said. "What's not to like?"

"What's not to like?" Esme said. "It's delusional. It makes no sense." She turned to her mother. "Are you going to get to the part where you tell us he was *a spy*?"

Augusta sat down at the kitchen table and pursed her lips.

Ru feared her mother was retreating, and so she jumped in. "He was a spy," Ru said flatly. "He was. People are spies, you know. It is an actual occupation and there are those, in reality, who do the work. CIA, NSA, FBI. These aren't just organizations made up by the entertainment industry."

Atty piped up, "Alicia Spitz's dad is in the CIA." She went ignored.

"How would you know anything about our alleged father?" Esme said.

"Yeah," Liv said, rubbing balm from a metal tin onto her lips. "Why are you saying things like this, Ru? I mean, where's this coming from?"

Augusta knit her hands together. "How *do* you know about the flag, dear? I've never told anyone about the flag."

Ru stood up, walked to the cupboard, and pulled out a small

juice glass. "Not one of you, not one, ever asked me where I went. Not one!" She was surprised how quickly the anger flared.

"You went to Vietnam," Esme said. "You told us."

Ru spun around. "No! I was sixteen years old and gone for three days—three whole days—before you even realized I was gone."

Liv laughed. "I know. Right? Three days. That's *hilarious*. I mean, that is *classic* Ru's Poos. It would only happen to her."

"*Classic* Ru's Poos," Atty said, wagging her head—obviously familiar with the phrase.

"What do you mean? *Classic Ru's Poos*? What the hell?" Ru said. "Is that something you say behind my back?"

"No, dear," Augusta said quickly. "I'm sure that's something they've said to your face. It's a full-family joke. Isn't it, Esme?"

"It is. Absolutely. I mean, we started saying that when you were really little."

"I remember you two saying that one time when I was like thirteen and we were playing Risk, but I cried and you swore you'd never say it again."

Esme looked at Liv, who then nodded. "That might have been when the saying went underground, but you do these classic Ru's Poos things. And our hands are tied."

"Screw you, Liv! At least my classic moves don't land me in rehab." On the car ride home, Ru had pieced together that the spa that Liv was raving about wasn't really a spa.

"Don't attack Liv!" Esme shouted. "That's not a fair fight."

"Oh, because I've hit a low point, Esme? Like I'm the one made of dish soap bubbles?" Liv said. "And I'm just going to pop to death if I have to take a jab?"

"That's not what I meant!" Esme said. "I was sticking up for you!"

"By putting her down!" Ru countered.

Atty's heart was skittering in her chest. She put the Nancy Drews on the ground just in case this got physical. She wanted to be ready to participate.

"Is this because I pooped in a shoe once as a two-year-old?" Ru said, holding her head with both hands.

"We've seen you poop in a shoe. All of us. Me, Esme, Augusta, and even Jessamine. We saw it."

"If you pay attention to the rest of the story," Ru said, stiffening, "you'll recall that I really only had one accident."

"I think it's the image that just sticks with you," Esme said.

"It's kind of a first impression," Atty added—as if Ru needed more people lining up against her. "And first impressions are important."

"Basically, I could win a Nobel and this is the way you'd think of me, still, as a shoe-pooper."

Liv raised her eyebrows and froze for a moment. "Really?" she snorted. "Now you're going to win a Nobel?"

"Screw you!" Ru said.

Augusta raised her hands in the air and shouted, "Enough! Enough! Enough!"

The kitchen fell silent.

There were some short sighs, huffy breaths, the scrape of a chair against the floor as Ru took a seat, pulled back from the table, holding her empty juice glass.

"We made light of your disappearance because it was a horror. We joked because the love and fear we felt overwhelmed us. And we believed you when we found the note you wrote that you'd come back soon!" Augusta sometimes relied on the tenets of the old lost Personal Honesty Movement, by offering many simple statements in a row.

"I looked him up," Ru said.

"Who?" Liv asked.

"Our father."

"You looked him up?" Esme said.

Augusta was stunned. "And you found him?"

"Yes."

"Where?" Liv asked.

"In Guadeloupe."

"You made it to Guadeloupe?" Augusta said. "You didn't have a passport, did you? That's international travel!" Augusta seemed retro-actively terrified.

Ru didn't want to bog down in details right now. "I found him and we talked in a bar. He's real."

"Our actual father," Esme said aloud—half question, half state-ment.

"And you never told us?" Liv asked.

"You didn't ever ask where I'd gone!" Ru said, trying to keep calm.

"Right," Liv said, and she sat back. "I get that. We didn't deserve to know."

"Right," Ru said, relieved.

"Nineteen ninety-two," Esme said, doing the quick math.

"How did he look?" Augusta said, a little defensively, as if she might have wanted him to look forlorn and lost without her.

"Like a middle-aged man," Ru said.

"I don't even know his name. What's his name?" Esme asked.

"Nick Flemming," Ru said.

Esme glanced at her mother for confirmation.

Augusta nodded.

"What was he wearing? Did he know you'd been hunting him down? What did you talk about?" Esme asked.

"We talked about the past, about his relationship with Mom, about his regrets and failings."

Liv stared at her mother. "Wait. You had three children with this man. Not just one or two but *three* full children."

Augusta sighed. "It's a long story. You don't have to understand it. In fact, I don't expect anyone to ever understand it."

Esme pounded the table. "Ru! What happened? What *really* happened?"

Ru lined up the salt and pepper shakers. "I asked him to leave my life alone."

"What do you mean—leave your life alone?" Liv asked.

"He'd abandoned us," Esme said, and then she knew why she'd decided he didn't really exist. If her mother had invented a fake father for them—a supposed spy, no less!—she didn't have to deal with the fact that either one or three men had, in fact, abandoned the Rockwell girls. In her personal narrative, Esme's mother had, most likely, seduced men from good stock, gotten pregnant, and never informed the fathers. Esme's abandonment issues were pristine—it was as if they'd been there all along, just like this box of letters that bobbed up from some basement during the hurricane—and now someone was taking off the lid. She could feel herself reprocessing being abandoned by her husband—as if it hadn't been painful enough. The problem wasn't that her mother was delusional or simply that her husband had some sort of breakdown. It was that she, Esme, was *ultimately* abandonable. "Our father had already clearly left our lives alone!" She rubbed her ears. Her own voice sounded muffled in her head. "Am I shrieking?"

Ru wasn't sure what her mother knew, what she was willing to admit, how far this conversation was going to go. "It's your turn," she said to her mother.

Augusta tried to smile. She lifted one hand as if about to offer a benediction. "It turns out, your father never really abandoned you girls at all. He's been very . . . involved in your lives." Her expression shifted then. The smile faded. Her voice tightened. "Your lives aren't completely your own."

CHAPTER *12*

Over the course of Ru Rockwell's sixteenth summer, she devoted herself to learning the outdated communication methods of spies. If her father was a spy—and that's really all she knew about him, true or false, so she had to begin there—and he had, in fact, sired three children with the same woman, Augusta Rockwell—who may or may not have had intimacy issues (only Esme seemed to give a crap about that)—then her father and her mother had to have stayed in touch, in some manner, for at least fifteen years. If the first child was conceived in the spring of 1969, as indicated by Esme's date of birth, then that's when the spy would have set up some method of communication that Augusta would have learned to put into practice.

At sixteen, Ru was leggy and tan. Doing touristy things was thought beneath most of the year-rounders and the Rockwells in particular—but she was a secret beach reader. She flopped on her towel in her bikini, hauling her books to the beach in a cooler, to keep them from collecting too much sand.

By this point, Esme was already married to Doug, and Liv was pretending to be a socialite in New York City while generally snorting too much coke. Ru was the only one left at home with Augusta, who was distracted with her peculiar buckshot brand of activism. They were both lonesome, Augusta and Ru, but they were also wary of bonding too much at this point; Ru would be off at college in two short years. What was the point?

Ru bailed on field hockey summer camp with her team—where she was the highest-scoring forward—claiming shin splints. This allowed her to spend her days in the dusty stacks of the Ocean City Public Library and haul said books to the beach in her cooler.

She wasn't sure if her mother had gotten involved with an old spy or a young spy, but in any case, any spy of her mother's generation likely would have been involved in Vietnam, if not having been embedded at some point early in his career. William Colby, who would become the infamous head of the CIA post-Watergate and mid–CIA scandal—oh, the wiretapping of US citizens, assassinations, hidden prisons for suspected double agents, mind-control experiments on unwitting test subjects, et cetera—was already living in Vietnam by 1959 and out by 1962, at which point he oversaw the war from afar. In 1961, the year her mother first arrived in Washington, DC, and the earliest moment she likely would have met a young, even still-aspiring spy, things were about to get very messy, and by 1969, during Esme's conception, things had only gotten worse.

At one point, on the beach, Ru looked up from her book to see some children putting crackers on the bare pink chest of their father who was dead asleep. The kids then backed away and, as the seagulls swooped in, batting around the man's head, eating the crackers from his chest, the man woke up, terrified, flailing wildly, and screaming.

She imagined her own father—cool and collected—a man who had the foresight not to want to get married and raise a family as a spy. Despite the Cold War's supposed code of ethics not to kill a spy's family members, he might have opted not to have a secret profession kept from his family, but a secret family kept from his profession. This made sense to her.

Eventually, she uncovered the most likely method of communication for her father's era—the dead drop. It was a standard method by which two parties—not ever having to meet in person—could arrange for a letter of some sort to be dropped at a location. The place would have been agreed upon. A sign would go out that the communication was ready for pickup. The book gave specifics on the kind of signs that might work, one of which was a brightly colored towel draped over a balcony railing.

This, of course, made Ru think of the Rockwell flag. Her mother would clip it to the flagpole throughout Ru's early childhood with no seeming rhyme or reason. She might fly it during a rainstorm or the dead of winter.

And then she stopped flying the flag altogether.

Ru thought about when she might have last seen the flag. Her eidetic memory helped her isolate an approximate date—around Christmas 1984, just months before her mother founded The Personal Honesty Movement, which, for Ru, stood out as crucial—especially to a woman who had a husband of some sort whom she couldn't talk about, a woman forced to keep secrets. And after the movement's quick demise, there was that one summer day in 1985 when Augusta taught her daughters to conduct a storm—set to Berlioz's *Symphonie Fantastique*—and Esme accused her of sleeping with strangers. That was the last time Augusta ever spoke of their father. Her silence was read by Esme as vindication. Liv was more interested in the lives of other families than figuring out her own. But Ru held that strange argument in her mind forever. It couldn't be erased. It was loaded like a steamer trunk.

Sitting on the beach, Ru wondered what would happen if she flew the flag now.

Surely her father or his local sub-spy would have given up looking for it after seven long years.

Still, it was a valid question.

She also thought that there could be a dead-drop location packed full of communications that her mother refused to pick up.

And too, she was smart enough to consider that her father was dead.

She questioned Jessamine, of course, but the woman was a vault or knew nothing.

Ru asked her mother if she could fly the Rockwell flag for her upcoming birthday.

"Why on earth?" her mother said and then added, "It's lost. I haven't seen it in years."

But while her mother was out one afternoon, Ru snooped through her mother's bedroom and found the flag in three minutes, folded neatly in a cedar chest at the foot of her mother's bed.

Ru left the flag there and walked to the third floor. She opened the window closest to the flagpole and leaned out into the salty wind. How many windows in other homes had a view of this flag? Her father had to have gone local with his pick for a go-between. In fact, using local culture to create alliances (and rout out the enemy) had been fundamental to the approach in the Vietnam War, as Ru had read.

She made a map of every house with a view of the flag, and then, one by one, she got to know the neighbors as well as she could.

It only took her two weeks—eating pastrami, playing canasta, gossiping, babysitting twin two-year-olds, applying eyedrops to an aged schnauzer—to zero in on Virgil Pedestro. He was the grown son of a widow who lived across the street and two doors down. The Pedestros were year-rounders, and, like the Rockwells, inheritors of their house on Asbury Avenue. Virgil was quiet and stoic. One eye was slightly droopy, and maybe this was what made him a bit shy. He might have been gay, but that could only be considered vaguely by Ru. Being gay was still relatively covert and remarkable back then. If one was not bold enough to make it to a big city, gayness might make one hole up in one's parents' home.

If her father had dirt on Virgil, he'd likely agree to almost anything.

Shortly thereafter, on a Thursday in early August, her mother went to put up flyers about her latest movement, The Inner Identity Movement, and Jessamine had gone to the butchers. Ru flew the flag.

Augusta didn't notice it on her return. But while trying to fall asleep with the windows open, she heard the rumpled rattling. She got out of bed, looked out the window, and stared at the flag. She stayed like that for a moment and then called Ru's name.

Ru shuffled in, pretending to have been asleep, but really she'd been watching the Pedestro home through a pair of binoculars.

"Did you put the flag out?" Augusta asked her.

"Do you think someone else did it?" Ru countered.

Her mother stared at her sharply. "Why would I think that?" Ru was sure that her mother had, for a brief moment, wondered if her spy had somehow snuck in and done it himself.

"I don't know. Why *would* you think that?"

"I didn't! *You* did!" She pointed out the window. "Take it down."

"Why? I like it. It shows pride in our ancestors."

"It's a fake crest! They just made it up!"

"All crests are made up by someone at some point in time, though, right? They are man-made."

"Take it down now!"

Ru obliged.

But the flag seemingly did the trick. Later that night, Virgil Pedestro walked out of his house wearing salmon shorts, a blue blazer, and boat shoes, and Ru followed him three blocks to the back door of a squat bungalow with its curtains drawn.

Ru wasn't sure what to do now. She'd expected Virgil to check a hiding place—somewhere nooky and private—where one could hide a letter, and that she'd never have to confront him at all. She'd brought a letter with her—one that she would plant in the hiding place later, after fishing around for letters from her father.

But then the drawn curtains of the bungalow lit up, just for an instant. It happened again and again, drawing Ru from her hiding spot, closer to the house. It was happening so quickly that Ru imagined her father was inside being tortured by electrocution. She'd read about such things. Of course, it couldn't be her father, but still she felt strangely responsible—as the sole witness—and so she ran to the back door, knocked loudly, then jerked the knob. The door was unlocked. It flew open.

And Ru found that she'd flung herself into a bedroom—a woman in a red satin teddy was on the bed, and Virgil, wearing *only* his blue blazer—the salmon shorts and polo shirt and boat shoes were stacked on a dresser—was standing behind a tripod with a camera, pointed at the bed.

This was the first live and in-person penis Ru had ever seen and the head of it reminded her, briefly, of the head of a Ken doll, possibly airless and surely rubbery.

"Good God!" Virgil shouted.

"I'm so sorry!" Ru said. "I thought this was about something else."

"Aren't you one of the Rockwell girls?" Virgil asked.

"No!" Ru said. "I'm not a Rockwell."

"You are too," Virgil said.

"What's a Rockwell girl?" the nude woman said, as if insulted that she wasn't a Rockwell girl.

Ru turned and ran from the room stunned that she'd seen Virgil Pedestro's penis, standing at full attention.

She jogged home, but once she got to her street, she saw Virgil's mother pulling into the driveway. She'd been out and now she was back.

Ru watched Mrs. Pedestro scurry up the walkway to her house.

Mrs. Pedestro looked up at Ru, standing in the full glow of a streetlight. Mrs. Pedestro stopped, arms crossed on her thin ribs. She glanced at the empty flagpole and then back at Ru.

That was all it took. It wasn't Virgil. It was his mother.

Ru pulled the letter from her pocket, walked up to Mrs. Pedestro, and without a word she handed her the letter and then ran the rest of the way home.

The letter was bold in the way that sixteen-year-olds who are overly smart can be overly bold.

She addressed her father this way—Dear Father—and she announced that she was his daughter, Ru Rockwell, and that she knew about his secret life. She told him that she wanted to meet. She gave a date that was two weeks away and a location: the Cathédrale Notre-Dame-de-Guadeloupe de Basse-Terre on the island of Guadeloupe.

Why?

Well, first of all, she had low expectations that she'd ever communicate with her father. She was also pretty sure he was dead. And if, by some miracle, she did get a message to him, she wanted to seem worldly. Why not offer to meet him in the French West Indies?

Her choice did have one thing going for it. Her friend Jenni Howell had gone on a Caribbean cruise, and because it began and ended in Atlantic City, no passport was necessary.

Two days after Ru gave her letter to Mrs. Pedestro while mainly trying to recover from the sight of Virgil Pedestro in nothing but a blue blazer, Mrs. Pedestro showed up at the door and asked Augusta if Ru could do some weeding for her.

Ru weeded for two and a half hours.

Mrs. Pedestro paid her a little over minimum wage for her efforts and, as she handed her the money, she simply said, "It is agreed."

Ru put the money in her pocket but didn't react. She was trying to be coy.

Mrs. Pedestro, who was never much of a go-between to begin with, said, "Did you hear me?"

Ru nodded.

"You'll like him," Mrs. Pedestro added.

"Thanks," Ru said.

Coincidentally, Liv and Esme were visiting at this point. Doug was on a golf weekend with college friends, and Liv's apartment was being fumigated.

Ru packed a duffel bag and put a note on the side of the fridge where the family often communicated shopping needs, mainly toiletries and feminine products.

The note told them not to worry. She'd be fine and back in less than a month.

No one saw the note and so began the now infamous three days of her unnoticed absence, followed by eighteen days of Esme, Liv, Augusta, and Jessamine's fear and anxiety set to a strange background noise of quiet confidence. Ru would be fine. She'd said so.

# CHAPTER 13

Augusta doled out the news. She hadn't planned to and she wasn't ready, but she never really would be.

"The box of letters from your father to Herc Huckley over the course of many decades shows that he was actually present for many events in your lives—a combination of graduations, plays, choral concerts, athletic events, even a wedding or two." She glanced at Esme and Liv.

"Which weddings?" Liv asked.

"Esme's first and your second, at least."

"Holy crap!" Atty said. "What about me?"

Augusta nodded. "He was at that multicultural pageant where you danced like a Japanese person with an umbrella."

"I was a wisteria maiden," Atty said.

"He was there?" Esme's eyes teared up.

"I don't know why he chose to come to that event in particular," Augusta said, obviously disappointed.

"That one girl, Sadie Worthaus, was always spinning her umbrella the wrong way," Atty said. "I was actually pretty good."

Ingmar was still roaming anxiously. "Sit!" Esme shouted at the dog. "Sit!"

For a moment Ru thought her sister was yelling at her and she almost shouted back, *I am sitting!* but then stopped herself, realizing her sister was ordering around her dog.

"There's a larger point here," Liv said flatly to Atty. "I want to know what my mother means by the phrase *our lives aren't our own.*"

"And the words *very involved in our lives,*" Esme said.

They all looked at Augusta, even Ru, whose reconnaissance didn't reach this far. "It seems he respected your request," Augusta said to Ru.

"It wasn't a request as much as it was an ultimatum," Ru said. "All-in, full transparency. Or out. For good."

Augusta was stunned by this confession. Her daughter had put this to Nick at age sixteen? It had taken Augusta nearly two decades to get there.

"What about me?" Esme said. "And Liv?"

Augusta turned to Liv. Hers was easier news to deliver. "He gave you gifts," she said.

"Gifts?"

"Well, scholarships and contest winnings and that little windfall from the woman in your building who died and you didn't even remember her."

"Like in the game of Life, bank error in your favor," Atty said. She wanted to tweet this very badly—and a bunch of other one-liners—but she was too afraid she'd miss something genius in the process.

"Jesus H. Christ," Liv said. "Do you mean to say that I'm *not* lucky? I've been just . . . coddled?"

"You're lucky to have been coddled," Atty said. "That's true of white privilege everywhere."

"Don't give me your boarding school regurgitation right now, Atty, okay?" Liv said. "I'm the only one here who's also been educated in one of those elitist prisons, and I know what's what."

"God. Fine!" Atty said. "I was just trying to help."

Liv stood up. "I'm going to go smoke three cigarettes," she said, and she walked toward the back door that led to the small stone patio. Ingmar got up and followed her as if he wanted to smoke too.

"Don't you want to know what he did to me?" Esme asked her sister.

"Not really," Liv said.

"Liv," Ru said. "Just stay."

Liv stopped by the back door and fumbled through her pocketbook for her pack of cigarettes and lighter. "Okay. Go ahead."

Augusta put her elbows on the kitchen table and then let her fists drop, not with anger, only a kind of exhaustion. "Well, it turns out you might have gotten into some Ivies," she said to Esme, "if not for your father's interference."

"What?" Esme said.

"Your father doesn't like Ivy League educations. He thinks they breed overbreeding and an overly inflated sense of self."

"I knew it!" Esme said. "I knew I was good enough for those schools!" She felt vindicated, almost gleeful. "See, Atty! I always told you that it didn't make sense!" She wanted to call Doug and Big-Head Todd and a number of teachers at the boarding school, including Little-Head Todd, who'd gone to Princeton and wore its gear relentlessly. It took a few seconds for her to realize that she'd missed the Ivy League education itself. That it was gone, forever. Her face went a little slack as the realization washed over her.

"And he might not have liked all of your choices in boyfriends," Augusta said.

"Excuse me?" Esme said.

"He liked Doug," Augusta said. "He ran checks on him and his family. And he approved. Wholeheartedly, it seems. But . . ."

"Who didn't he like?" Esme asked, but she knew.

Darwin Webber.

The way he'd disappeared not only from Esme's life but also his own. Just, one day, gone. Esme had been wrecked by the news. She'd come home and missed classes for two weeks. Her mother told the school that Esme had a form of mono.

Liv looked at Ru and shook her head, trying to telegraph to Ru to stop Augusta. Ru was closer. She could reach out and cover their mother's mouth.

But Ru was stricken too. She muttered, "No. Don't."

It was too late. Esme stood up so fast that the kitchen chair kicked out behind her and fell backward, slapping the floor.

"Who was it?" Atty asked.

Esme's sisters were eyeing her with such pity and fear that they confirmed it. "Was it because he was black?"

"Was he black?" Augusta said. "I thought he was German."

"He was of African descent, somewhere in the mix, I think," Ru said. "But also German."

"He wore really brightly colored polo shirts," Liv said, apropos of nothing.

"What *boyfriend*? Who are we *talking* about?" Atty said.

"No one you know," Esme said and walked to the doorjamb leading to the dining room. She steadied herself and then pushed off, away from them, reeling.

CHAPTER *14*

Augusta said, "I've learned that when grief is kept to yourself, it expands. If it were a dog, I would take the dog out on a leash and walk it around the neighborhood and people would pet it or scold it for eliminating where it shouldn't. But grief isn't a dog and I couldn't share mine and it just got bigger and bigger inside of me, like it was forcibly pushing my other organs around. It applied so much pressure to my lungs, my breathing went shallow. I could only eat little tiny meals because my stomach felt flattened against some other interior organ. It was all too much. I thought that if I called it off, the grief would go away, but it didn't."

Liv had gone out the back door to smoke.

Esme had stumbled from the kitchen, her shoes clomping on the stairs slowly as if she were climbing a steep rocky precipice.

Ru wasn't listening. She wanted to follow one of her sisters, but she wasn't sure which one would want to be followed at the moment. She felt culpable. Maybe she hadn't told them because she'd been trying to protect them. But she hadn't protected them. She'd asked for her own freedom from her father's interference when she should have negotiated a deal for all of them.

Atty was still in the kitchen, rubbing Ingmar's congenitally compromised hips. "I get that," she said to Augusta. "I know something about grief—what with my father's indiscretion."

"My grief was about loving someone you can't actually be with, someone you can't even acknowledge."

"Our griefs have a lot in common then," Atty said.

Augusta was startled. She had shared her grief and Atty had accepted it as a recognizable version of her own. Easing up, that's what she felt.

Easing.


Liv stood on the back patio, still holding an unlit cigarette. She'd blamed much of her life's failings, her personal weaknesses, her inability to want things that other people wanted and to attain them in honest ways, on her father's absence.

Even smoking. She'd always thought she wouldn't have been a smoker if she'd had a real father.

But, well, shit. Turned out she'd had a real father and he gave her gifts. He actually made her life easier. But this upended the things that she'd used to build the foundation of her life. If the universe didn't love her and her father did, it meant that—in one fell swoop—she was vulnerable in the world because her luck was no longer a shield, and she'd lost her scapegoat.

She looked at the cigarette then she lit it and for the first time in her life, she wondered if she didn't have anyone to blame but herself.


Upstairs, Esme lay down in her canopy bed and stared up at the metal framework. She could smell Liv's cigarette smoke through the screened window. She wished that Ingmar weren't so suspicious of stairs and were the type to jump on a bed and snuggle with her. Why couldn't he be more like Lassie, an archetype of American dog-heroism? It's why she'd been drawn to collies to begin with.

She thought of Doug and for no reason she could negotiate, she missed his body, his broad calves and thighs and then dainty knees like doorknobs on a house from the colonial era. She missed his chest, only lightly furred, and his hunched shoulders, as if bent to create a curtain of his shirt in order to hide his subtle paunch. It was a pretty strong yet humble body. She wanted to curl up next to him and punch the soft dough of that paunch, knee him sharply in the groin . . .

And she wanted to whisper to him that she'd loved him, but she'd loved Darwin Webber more, and so, in a way, she'd cheated on Doug in spirit before he ever cheated on her in reality because she didn't even head into their marriage with the kind of love she knew she was capable of.

Her father was worse than she'd thought. He was worse than the idea of her mother having sex with strangers. He was worse than abandonment too. He'd ruined her life.

And she thought of finding him and yelling at him in public — perhaps on a putt-putt golf course. Augusta would never have allowed something as touristy as putt-putt golf — the Rockwell girls were already too vicious for croquet; what would happen with an audience? — but surely a dad would have insisted on putt-putt, maybe even annually.

And then she only thought of Darwin Webber as she last saw him — running toward her after a game of pickup soccer, popping the ball toward her but catching it in his locked elbows. A trick.

And then he was gone.

Never even a blip on the Internet. No data. Nothing.

What had her father done to him? Where was Darwin Webber now? What had become of his life? What would become of all of their lives now that they knew the truth?

# Part Four

*In which the old spy returns.*

CHAPTER *15*

Ru's book signing wasn't held at a bookstore after all. It was a book talk at the local library where Ru had once spent a summer checking out books about espionage.

When Maska Gravitz called to tell her about the venue—just hours after Augusta had come clean about Ru's father—she pretended to have misspoken. "Did I say bookstore? No, no. I meant the gig was in a library. In French, the word for 'bookstore' is something like *library*."

"Really?" Ru said. "*That* was the confusion."

Gravitz only gave her a two-day lead-up to the event. "So you don't have time to make an escape plan." She was referring to her months in Vietnam, which had entailed calling off three highly visible readings, one of which came with an award of some kind.

"I'm not making any escape plans," she said and she meant it. She was tired. She had family to deal with. They'd all been struck by the news and were walking around with unusual politeness. She was bracing herself for the real reaction—a blowup of some sort.

"Remember to be nice to the people," Maska said.

"I'm always nice to people," Ru said.

"Yes, but don't slouch. Don't look so pained by it all."

"Right. Okay. I'll try not to."

As indebted as Ru was to libraries—they had allowed her to track down her father—she found the talks she gave in them were usually poorly attended and, although she hated herself for it, libraries sometimes made her feel like a stripper wearing a bikini on a beach—giving away for free what she hoped to sell in order to make a living. Then again, she felt conflicted in bookstores, too, which sometimes felt like visiting an animal shelter—all those books gazing at you with sad doggy eyes; you can't save them all, and you know what's going to happen to them.

She was conflicted about her career in *most* ways. She felt guilty about killing trees and about the exploitative mining process necessary to make wiring for e-readers. She didn't like criticism—who does?—but she also found praise paralyzing. If a bookstore had a lot of copies of her books, she assumed they couldn't move them, and if they had too few, she assumed they hadn't ordered many to begin with. She got nervous about a reading only after it was over, but the nervousness was the physical sensation of her bones wanting to get out of her body. Sometimes she threw up.

All in all, publishing a book felt like an exercise in public failure even when it seemed like a success. Ru's editor, Hanby Popper, though delighted by Ru's success, had said—more than once—that they just couldn't figure out why the books hadn't sold 20 percent more. And the look-at-me that authorship demanded made her feel like both hawker and product, both pimp and whore. There was no deeper sense of self-loathing for Ru than sitting behind a table, trying to talk people into buying a book she'd written. More than once, a bookstore didn't really advertise she was coming and no one showed up so she'd left her post and, being mistaken for store personnel, had walked people around the aisles, making fun of her own book and suggesting others instead.

No matter how well things were going, she was self-assured about only one thing—the persistent and, by now, comforting sense of her own personal failure.

It was raining. Ru and Atty left their umbrellas propped in the lobby of the library with the other umbrellas, all pooling. Atty had insisted they stop by an antiques/secondhand shop on the way there to see if they had any new arrivals of old Nancy Drews. The woman behind the counter knew Atty well, and had set aside twelve books—not first editions and not mint condition, but still the old-fashioned hardbacks that Ru remembered from her youth. Atty found five that were missing from the collection she was restoring.

"How many more until you have the complete set?" Ru asked.

"I'm only missing twenty-four through twenty-six, forty-eight, forty-nine, and seventeen."

She paid for the books from a wallet kept in a black fanny pack hooked around her waist. The fanny pack was inexplicable on a girl Atty's age, but Ru let it go.

Atty was the only one to come with her. Liv had bowed out: "I've heard you speak a million times."

"I don't remember you ever coming to a reading I've given," Ru said.

"No, but you've been speaking all your life. I mean, am I going to hear something new?"

Esme shrugged off the invite and ate ice cream straight from a Häagen-Dazs container, and Augusta pulled Ru aside. "I'm keeping an eye on everyone," she said. "Otherwise I'd be there."

Atty invited Jessamine, who was yanking the plastic bag of innards from the cavity of a chicken she intended to roast. "Me?" she said. "Oh, no. I couldn't." Ru assumed that she meant that it would break some rule she and Augusta had set up ages ago in order to create a healthy necessary distance.

Ru saw small announcements of her reading, photocopies taped up on the library's various bulletin boards. They each had thumbnails of the movie poster, not her book, and an old photo of Ru, staring into a small fishbowl—a shot that Maska Gravitz told her would be memorable. "Gary Shteyngart has that photo of him with that bear on a leash. So bears are out and hard to acquire anyway. I looked into your typical big cats too—tigers, lions, leopards. All kinds of permits required by state law. But a fish—who doesn't like a fish?"

Ru didn't recognize any of the staff.

But as the woman running the event ushered her through the stacks to the place where she was going to read, the smells brought back full-body memory. Ru's memory was so precise, this rush made her feel off-kilter. Her breathing ran shallow.

"Excuse me," she said. "Just a minute." She veered down an aisle and then took another turn and found herself in a nonfiction section where she'd spent hours uncovering books on the CIA, FBI, NSA, and international espionage. She recognized certain spines but didn't touch them. She just breathed the dusty air.

"The reading's going to be held in one of our discussion rooms," the librarian added.

"Right," Ru said. To get to Guadeloupe, she'd talked a guy in a cruise ship band into letting her tag along as a kind of roadie. The targets of his impersonations ranged from Elvis to Hall, but not Oates. She fooled around with him naked in his bunk, trying to erase the image of Virgil Pedestro's penis as the sole penis she'd ever seen live.

She arrived in Guadeloupe two days before she was to meet her father and staked out the bar and its environs. It was possible that her father was already in town too, but she had no way to recognize him.

When the time came, she did recognize him, of course.

He was the white guy in the back corner, facing the door, and as she got closer she saw that he was wearing a pin sold at the concession stands of her private high school.

She walked to his table, sat down, and pointed at the pin. "Is that some kind of a joke?"

"No," he said. "Of course not. How could it be a joke?" He recounted a few of her field hockey matches with exacting detail. He was proud of her and eventually he said, "I'm impressed, Ru. I mean, you're a lot like me, you know? Tracking down a mystery, seeking adventure. I wouldn't pursue it as a career. That would be my bit of advice, if you don't mind." He kept sweeping the place casually with his eyes, the habit of a spy.

"I do mind. I mind a lot," Ru said. "Don't come to my field hockey games anymore unless you tell me you're there. Don't act like my father unless you're willing to announce it. You're either in my life with full transparency. Or out. For good. Okay?" She was fierce for her age or maybe because of it.

"I can't be fully in, Ru. That ship has sailed."

"Then stay out. Completely."

He agreed.

Augusta would know all about this trip if she'd read Ru's college entrance essay. It was the only time Ru had written memoiristically. She didn't get into her top picks either and vowed to never reveal too much of herself in writing again.

As Ru and Atty followed the librarian down a flight of stairs, Atty asked her about their Nancy Drew collection. "Do you have all the books in the original series?"

"We do."

"But no actual original hardbacks, right?"

"Ah, no. They've all been reordered dozens of times by now."

She ushered them into an anteroom filled with a modest ar-rangement of twelve folding chairs.

"Do you want a mike?" she asked.

"Did Jesus need a mike while speaking to the apostles?" Ru said, and then remembering Maska Gravitz's advice, she stood up straight and smiled.

"That's a joke," the librarian said, and Ru noticed her small cross necklace. "I guess I'm not partial to religious humor."

"It was really humor about the lack of a need for a mike while speaking to only twelve people, potentially," Ru said, smiling some more. "I don't need one. Thank you."

Atty laughed a little and when Ru shot her a look, she noticed that Atty was clutching a Nancy Drew mystery that she must have dug out of the bag from the secondhand shop. "What's with the book?"

"Just in case I get bored," Atty said.

"But I'm going to be reading . . . from a book."

"I know. I brought a *different* book."

Ru said, "Why is someone your age wearing a fanny pack? It seems like a desperate act of social suicide."

"It's ironic," Atty said. "I'm wearing it *ironically.*"

"I see." Ru did not see.

As the audience members arrived, the librarian introduced them to Ru. There was a sum total of five, not including Atty. Three were bloggers, as Maska had suggested. They wore baggy T-shirts. Two were pale and one was bright pink and freshly blistered by the sun. Two older women were members of a book club that had been around since 1973. They shook hands with Ru, explaining that their first book had been *Fear of Flying* by Erica Jong.

"Luckily it's a rainy day! That's why we've gotten such a good turnout," the librarian said. "When it's sunny, almost no one comes."

Ru had the desire to slap someone.

Atty muttered, "This is my definition of almost no one. What's yours, sister?" And Ru was glad she'd brought the kid. Ru had heard from Liv that Atty had almost been arrested for carrying an antique gun around on campus. From Liv's description, Atty had left the boarding school in disgrace. *People treated her and Esme like mother–daughter Unabombers.*

"Okay," the librarian said. "If you need anything, just wander back to the help desk."

"You're not staying?" Ru asked.

"We can't leave the help desk unstaffed," the librarian said and then she wished Ru luck and left.

"Hey," Atty said. "Look. I can at least live-tweet this so it's not just all wasted on this minuscule audience."

"Oh, good," Ru said, trying not to sound insulted and jaded.

As Atty held her iPhone, her thumbs flitting madly, Ru read a small portion from her novel and then gave a talk. She could only stomach reading to strangers as if they were children for so long. Ru's mini lecture was on the creative process and the adaptation of the novel for the screen, and of course all of the questions were about meeting the various leads in the film.

Atty never did open her mystery. In fact, for a good bit of the talk she wasn't tweeting at all, but eyed Ru with a grave expression as if Ru were suddenly foreign. Her aunt was actually a little brilliant and obviously undervalued, and this was news that Atty took to heart. Because she was pretty sure that she herself was a little brilliant and undervalued.

After twenty minutes, Ru was trying to wrap up the Q and A. "One more question?"

A man in a yellow slicker stepped into the room and found a chair, and for a second Ru thought it was her father finally ready to announce that he was her father. But that made no sense.

Then he pulled off his hood and Ru recognized him immediately— Teddy Whistler. One of his eyes was red and puffed-up.

He took a seat. "Sorry I'm late." Again with the being late and the apologizing for it. His hair was wet but unlike last time when he'd pushed it back in a delicate way, he used his whole hand instead and roughly shoved it. His face was flat, empty of expression.

Slack.

Was he sad?

Jesus. Was he going to start crying?

Had things gone badly with Amanda? Had he kind of lost his shit again? On the plane, he'd seemed relatively sane—if not a little more overtly hopeful than most people in the world—but had Ru misread him? She imagined how he must have leaned over to the heavyset salesman from Kansas and talked him into changing seats. What had he told the guy? "That woman, right there, wrote a book about me that was made into a movie. I'd kind of like to call her on it."

"Okay," Ru said again. "We have time for just one question." Ru stared at the original audience, hoping Teddy wouldn't raise his hand. She assumed he'd either Googled her and found this event online or had seen one of the shitty little flyers taped up somewhere around town. Was he a stalker? Did the rain require an entire slicker?

Finally, Atty raised her hand. "Who's the guy in the Gorton's Fisherman rain gear? What's up with him?" she asked while snapping a picture of him with her iPhone and Instagramming it.

Ru looked at Teddy again. "I wrote something for him."

"A commissioned piece?" Atty asked while typing into her iPhone.

"Kind of."

Atty swiveled in her seat. "Are you happy with her work?"

The bloggers and book clubbers turned around and stared at him too.

"Not really. It went badly."

"How?" Atty asked.

"It went badly at a New Jersey party-boat engagement brunch."

Atty tweeted *Guy in yellow slicker shows up. Things went badly on a NJ party boat. #nosurprise*

"Did you crash an engagement brunch?" Ru asked.

"I rewatched your movie," Teddy said. "Your Teddy Wilmer win-back was public—to great effect."

"Did you write him a win-back?" the pink, blistered blogger asked. "You won an award for those. Didn't you?"

"I did," Ru said.

"Teddy Wilmer's win-back is so public," a pale blogger added. "I mean it had to be!"

"You look like someone punched you in the eye," Atty said.

"That's because someone punched me in the eye," Teddy said.

"Oh," Atty said. *Jersey party-boat-goer was punched in the eye. #Njpartyboatingisacontactsport*

"It's over anyway. She won't speak to me again," Teddy said. "The wedding is next weekend. I'm done."

"Do you love her?" Atty asked, resting her chin on the back of the metal folding chair.

"Yes," Teddy said. "Very much."

"Oh, honey, your win-back backfired on him," one of the book clubbers said to Ru.

"You have to fix that!" the other finished her thought, as one could only after forty years in the same book club.

"I don't think it's my responsibility," Ru said.

"But you screwed him over," Atty said. "I think you have to try to make it right."

Atty didn't even really know exactly how much she owed Teddy Whistler. Still, Ru tried to back out of it. "If she's not going to even speak to him again," she said, "I don't think—"

"You either believe in the stuff you write or you don't," one of the bloggers said.

"I don't," Ru said. "It's fiction."

*Ru Rockwell doesn't believe in her own work. #itsfiction*

"But in your speech, you said that fiction speaks to a larger truth," a pale blogger said, holding up her iPod. "I taped it. Just audio."

"Are you shitting me?" Ru said. "You didn't ask me permission to do that."

"I'm taping *this* too," the blogger said with a warning tone.

"You have to do something," Atty said. "I mean, what's the point of being an author if you just screw up people's lives?"

"You owe it to him," the pink, blistered blogger said. "Look at him."

And there sat Teddy Whistler in his wet yellow slicker and she remembered him that night when she was just a little kid in her pajamas, looking down at him from her open bedroom window, the wind gusting around her. He was a little older and tragically in love and drunk, beautiful, sad, and crazy.

Ru took a deep breath and was about to say no, and storm off. In other words, she was going to run away, but she thought it was time she stopped running away. Instead, she heard herself saying, "I'd help if I could, but what could I possibly write for him now?"

"You could just make it up to him and invite him to dinner," Atty said.

"Dinner with the Rockwells," Teddy said. "Who'd be there?"

"Both of my sisters are in town."

"Huh," Teddy said. "You know, I'd love to be invited to dinner with the Rockwells." He'd been denied this in his youth.

Ru was sure it would be a mess, but on some level she felt like Liv was owed a little surprise like this—for bitching at Ru about writing the book to begin with, as if Liv's drama hadn't drowned out much of Ru's own childhood, and for all the baby comments, and Ru's Poos, and for not even coming to baggage claim to pick her up, and for a lifetime of beating Ru down at any chance. She could dress this up as something she was forced to do. She might even be able to pass it off as a good deed. Plus, young Teddy Whistler probably should have been invited to dinner way back when. I mean, all he did was fake being a hero. Isn't that what we all do?

And then, in a flash of precise memory, Ru remembered how it felt to be poised at the window on the night he showed up drunk on their lawn.

Ru, just a girl, staring down at this beautiful, raw display, with her recording device of a brain, with her big wet eyes.

Ru, absorbing the declaration of love.

"Okay, yes," Ru said softly. "Come to dinner."

CHAPTER *16*

Esme had googled Darwin Webber countless times since the dawn of the Internet. None of the Darwin Webbers was *the* Darwin Webber.

After hearing that her father was responsible for Darwin's disappearance, she googled him on Atty's iPad in her canopy bed and once again found no matches.

She tracked down two of his friends from college on Facebook. This wasn't her first time asking them about him, but she tried again. One told her that the man had fallen off the face of the earth. The other didn't respond at all; a glance at his embittered posts revealed that he was going through some personal shite — maybe a custody battle of some sort.

Jesus H. Christ, she wondered, did her father kill Darwin Webber and dispose of his body? Was Nick Flemming a spy or a mobster?

She looked up Darwin's older brother, Phillip, whom she'd called many times after Darwin was gone. At first, Phillip had been distraught, but he had always seemed to know something she didn't. The family never put out a missing person report and when Esme confronted Phillip about it, he finally told her to let it drop and to stop calling. That was when she took it the hardest. Whatever had happened to Darwin, he didn't want anything to do with Esme. It was over.

She knew, in a way she couldn't explain, that Darwin wasn't dead. If he were, she'd have felt it. She didn't make a habit of believing in this kind of mysticism, but this was beyond rational thinking, and she accepted it because it comforted her.

Her mother might not have known he was partially black—it was just a small wedge of the total pie—but her father would have, what with his practice of vetting people. Was her father a racist? Was that the problem? Was Darwin not rich enough or from the right family? His parents had been hippies. Did Nick Flemming have something against hippies *and* Ivy League schools?

She spent the rest of the day looking up the coveted details of the Ivy League educations she'd missed out on—a recent Princeton reunion where Bon Jovi gave a concert, the significance of the three-legged chair for Harvard's president at graduation, Yale's secret Skull & Bones society.

She rode spikes of anger. Augusta had betrayed her daughters. She'd told some smidge of the truth but allowed it to be interpreted as a lie. That was as bad as lying, wasn't it?

Esme wanted to know how her parents met, why they'd had three children if they couldn't even manage to get married—who did that nowadays, much less back then?

But most of all, she was stunned that her mother had fallen in love at all, ever. Augusta seemed resolutely solitary. She was annoyed at Esme's wedding. Almost disapproving. Augusta didn't care for the extravagance of it all, but, to be honest, it hadn't been an extravagant affair. So what were all those snide comments about? At the time, Esme had suspected Augusta was jealous. A woman who had sex with strangers instead of entering into a committed relationship would be jealous, right? But now she knew her mother had been in a relationship in some weird way for a long time. How in the world did it start and then, of course, why did it end? She was particularly interested in endings since her own marriage was mid-demise.

And though it might seem petty, what the hell were her father's family's health issues? Her whole life the paternal side of her medical history had been blank. What if she'd had an aneurysm or gall-bladder issues or came from a line of hemophiliacs and never knew? Why hadn't her mother told them this?

And then Esme remembered her uncle. Uncle Vic. A dim memory of fishing on a dock. There'd been a bucket of worms, a hook—shiny and sharp—and this man teaching her how to cast and reel though she was much too young. How young, she couldn't remember. Her mother had been an only child. So Uncle Vic had to have been from her father's side of the family? Where were all of those relatives?

Her biggest regret was her father running off Darwin Webber, but the Ivy League education was a close second. Most of the faculty members at the boarding school, because of their elite educations, had a permanent shield to protect them from any insult the world flung at them. Esme would never be able to prove that she belonged among them.

And she *did* belong among them. She was owed another life altogether. She could feel the other life; that was the problem. She could sense it riding alongside the one she was in right now—betrayed by her husband, trying to get a divorce, kicked out of her home, unemployed, and raising a daughter who may or may not be imbalanced, but who'd proven to be emotionally volatile. My God, she worried about the effect this year had had on Atty.

Actually, to be honest, she'd felt the other life all along. When she was marrying Doug, she imagined—with visceral exactitude—what her wedding would have been like with Darwin Webber, down to the details of his older brother's toast. She imagined their first apartment, how they'd have had a few more kids, and dogs, and taken in stray cats. It was so real that she felt it could almost be explained by physics. Physicists believed in things like alternate universes, didn't they—even though it was embarrassing for them to admit?

She lay back in the bed. The breeze from the open window made the thin gauzy material of the canopy breathe lightly.

Screw her possible genetic weaknesses, her lack of relatives, her lost childhood with two parents, and even the Ivy League. There was no way to get any of that back. It was behind her now. She wanted one thing—to know what happened to Darwin Webber, maybe to see him again with her own eyes. She'd exhausted her investigative skills.

Then it hit her that Ru, at sixteen, had somehow found their father.

And then she thought of the old man himself.

If she was owed another life, her father was surely her debtor.

The flag was on display. If there were any ties left, this was a signal that should draw him back.

# CHAPTER *17*

Once the clouds broke, Liv walked out the back door, pulled a beach chair from the thickly webbed shed, carried it upstairs, and shoved it out the window overlooking the flat roof of the back porch. Then she put on a bikini, oiled herself up, grabbed all of the engagement pages she'd stolen from her mother's newspapers, took Atty's iPad sitting on the bottom of the girl's unmade bed, and set herself up in the beach chair to catch some sun.

She'd thought her luck would last a lifetime. Fathers, on the other hand, die. She was shaken, in all manners. She had to pull herself together and this was how she'd always done it—cherry-picking. To ensure some measure of calm, she also popped a Xanax, only vaguely aware that she was taking too many and should probably pace herself or she'd run dry.

She sorted through her options quickly. There weren't many really viable men to choose from, and when she decided to look up Clifford Wells, she told herself she was doing Ru a favor. "I'm not Gong Gong," she said aloud. Something was up with Ru and Cliff. Things hadn't been good for a year. Who would take off to Vietnam, post-engagement, and then choose open-ended quality time with family? Why hadn't he picked Ru up at the airport?

She watched Ingmar who bounded out onto the back lawn and squatted to pee-pee, like a girl. Had he too lacked male role models? she wondered.

"What are you doing out here?" Atty asked, popping her head out the window.

"Catching up on world affairs." Liv was wearing oversized sunglasses. She put the iPad down and picked up one of the newspapers, a fine-point Sharpie in hand. "How was Ru's reading?"

"Weird."

"Good weird or bad weird?"

"No-judgment weird," Atty said. "Mind if I join you?"

"Free country," Liv said.

Holding a Nancy Drew mystery and her smartphone, Atty climbed out the window and sat on the shingles, still wet from the rain. The sun was warm and blinding.

It was quiet for a moment and then Atty asked, "Are you lonely not being married?"

"I'm most lonely when I'm married."

"That doesn't make sense," Atty said.

"It doesn't have to." Liv tilted her face to the sky. "I do miss Icho some. He was my first husband and very attentive. I was pretty coked out during the second marriage—and so was Sven—so I don't remember much, but Owen was pretty charming. You know, he had a sense of humor at least."

"How do you feel when you're dating someone?"

Liv folded up *The New York Times.* "I had a torrid thing with a fellow resident last month. I think it felt . . . good."

"By *fellow resident,* do you mean a drug addict?" Atty asked.

"Actually he was in for something else," Liv said. "And I'm not a drug addict. I abused prescription drugs. It's an important distinction. It's the equivalent of insider trading, a white-collar crime." She went back to the engagement photos of the men. None of them seemed to wear *that* smile: the kind that seemed to grip his face like a claw.

"Do you have some goals?" Atty asked like some shitty prep school college counselor.

"Well, I was very good at my old job—I was a marriage-profiteer—but I'm supposed to stop doing that."

Atty nodded and it was clear that Esme had told her daughter something about Liv's marriages; *gold digger* was a term Liv found offensive. Still, Liv was supposed to try to be more honest with herself and others so she chose not to equivocate.

"Are you going to stop?" Atty asked.

"I don't think so." She took a deep breath, opening her ribs and imagining the breath moving through her. She was supposed to do this too, think about breathing.

"What about the fellow resident?"

"It was amazing really. All this dirty talk."

"I don't understood dirty talk," Atty said. "I think it'd be hard to do without laughing."

"Men can take laughter personally, I've found."

"But talking dirty seems *complicated*."

"It's not. You know, like baseball announcers—how one's supposed to do a play-by-play and the other is supposed to add colorful commentary?"

"I guess," Atty said.

"Well, really a play-by-play is fine," Liv said. "Men with hard-ons are very basic creatures. A plain voice-over narration of what's happening will do—you know, like a flight attendant explaining how to work a seat belt."

"Are you going to see him again?" Atty asked.

"Who?"

"The fellow resident."

"I don't know. We did have the safest sex in history, a fresh condom for every orifice. It was like waking up in the Bois de Boulogne, condoms everywhere."

"What's the Bois de Boulogne?" Atty asked.

Liv opened her eyes and blinked at Atty as if realizing for the first time that she was talking to a minor and should probably keep this clean. "It's a park in Paris."

"Oh," Atty said. "France is kind of a sour subject for me, what with my father's indiscretion."

Liv closed her eyes again. "Sorry about that, by the way."

"That's okay."

"Normally, I'd one-up you by saying that I never had a father at all, but that's no longer a weapon in my arsenal."

"I'd like an arsenal one day."

"I heard about the musket incident." Liv had endured her own pheasant-hunting gun incident. She knew how wildly people could overreact to such things.

"I meant that I want a *figurative* arsenal—of comebacks to one-up people with."

"You have to work up to an arsenal, gun by gun," Liv said. "And it's not just about comebacks. It's much deeper than that."

"What did my mom tell you about the musket incident?"

"I think she said it was *regrettable*."

"She's lying."

"You don't regret it?"

"I regret it, but she doesn't."

"You think so?"

"I know so."

"It must be nice to be so sure of things."

"It's one of the few things I have going for me. I'm very decisive," Atty said. "My mother says I'm an oak and I should be more of a willow."

"Where has being a willow ever gotten your mother?" She dipped her sunglasses to the tip of her nose and stared at Atty. "And she's not a willow anyway." She pushed the sunglasses back into place and added, "You should be a carnivorous plant, if anything."

"Like a Venus flytrap?"

"Or whatever."

"What did you write your college entrance essay about?" Atty asked.

"Profiteering," Liv said. "I was in favor of it. I might have also mentioned that I thought being a productive member of society, by society's standards, was overrated. What will you write about?"

"It might not matter because I think I'm pretty screwed, collegiately, what with my personal history."

"My second husband, Sven, didn't go to college. He's an inventor. He holds tons of patents. College is kind of contrived." Liv pressed her eyebrows flat with a thumb and index finger and then said, "I should take you under my wing, Atty."

"I don't know what that would be like."

"No, of course you don't."

Atty seemed to think about it. She pulled her knees to her chest. "A man's coming to dinner."

"We're too competitive to handle a man coming to dinner. It's like musical chairs being played out by your prep school pals, all gunning for valedictorian—only one can win enough attention."

"Like in a game of Spoons." Atty picked up the tanning oil. "Are we going to play Spoons?"

"I think we banned parlor games, wisely. The last time we played Spoons was when your mother brought home Darwin Webber from college."

"Who *is* Darwin Webber? She won't tell me." Atty popped the oil's lid, dribbled some on her arm, and started rubbing it in.

"He was her boyfriend," Liv said. "I think he might have been good."

"What do you mean *good*?" She stared at her shiny arms.

"I mean it in the most basic way. Good. What do you mean what do I mean?"

"So was he an African German American or a German African American?"

"I don't know. He was one of those people who looked like almost every nationality. A globalized face."

"Oh."

"What kind of man is Ru bringing here?" Liv asked. "Did he seem rich?"

"How can you tell?"

"It takes an eye," Liv said. "Why's he coming here?"

"Ru promised to help him win back this woman he's in love with. She invited him over to meet everyone. I think she knew him when she was younger."

"A man in love?" Liv laughed.

Atty nodded.

"Easy pickin's."

Atty laid back, propped the Nancy Drew behind her head as a stiff pillow, and closed her eyes. She'd been planning on reading more of her Nancy Drew mystery. She hated Nancy, to be honest. Her lawyer-daddy buying her a car, her blond hair and blue eyes, her earnest soul. Wasn't there some regret pawing just beneath her cardigan sweater? That was the real fucking mystery. "If you take me under your wing, will you teach me how to have an arsenal, a deep one."

Liv nodded. "Gun by gun, my dear. Gun by gun."

Atty flipped to her side, facing her aunt. "Give me my first gun."

Liv said, "Never ask for favors."

"Sorry," Atty said, hurt. "I thought you'd offered."

"No," Liv said, "that's the first gun. The point of an arsenal is that it's not just some pawnshop pistol you wave at an intruder. The arsenal speaks for itself. It looms. The point of an arsenal is that you seem so heavily armed, no one messes with you to begin with."

"Got it." She wanted to tweet all of this, very badly, but she knew that if she pulled out her iPhone, it would scare Liv off.

"You make people think they thought of the thing you want them to do for you all on their own. If they think of it, you don't owe them. It's best to walk through this life debt-free, emotionally speaking."

"Debt-free," Atty said, trying to memorize it for future tweets. "Emotionally. I like that."

"In rehab, I gained a lot of wisdom. I'm glad I can pass that on." Liv glanced at Atty. "Sometimes you remind me of a young me. You know that?"

Atty looked teary-eyed suddenly. She reached up and pinched her nose. "Would you have stolen a musket and lost it in front of your whole school at parents' weekend?"

Liv wanted to ask her why she'd done it. She was afraid that the story was scarier and darker than Esme had let on. Had Atty stolen it with an intention to hurt herself? Rehab had been full of suicidal types. Even Liv had been pegged as one and, for a time, she'd been in group therapy for it—as if someone had reported that she might have been planning on turning her ex-husband's pheasant-hunting gun on herself. She remembered how the therapist requested they steer away from what could be "trigger words"—*crazy, nuts, insane.* Liv wanted to say, *What if* trigger *is your trigger word?*—I mean, her supposed incident had involved a gun after all. She refrained and instead talked her way out of more sessions.

"You know," Liv said, "under the right circumstances, I might have reacted the same way you did. Sometimes it's the world that's crazy, not us."

Liv's own life felt tremendously fragile right now. She had the sudden urge to eat too much birthday cake and cry too hard. In fact, she felt like she was crashing back through her life and landing—emotionally speaking—in her tumultuous teen years. She kept all of this tightly wound inside of her.

And so she gave Atty what she'd asked for, her arsenal. "Don't be vulnerable," Liv said, "unless you're using your vulnerability to get what you want. Learn to cry on a dime, but never let someone see you cry for real."

"I can give that a try."

"And remember it's easier to steal another girl's boyfriend than it is to take a boy who doesn't want a girlfriend and turn him into someone who does."

"Really?" Atty thought of Lionel Chang, kissing her. She felt—in a flash of memory—his hand fondling the front of her padded bra. Lionel had been dating Maeve Brown at the time, but that hadn't stopped him, and Atty hadn't won him over. In fact, the whole thing was the start of her ruination. Even now, one of the reasons she tweeted so much was that Lionel Chang was a follower. (She had 3,904 followers—a number she was proud of.) Maybe Lionel saw her tweets. Maybe he didn't. But still she wanted to prove to him—and others, including the vicious Brynn Morgan—that she was doing just fine. Thank you very much.

"Absolutely," Liv said. "I've built a solid career on that realization alone."

Atty stiffened but accepted the advice. "Okay," she said, taking a short breath in and then out. "What else?"

# CHAPTER 18

Augusta went to Jessamine for advice. She'd never done anything like it before. She didn't ask people for advice generally because she'd never been impressed by the kind that people gave unbidden, but ever since she and Jessamine had endured the hurricane together—the ripping wind, the ferocious tide, the fear of death—things had changed between them. After the storm, they'd trudged through the wreckage of the first floor together wearing hip waders left behind by some long-dead Rockwells. Jessamine never brought up her husband again, and Augusta surely didn't ever speak a word about her own ex-husband of sorts, but things had opened up between them—for God's sake, they'd huddled under the old oak table on the third floor, clutching each other for dear life at the height of the storm—and there was no way to ever completely go back to the invulnerability of their previous relationship with its elaborate system of privacy fences. Perhaps Augusta had been looking for a reason to seek Jessamine out as a friend, a confidante, and this was the opportunity.

Augusta found Jessamine in the laundry room off the kitchen pantry. Not used to interacting with people on intimate issues, Augusta started awkwardly in the middle of her thought. "They'll eat him alive," she whispered to Jessamine. "I've written him a letter and dropped it, but I think I should call him off. What do you think?" She assumed that Jessamine had absorbed enough of the current crisis by simply breathing the same air. If she'd really thought about it, she'd have realized this made no sense. She sighed and rubbed her hands together. "Maybe he'll never get it. The lines of communication are old and, to be honest, I've never understood how they worked." And then in a rare moment of self-awareness, Augusta said, "Are you following me?"

Jessamine *was* following her and *did* know how the lines of communication worked. In 1983, the year before Augusta called it quits with Nick Flemming and later made a commitment to personal honesty, Jessamine had found the stash of toys Nick had bought the girls over the years—board games from the Soviet Union, blocky Russian lettering over a man in a red gas mask, spraying an industrial city with green chemicals; cloth dolls from Vietnam in wide straw hats and silk dresses; handheld fans of lace trim made in Cuba. The stash, hidden in a hamper in the back of a closet, made the stories of the long-lost-husband-as-spy a little more believable. And Jessamine and her husband, before his death, pieced together a feasible history of the secret relationship, which, one time, included Jessamine following Augusta to the location under the boardwalk where she hid her letters, and Jessamine's husband taking a day off work once to keep an eye on the hiding spot, from afar, snapping pictures of Mrs. Pedestro picking up the letter. From there, they lost track of what Mrs. Pedestro did with the letters exactly but they assumed that she had her way of getting them to Nick Flemming because after a week, Augusta returned to the location to pick up a new correspondence from him. Within a few days, she made plans for Jessamine to watch the children so she could allegedly visit her friend from her old days in DC, a woman named Cloris Branchwell, an invalid who could never come to visit Augusta. When Jessamine and her husband dug through the white pages of the DC phone book in the library, they found no Cloris Branchwell.

Jessamine required no lead-up to Augusta's confession in the laundry room. "They need to meet him. He needs to meet them." The air smelled of dryer sheets. "It's beyond you now."

"Beyond me?" Augusta's reach into her daughters' lives had never had a border before—or if it had, she wasn't aware of it.

Then suddenly Augusta remembered having sex with Nick for the last time. A piece of shrapnel had worked its way out of his body—on his chest, the right side, not over his heart. After it was over, she felt the wetness on her collarbone and touched the spot. Her fingers were smeared with blood. She drew in a breath.

"Sorry," he said. "It happens. You know, I've taken a few bullets over the years." He walked to the bathroom and, with the door open, picked a few shards from his chest.

And she realized that he was lucky to be alive. She loved him so much she couldn't speak. She lay there, shaking, knowing that she couldn't go on like this—seeing him only here and there, falling into intimacy and then nothingness over and over. It had worn her out. She was done. "If I loved you less," she said, "I could keep going."

It was the truth and he knew it. "I understand." He said it so easily she assumed that he felt it too.

He sat on the edge of the hotel bed while she taped gauze over the wound. By the time they were saying their goodbyes, parting in a crowd of tourists, it had bled through the gauze and his shirt bloomed like he was wearing a red boutonniere. He stood still, watching her go, and when she glanced back, the tourists were pouring around him. He was waiting for her to change her mind, to rush back to him, to cry a little and maybe even bite his shoulder—a habit that made him seem real to her.

But she didn't turn back. She kept going.

"What are you two whispering about in here?" It was Ru. She'd swung into the door frame.

"You're back!" Augusta said. "How was the reading?"

"Fine," Ru said, and she stepped into the laundry room with them. Suddenly Augusta felt smothered. There wasn't enough room for all of them. She started to push past Jessamine toward the exit but Ru had her blocked.

"I spent the last nine months in a one-room hut with seventeen people—well, then there was a new baby so eighteen people. Four generations. I miss small spaces."

"Well, I've been living in a three-story Victorian basically alone for a very long time. I like a little air." Augusta moved for the door again.

But Ru kept the gap closed. "You didn't answer my question. What are you two whispering about?"

Augusta didn't want to confess she'd asked Jessamine for advice. It could be taken as a sign of weakness. So she said, "I'm just waiting for word, that's all. I hope your father gets in touch."

"Have you asked Mrs. Pedestro?" Ru asked.

Augusta tightened her expression. "Mrs. Pedestro? Why would I ask her anything?"

"She's the go-between," Ru said. "You knew that, right?"

Augusta's head shook ever so slightly. "Mrs. Pedestro . . ."

Ru turned to Jessamine. "She had to know it was Mrs. Pedestro! I mean . . . surely!"

Jessamine gave a tight-lipped smile and raised her eyebrows.

"I mean, you know all about this, don't you, Jessamine?" Ru said. "You know all of our secrets, right?"

Augusta whipped around so fast that her elbow knocked a canister of Spic and Span off the shelf. It fell to the ground, giving up a little puffy green cloud. They all stared as it rocked back and forth for a moment, then slowly Augusta looked at Jessamine. "Well?"

Jessamine folded her arms on her chest. "After a few decades, you piece things together."

"You know," Ru said, "Jessamine came the closest to asking where I went when I was missing for twenty-one days."

"What did she say?" Augusta asked and then turned to Jessamine, putting the question to her directly. "What did you say to Ru?"

"I don't remember exactly." Though she had an inkling, she preferred not to get into it.

"She asked me if I'd gone where I needed to go and done what I needed to do," Ru said. "It was simple."

Augusta felt completely rattled. All of these people with all of these lives. Augusta had thought she'd cornered the market on secrets, but evidently her family was full of them. She rubbed her lips with the back of her hand as if she were suddenly aware she'd put on too many coats of lipstick. "Okay, then. Okay!" she said, and she reached for the door frame and pulled herself out of the pantry. "We'll ask Mrs. Pedestro! We'll find out if the bastard is dead or alive!"

# CHAPTER 19

When Ru came home after running away to find her father, Augusta sent her to a therapist, a tall woman with deeply inset eyes. Before the woman became fascinated by the exactitude of Ru's memory functions, she focused on Augusta. Ru described her mother as "a baby, a doll, fragile like that."

"Really," the therapist said. "And so you think of your mother as a baby doll you must protect?"

"No, no," Ru said. "She's a baby on the outside but on the inside she's more like a mobster. She might be powerful beyond measure."

"And so she's a mobster baby?"

"No," Ru said, "maybe more of a baby mobster."

And this was a perfect example of the baby mobster: Standing in the pantry, Augusta proved in one moment to be incredibly naïve — she'd never assumed her housekeeper for the past few decades understood anything about her private life? — and then in the next was storming out of the house to confront Mrs. Pedestro about her role as a top-secret messenger and to find out if the father of her children was dead or alive.

"She's on the move!" Ru shouted to her older sisters as Augusta banged out of the front screen door. It was an expression they'd used as children to explain the flurry that followed one of their mother's inspirational ideas about founding a new movement. "I repeat: She is on the move!"

Ru ran after her mother across the busy street as Liv and Atty ran downstairs together and followed.

Esme appeared at her bedroom window. "What's going on?"

Ru shouted, "She's going to ask Mrs. Pedestro if our father's dead or alive!" Ru's plan had veered off-course. She'd walked into the pantry to tell Jessamine and her mother that she had a guest coming to dinner—one sad and forlorn Teddy Whistler—but she'd missed that window now. Everything had careened out of control.

"How would Mrs. Pedestro know if our father's dead or alive?" Esme shouted back.

Jessamine stepped out of the front door onto the small lawn and looked up at Esme. "She's been the messenger between your mother and father all these years."

"How do you know that?" Esme asked.

Jessamine shrugged.

Augusta knocked on the Pedestros' front door. By the time it opened, Ru, Atty, and Liv had formed a semicircle behind her.

Virgil Pedestro answered. His hair had thinned and grayed, but he had the same nervous smile and wore a polo shirt with the collar up. "Who do we have here?"

Ru looked at the ground, hoping he wouldn't recognize her from the night she barged in on him, naked except for a blue blazer, standing behind a tripod.

"Where's your mother, Virgil? Is she here?"

"Maybe she is and maybe she isn't."

"Like I have time for this shit, young man," Augusta said. "Tell her I want to talk to her right now."

Virgil opened the screen door a little, dipped down, and peeked at Ru's face. "Are you Ru Rockwell?" he said.

Augusta reached out and grabbed Virgil by the short row of buttons on his shirt. "Get her now. Do you hear me?"

"Hey, hey!" he said, lifting his arms in the air. "Ma! Mrs. Rock-well's here to see you! Ma!"

Mrs. Pedestro appeared behind him, looking exactly the same as the night Ru handed her the letter she'd written to her unknown father. Her hair was still puffy and pinned back on one side. She was wearing the same kind of clothes—well fitting and nearly sporty. She'd just washed her hands, it seemed, and was drying them with a sand-dollar-appliquéd hand towel.

"Augusta," she said, sensing alarm. "What is it?"

"I want to know if Nick is dead or alive."

"I can't say anything like that. I can't . . . You know . . . It's not . . . There are rules."

"Is he dead then?" Augusta said, nodding curtly. "He's dead. Isn't he?" She reached out and grabbed Atty, who was closest. The girl's eyes went wide. "He's gone. That . . . triple asshole! He's dead!" Their mother wasn't accustomed to cursing so when she did, her expletives were often strangely vivid and inventive.

Here, again, was a perfect moment when the line between baby and mobster was blurred beyond distinction. Was her mother a baby about to break down wailing on Mrs. Pedestro's lawn, or was she faking it, using the threat of explosion to bully Mrs. Pedestro into telling her the truth?

"No, no!" Mrs. Pedestro said. "He's not dead! He lives in a retire-ment complex in Egg Harbor. He's got a shih tzu named Tobias. He's fine!"

"Egg Harbor?" Augusta said. "What's in Egg Harbor?"

"He has a shih tzu?" Liv said, laughing. Ru wasn't sure if it was the fact that the term *shih tzu* was inherently funny or that the small dog seemed to emasculate their father's image—or both.

"Why'd he name it Tobias?" Atty said. "After the novelist Tobias Wolff?" Raised on a boarding school campus, Atty was inculcated in the art of naming pets after writers.

"Is he still *with it*?" Ru asked. "Mentally?"

"Let me put it this way," Mrs. Pedestro said, tucking her chin to her chest. "There's a sign in his room that reads: IN CASE OF EMERGENCY: DO NOT WAKE ME UP BY TOUCHING ME OR EVEN SHOUTING WITHIN TEN FEET OF THE BED."

"I don't know what that means," Liv said.

"He was trained to wake from a dead sleep, disarm, and pin an intruder down," Ru explained.

"Cool," Atty said, gripping her iPhone then quickly tweeting.

"How do you know what's posted *in his bedroom*?" Augusta asked Mrs. Pedestro.

"I've visited him. He gave me a tour," Mrs. Pedestro said defensively. "He was surprised to hear from you after all these years, Augusta. He was sure it was over."

"It is over."

Mrs. Pedestro looked at Augusta as if she felt sorry for her, and then she turned and pulled a small envelope from a drawer in a hall table. "I was going to slip this in our mutual hiding spot, but I guess that's not necessary anymore."

Suddenly it felt like Mrs. Pedestro and Augusta were the ones who were clandestine lovers all these years. A wash of self-consciousness seemed to make Augusta blush, a rarity. She didn't reach out and take the letter. It was as if she'd have to admit Mrs. Pedestro's intimate role in her life, and she couldn't do it.

Ru took the letter. Liv then ripped it out of Ru's hands, opened it, read it, and then handed it off to Atty, who read it aloud.

*Augusta,*

*Of course I want to see the girls. You've told me to show up and that's what I'll do.*

*As for my enemies, you're right. They're mostly just beset by nostalgia not vengeance.*

*Love,*

*NF*

"He could show up at any time," Ru said and it dawned on her that her mother must have thought she was seizing control of the situation by demanding Nick Flemming show up at their house— but by not setting a date and time, she'd actually relinquished all control. It was a grave tactical error.

"What's *NF* stand for?" Atty asked.

"Nick Flemming," Liv said, in a soft motherly tone Ru had never heard from her before. "Your grandfather."

"Enough!" Augusta turned and started to head back to the house, but she took only a few paces before she stalled and looked at Jessamine in the yard and Esme still propped in her bedroom window. She glanced back over her shoulder at Liv, Ru, Atty, and Mrs. Pedestro.

Then her eyes went back to Jessamine. In some strange way, Jessamine knew Augusta best of all. Augusta searched Jessamine's face and she saw sorrow there, but also courage. Jessamine looked at Augusta steadily. *Cherish this,* that's what Jessamine's face seemed to say. Jessamine's husband was now dead. Augusta had been preparing herself for change, thought she was open to it, but this was too much at once.

A car pulled up—a little economy number—and a man stepped out. Teddy Whistler. He looked at the family looking at him. "Hi!" he said and waved.

Ru felt a strange desire to trumpet—it was how the elephants reacted to a surprise or when they were excited. On top of everything else, here was Teddy Whistler, returning to the Rockwells' front lawn where she'd seen him so dizzy and dazed, professing his love for Liv. Ru knew that she shouldn't feel like trumpeting when she saw Teddy, but she did, instinctively. She piped up from the Pedestros' lawn, "Oh, and Teddy Whistler's coming to dinner!"

"Teddy," Liv whispered.

"Yes," Ru said.

Liv turned on Atty, angrily. "*This* is the man you told me about! Why didn't you say his name? Why didn't you—"

"She doesn't know," Ru said.

Atty glanced between Liv and Ru. "Who is he?"

"Teddy from Ru's book," Liv said. "She didn't make him up. He was already real." The last time Liv had in any way acknowledged the existence of Teddy Whistler was the angry voice mail she'd left for Ru after reading the summary of her novel in *The New York Times Book Review*. The truth was that Ru had listened to the message, but was simply too ashamed to bring it up. She'd been waiting in line for a friend's retro punk rock concert and when Cliff asked who it was, she hit DELETE. "Just my sister Liv, confusing life and art."

"A spectacle!" Augusta whispered. "After all those years of hiding and fixing and keeping it all together, it's just a spectacle!"

And then Ingmar started barking, deep inside the house.

Augusta's back went straight and she started loping, which turned into a very slow and heavy jog. She raised her hands in the air, stopping a bit of traffic, and then she was running. She'd always told her daughters she'd been very fast as a child, but the girls had doubted this. It seemed, for a moment, that she was charging Teddy Whistler and so he took a step toward the driver's-side door, but she veered, rounding the car.

"What is it?" Esme shouted.

"That son of a bitch! Your father!" Augusta said, raising her fist in the air.

Augusta could feel him. He was already in the house. She was sure that's what had alarmed the dog but also she just *knew*. The moment before she'd ever laid eyes on him—that first time— she'd sensed his presence running alongside the downtown bus. She sensed him each time they met in public—a crowded train station, a bookstore, an airport bar. In all of those various hotel rooms, she knew he was going to knock just moments before he knocked.

Liv, Ru, and Atty took off after her.

Esme made a Statement of Personal Honesty. "My life is a shit show," she declared, and she dipped back in through her bedroom window and headed for the stairs.

And soon enough all of the Rockwells were gone, leaving Teddy Whistler and Jessamine. He walked up to her and extended his hand. "Hi," he said. "I think I was invited to dinner."

Jessamine smiled. "Welcome to the Rockwells'."

# CHAPTER 20

Augusta was right. When everyone flew into the dining room, Nick Flemming was standing on the other side of the table, in front of one of the chairs, waiting to greet them. Ingmar was eating some kind of doggy biscuit that Nick had brought with him for the purpose of subduing him. Nick was wearing a light-blue guayabera, his gray hair slicked back.

"You look like a Puerto Rican barber," Augusta said breathlessly.

"That's racist," Atty whispered.

"I've missed you," Nick said to Augusta.

"Screw you," Augusta said.

And then Nick Flemming made a gesture like he'd studied dance, or like, at the very least, he'd raised daughters who'd studied dance. (All the Rockwell girls had studied dance.) His arm swept out very slowly. His eyes teared up. "Look at my daughters." His eyes fell on Atty. He whispered, "And my grandchild."

And then he fell back into his chair like the backs of his knees had been hit by a bat, and, just like that, he was seated. The table was set for six. The plates stared up blankly. Ingmar nosed his empty hand, ready for another treat.

Jessamine cut through the dining room to get to the kitchen.

Teddy appeared in the door frame and said, "Hello. I'm—"

"This is Teddy," Ru jumped in.

The girls took little notice of him, and Nick only glanced at him, giving a perfunctory, "Nice to meet you."

Teddy nodded but kept quiet.

Jessamine bustled in, setting an extra place for Teddy.

"I hope I'm no trouble," Teddy said.

No one assured him he wasn't. Ru wanted to but stopped herself. The comment hung in the air.

Liv wasn't even all that interested in Teddy, not in the presence of her father. She was struck by her father's full head of hair. She decided that if she were a son not a daughter this would be a great relief to her. She thought he looked fit and, as she had an eye for wealth, she figured he'd done well but wasn't showy about it. She wasn't emotional as much as she felt giddy, and the giddiness reminded her of being a little strung out, which made her feel like she had to fight such associations and so she felt tired. She said, "I picked a pretty time in my life to kick Klonopin." It had been the toughest to let go of, Xanax had proved a pitiable substitute, and she was now hoarding her Valium, saving her antiques for a very rainy day.

Esme felt completely uprooted by the sight of her father. He was shorter than she'd expected. There was something around his eyes that was familiar in Atty. She folded her arms, gripping them to reaffirm that she had nerve endings, which reaffirmed her existence.

It still wasn't clear what Augusta might do next. She seemed coiled, ready to strike. She said, "You already know Teddy. He's the boy who made our lives a misery when Liv was a teenager in love. Then Ru went and wrote that fictional book that was clearly not all fictional."

"*Trust Teddy Wilmer*," Nick said, then he turned to Ru and preempted. "I hope that's okay. It was available to the public."

"You know my work," Ru said, surprised. Sure, it was kind of a breach of their agreement, but he could keep up with her work without interfering, right?

"Of course he knows your work," Esme said. "He knows everything. That's the problem!"

"What did you think of it?" Ru asked even though she knew she shouldn't.

"I noticed the absent father figures, and I felt bad about that."

"Let's not get maudlin," Liv said. "Self-actualization comes when someone has the courage to examine their own life — not other people's. Plus, it wasn't realistic. That's not how it happened. Right, Teddy?" His name felt so familiar in Liv's mouth that she wanted to say it over and over.

"Some essence of it seemed true," Teddy said.

"Really?" Liv said. "It all rang false to me, personally."

Ru didn't care whether it was realistic or not. She wasn't even really stung by her sister's comment. Instead she was simply struck by her father's physical presence — the *all* of him. She remembered him most clearly in small parts from their conversation in the bar — his eyes, his hands, the stupid school pin he'd worn on his shirt. She remembered how he was so proud of her. He smiled so hard that his cheeks were shiny and his eyes were wet with tears. At one point, he looked down at his drink, swirled it with his finger so that the ice cubes clinked, and said, "You're the most like me, of the three girls, you know it?"

Esme was the one to drive to her point. "You owe me," she said to her father. "And the debt is so deep you can never, ever repay it."

"She's right, Nick," Augusta said.

"You think I'm right?" Esme said. Her mother never openly agreed with her.

And it felt like the entire family had always been barreling to this moment. It was inevitable that they would find themselves here — in just this way. Each of them somewhat shattered, full of longing, expecting something for so long but never knowing what form it would take. Here it was. At long last. Their father, Augusta's husband, the real man, returned to them, alive and whole.

"Would you believe that I had good intentions?" Nick said.

The girls looked at one another as if they could only answer as a unified front.

"You were there, Augusta." He reached out and grabbed the edge of the table. Ingmar standing steadfast at his side, already won over. "Right from the start. I *did* have good intentions."

"You could have given it up," Augusta said. "You could have walked away and made a family with us."

Nick leaned back and shook his head. "It had me already. It had me."

There was only the sound of breathing—labored breathing. It was coming from Esme. She balled her fists. "Did you kill Darwin Webber? What did you do to him?"

"Jesus!" Nick said, tilting the chair back. "He's a cabinetmaker. High-end. The man charges a shit-ton and has a summer house on Long Island. He just changed his name."

"To what?"

"Something simple. I can't remember."

Esme glared at her father. "Remember it."

"Uh, Parks, I think. Bob or Bill. Or Rob. Rob Parks. *Parks.*"

"What town in Long Island?" Her voice was gravelly and low.

"Um, that one . . . you know, where *The Great Gatsby* is set . . ."

"East Egg?" Atty said. She didn't think of herself as very pretty, and so she wanted to prove to her newfound grandfather that she was at least smart. "Or West Egg."

"No, the *real* place," Esme said. "Ru, you're the writer! Where was it?"

"Orgiastic," Liv said, noting the controversial word on the final page of *The Great Gatsby,* a bubble from some educational moment that rose to the surface and popped. It seemed to catch Teddy Whistler's attention. The two exchanged a look. (Teddy Whistler had made her orgasm in his neighbor's aboveground pool.)

"Great Neck?" Ru said. "I think it was in Great Neck. He and Zelda had a place there."

"Great Neck?" Esme said, glaring at her father. "Was it Great Neck?"

"Yes," Nick said. "Great Neck, for the love of God. Great Neck!" And then he pounded on the table and shouted, "We're all in the same room! For the first time! My God, can I—" He pressed the fingers of one hand together and lifted them as if holding something precious. His hand trembled in the air. "Can I enjoy that? Can I be allowed to *enjoy* it?"

"No," Augusta said.

It was quiet.

Teddy Whistler started to back out of the room as gently as he could. "Excuse me," he whispered.

"No," Esme said. "No one leaves."

And he stopped moving, except for his eyes, which searched the others for some counterindication. None came.

Jessamine walked into the room holding a piping-hot lasagna with oven mitts, and took control of the situation by making a simple announcement, one she'd made a thousand times before in this house. "Dinner is ready!"

Augusta latched on to its ordinariness and said something she'd said thousands of times. "Sit down. Let's eat."

CHAPTER *21*

When men arrived at the Rockwells' house, any guff of bravado wore thin quickly and they became stiff intruders. When they started to take a seat, someone would tell them that the seat was taken and would sit down in it. Sometimes as they made conversation, one of the sisters might burst into laughter for no apparent reason and another would nod at her encouragingly. The inside jokes were land mines.

The men were only invited one at a time. They were usually interrogated at first, eyed closely, and then an abrupt reversal would happen, and they'd find themselves pinned into the role of audience member—part of a larger audience that they were vaguely aware had come before them, and had failed to gain a foothold.

If one of the sisters clung to a man too closely, the others would sense weakness and things would go badly. It was best to let the man fend for himself.

Ru hadn't invited a man to the house since the cruise ship singer showed up during a break in the tour. He'd risked his job letting her be a fake roadie and stowaway; how could she say no? He was supposed to spend the night in the guest bedroom, but said he had to pee at some point during dessert and, wisely, left.

Liv had a string of boyfriends but she stopped the practice of bringing them home to meet the family once she hit college and dated a French foreign exchange student named Jerome. "We don't represent a typical American family," she said. "We'll only confuse him." But from then on, she'd never invited another man to the house on Asbury Avenue, not even her three husbands.

Esme only had *serious* boyfriends and, as the oldest and a rule follower and someone who wanted to rub her mother's nose in the benefits of engaging in a long-term relationship, she invited each to the house, including Darwin Webber, who was notable in that he was the only male visitor in the history of the Rockwell girls' suitors to win at a game of Spoons.

The last male visitor in the house had been Esme's soon-to-be ex-husband, Doug, seventeen years ago. That evening ended in a sour game of Scrabble—some argument about whether hoc as in *ad hoc*, was a legitimate word—but all had to agree that Doug was relatively likable. "Don't gloat," Liv had told Esme after it was over. "It was likability by default. We just couldn't really find anything tragically wrong with him."

His tragic flaws were now obvious.

And so for the first time in the family's history, there were *two* male visitors on the same night—one was their long-lost father, the other was Teddy, the subject of various controversies.

No one was quite sure how to handle the situation.

Jessamine had served the lasagna and salad, and sat alone at the kitchen table, holding her pocketbook, deciding whether to stay on to do the dishes or just go home. They could find dessert on their own. This was all so personal she felt she should go, but would Augusta need her? For God's sake, she'd asked Jessamine for advice. Advice! Anything could happen now.

Inside the dining room, Teddy also wanted to go but that seemed impossible. As he started to take a seat, Atty said, "That's my seat," as if she knew, instinctively, how to treat a man inside the Rockwell home.

"Where would you like me to sit?" Teddy asked Ru quietly.

"Anywhere," she said. "There are no rules." She meant there weren't any rules anymore. Everything was up for grabs. She sat down across from Atty, and Teddy followed and sat next to Ru. And she felt embarrassingly happy that he had, like a kid with a crush. This thought terrified her. Would her sisters sense that she *liked* Teddy Whistler? She had the sudden fear that someone was going to ask her if she just *liked* him or if she *like-liked* him.

But what was worse was that she glanced at Teddy, and her stomach flipped. What if she *like-liked* him?

Augusta sat at the head, where she always sat. Nick stayed in his seat to her left.

Esme and Ru flanked Teddy.

Atty put her head under the table and then popped back up. "Ingmar is lying at his feet," she reported, nodding to her grandfather. "It's like primal or something."

Esme dipped under the table. "Stop it," she said to the dog and when he just stared at her innocently, she said, "After all I've done for you." She reemerged, snapped her napkin, and laid it in her lap.

They began passing the lasagna and salad, one clockwise and the other counterclockwise. "What do you do for a living these days?" Esme asked Teddy.

"I run a company."

"That's vague," Liv said.

"How many brothers and sisters do you have?" Atty asked.

"Two older sisters." Teddy quickly turned to Liv. "What are you up to these days?"

"I'm trying to perfect my Zen." She said it so seriously that Ru laughed, thinking she was going for deadpan.

"What's funny about that?" Liv asked Ru.

"That was the laughter of joy," Ru said quickly.

Liv's eyes flicked around the table, as if she dared anyone else to mock her Zen.

No one did. It was quiet a moment. Atty Instagrammed her plate of food, and as if that were some kind of prayer, they all began to eat.

"So, having sisters, you're used to this kind of thing," Atty said to Teddy, but no one knew what she meant. What *was* this kind of thing?

"Nope," Teddy said. "Not at all."

Nick gestured to Teddy's freshly punched face with a fork. "How's the other guy?"

"I'd guess his knuckles are sore," Teddy said.

"Who punched you again? Context?" Liv asked.

"A groom punched me," Teddy said and then he took a bite, clearly refusing to say much more.

"Why did you invite Teddy Whistler again?" Liv asked Ru as if he weren't there. "I'm confused."

"I thought it would be a good thing," Ru said.

"Teddy and I are all good. Right, Teddy?" Liv said, and then she turned to Atty. "Teddy and I were in love with the *idea* of each other when we were around your age."

"I actually loved her," Teddy said to everyone at the table. "But I also loved the *idea* of her."

"Maybe it was like practice for real falling in love," Atty said, thinking of Lionel Chang fondling the edge of her padded bra and dipping his fingers inside of it.

"Maybe there is no real falling in love," Liv said. "That's something deep to really think about. Self-love, the love of others, which is which."

Atty nodded. "Right." She tweeted, *Maybe there's no such thing as real love. #love=santa*

"I want to know if you're going after one of my daughters, Teddy," Nick said. "What are your intentions?"

They all turned and stared at Nick.

"Excuse me?" Teddy said.

"You can't be territorial here," Augusta said, as if reminding him of a small rule in a parlor game.

Ru was wondering if she'd written the goddamn Teddy Wilmer book with its absent fathers in the hope that her father would read it and be stung by the absence of its father figures. She hated him and herself and being in this room.

"Which one of them would he be going after anyway?" Atty asked. The idea struck her immediately as gross. *Will my mother ever be on the market one day? #ew*

"That reminds me, Ru," Liv said. "When are we going to meet your fiancé?"

Ru's cheeks went hot. She didn't want Teddy to know she had a fiancé and she didn't have one, not really, but she didn't want to announce that either.

"Yes," Augusta said. "I've been meaning to ask."

"Fiancé?" Nick said. "I didn't know—"

But Esme stopped him cold. "Don't play dumb."

He raised his eyebrows and crimped his mouth.

"You're engaged?" Teddy asked.

"Can you miss that ring?" Liv said. "The shine of it could cure cataracts!"

"What's his name?" Teddy asked.

"Cliff," Ru said. Stating his name allowed her not to have to lie in a bold-faced way. "He'll show up at some point soon." She needed to return his voice message and set up a time and place to give back the ring.

"What do you have against the Ivy League anyway?" Esme asked.

"Nothing," Teddy said.

"Not *you!*" Liv said and she laughed and then Atty laughed too and Ru smiled.

Esme didn't. She looked at her father. "You. What do you have against the Ivy League?"

"I don't have anything against it," Nick said.

"But you derailed my entire Ivy League career!"

"Oh." Nick wiped his mouth. "That. Right. It's not good for a kid to think they're better than everyone else in America. Heavy mantle. Screws with your head. Either you can't stay hungry enough and kind of give up the ghost, or you live in fear that someone will find out the truth."

"What's the truth?" Atty asked.

"That you're a fraud," Nick said. "And we're all frauds. That's the trick. If you know that, you're ahead in the game."

Atty tweeted, *We're all frauds. If you know it, you're ahead of the game. #grampsisaspy*

"What if my true self was Ivy League and this self is the fraud?" Esme said.

"Well," Nick said, "that would be a real shame."

"Do you mean a miscalculation?" Ru said. "Because it feels more like it would have been a miscalculation on your part."

"Maybe a shameful miscalculation," Esme said.

"But your life went the way your life went and if it hadn't you wouldn't have had me," Atty said.

"Ha-ha!" Nick said. "See. You can't deny that logic!"

"After World War Two—a death toll of sixty-five million people—babies were born who wouldn't have otherwise been born," Esme said. "And I'm sure that many of those babies grew into great people. But still, should we just shrug and say, *Well*, that *worked out*? Would you like to argue with *that* logic?"

Augusta leaned over to Nick and said, "There's nothing I can do for you. And if there were, I wouldn't."

"Can you kill a man with your bare hands?" Atty asked her grandfather.

"The last time I needed to, I could. Yes."

"I have a question!" Liv said.

"What's that?" Nick said, obviously hoping for a better outcome.

"When my neighbor died and left me that cash and the car and she'd been an invalid most of her life. She didn't drive. And, moreover, she didn't like me. That was you?"

Nick rubbed the bridge of his nose. "I thought you needed it," he said. "I thought . . ."

"Why did you give Liv a fake inheritance?" Esme said.

"The inheritance was *very* real," Liv said. "Trust me. And thank you," she said to her father. "It came in handy."

"You're welcome. Of course, honey."

"Wait," Ru said. "When I said not to interfere with my life, I still thought things would be evened out through Mom. I still thought we'd keep this fair."

"No, no, no," Nick said. "You didn't say anything about keeping things fair. You told me—in no uncertain terms—not to be involved in any way. I honored that. Hard as it was. I did honor that request!"

"I'm going to go throw up," Esme said. She stood, looking blanched, and said to Teddy, "Let me warn you. There's no use trying to worm your way back into this family. Can't you see that all men fail at this. Look at *that* failure! See him!" She pointed at her father. "They all fail."

"I'm not trying to worm my way in. I'm here because Ru said she was going to help me because there's Amanda, and Ru writes winbacks and—"

"Amanda?" Liv said. "Are you back with Amanda?"

"Wait!" Nick stood up too. "Before you go, before this ends, wait. I just want to say that I've been here—I was standing off to the side, sitting in the balcony, gliding past the nursery glass to get a glimpse of my babies. I've been here all along, but not. You don't know me, but I know each of you in a way that no one else does or could. I know you distantly but I know your grace and your triumph and your sadness and your beauty. I know you. And that's worth something. When you get old, sometimes what you miss most of all is being known, in some way, being known and having

been known for a long time. Augusta." He turned to her. "Goddamn it, Augusta. Tell them that I willed them here. Tell them it
was me. Tell them how much I love them."

Augusta nodded. "He loves you."

"And I never stopped and I always will." He opened his arms
wide. "Tell me what I can do. Tell me what I have to do. Tell me."

Ru looked at Teddy. She was crying though she didn't even
realize it. She was moved by the artistry as much as her father's raw
emotion. She said, *"That*, Teddy—*that* is a goddamn win-back."

CHAPTER *22*

Esme stormed out of the dining room and everything fell silent for a moment.

Finally, Augusta said, "One of you go after her. She won't listen to me."

"I'll go after her," Nick said.

"Shut up," Augusta said. "You don't know anything."

"I'm going to take off, if that's okay," Teddy said.

"Let Teddy go after her," Liv said. "You invited him here just to fill out the story line to some sequel, right? Put him to use!"

"We ran into each other on the plane," Ru said.

"And *that* just didn't come up in any conversation you've had with me since I picked you up at the airport?"

"*You* go after her," Atty said to Liv.

"Sensitivity isn't my strong suit," Liv said. "Let the highly acclaimed writer, who's drawn comparisons to Ephron and Kaufman, go after her."

"Nice," Ru said. "Very nice."

Teddy stood up and tried to smile politely. "Thank you so much for everything, especially you, Mrs. Rockwell, and Mr. . . ." Teddy was suddenly boyish. This display of manners should have happened when he was sixteen and dating Liv, but Augusta had never accepted him—even now she was a little chilly.

"Mr. Flemming," she said to Teddy. "Certainly not Mr. Rockwell." And then she turned to Ru. "Walk him out. He's your charge."

Liv walked up to Teddy, and for a second Ru was sure that Liv was going to slap him—or kiss him. But she reached up and fixed the collar on his shirt. "You're all grown up," she said. "I had you frozen in time."

Teddy didn't move. He didn't say a word.

Liv patted his shoulders, and turned away.

"Poor kid," Nick said under his breath.

"I'll go after Mom," Atty said, pushing away from the table.

Atty ran ahead, up the stairs, and Liv said, "Hold on, Atty. I'll come too."


Ru walked Teddy to the front door.

"I don't know what I expected," Teddy said, "but not this."

"I don't know what I expected either. Obviously, things got complicated." Ru couldn't be falling for Teddy. For one thing, he was in love with someone else. But also, Ru didn't believe in falling for people in this way. She didn't believe in getting giddy around a man just because. She didn't believe that two people could meet and fall for each other. She didn't believe all that much in love— regardless of the ending of her romantic comedy and its much-lauded win-back. "Sorry about it all."

"That's okay," Teddy said. "I got a win-back lesson, right? Your dad is really something. Tonight was really—"

"You'll be fine," Ru cut him off. "Go with what you were going to say to Amanda. What you told me on the airplane."

"What was that?"

"You said you missed the way she looked at you, that that look could knock everything down and strip everything away. And then it was just the two of you." Teddy watched her lips as she spoke. "You said you'd been missing that look ever since you left and that you couldn't spend your whole life missing it."

"You remembered all that."

"I have an eidetic memory. I remember things I don't even want to remember."

"I thought you said it was cloying."

"But it's the truth. Just tell her the truth."

"Okay," Teddy said. "Thanks." He hesitated, then he stuck out his hand.

She shook it.

"Good luck in there." He opened the screen door then turned back around. "It's funny. Liv isn't the way I remember her, but you are exactly the way I remember you, and you were only a kid, but you're still you."

This made Ru feel inexplicably happy and weirdly desirable. He was flirting—it wasn't a flirty line but it *was* flirty in delivery. Ru laughed nervously. "You're still you, too," she said.

"Good." And then he walked out into the cool night.

Ru found Esme in the large attic room of the third floor, lying down in a square of light from the streetlamps shining through one of the large windows. Her arms at her sides, her feet lightly splayed. Liv and Atty stood nearby, not sure what to do.

"I'm sorry about inviting Teddy," Ru said. "I'm not writing a book. I swear it just kind of fell into place and—"

"It doesn't matter," Liv said.

"She's not talking," Atty said, staring at her mother.

"We don't have to talk," Liv said and walked over to Esme, got on her hands and knees, and lay down, putting her head next to Esme's at a ninety-degree angle.

Atty crawled over next, putting the top of her head against the top of her mother's, and Ru joined them, finishing off the strange cross.

"I bet this is how synchronized swimmers practice," Atty said. "You know, out of water, so that they can hear the instructions better."

"Probably," Liv said.

"We're sisters," Esme said, "and we don't even like each other."

"What if that's what we have in common?" Ru said.

"That we don't like each other?" Esme asked.

"No, that we're unlikable," Ru said.

"I'm very likable," Liv said.

"You're manipulative," Esme said. "It's different from being likable."

"I used to think I was likable and then I married Doug and watched people naturally like him. I've always had to earn it."

"I'm not likable," Ru said. "But I *am* occasionally lovable. Sometimes someone will love me and I don't know why, but I accept being unlikable."

"I'm not likable," Atty said.

"Yes you are!" her mother quickly corrected her.

"Maybe I could be if I wanted to." Atty had blamed her unlikability on her status as a faculty brat, but now she wondered if it might be genetic. She quickly tweeted *Likability is a gene?* "Anyway, I don't think siblings are supposed to like each other. I mean, that's not a belief that's widely held from what I can tell."

"Actually, a lot of siblings like each other," Liv said, "because they're the only ones who understand some kind of basic premise of their childhoods."

"Have we all agreed on a basic premise of our childhoods?" Ru asked.

Liv and Esme shook their heads, and Ru could feel the answer against her own.

"Our childhood seemed fucked up at the time, in a way, and it turned out to be more fucked up than we thought," Esme said.

"That might be a reigning definition of childhood," Ru said.

"I think you're right," Atty said, while tweeting *Fucked-Up Childhood in Retrospect is More Fucked Up. #sotrue*

"I'm mad at your father," Esme said to Atty. "I really thought we weren't going to screw it up."

"There are life lessons in the screwed-up-ness, though," Atty said, wisely.

"What happened with the musket?" Liv said. "Is this a bad time to ask?"

"You don't have to talk about it," Esme said.

"It's okay," Atty said, and then she cleared her throat. "The administration was having a hard time hearing me on this point I was trying to make about discrimination against faculty children. And the history teacher, who lived across the street from us, collects vintage firearms."

"Did you steal the musket?" Ru asked.

"I think I borrowed it, personally, but that was debated at the school hearing."

"Did you fire it?" Liv asked.

"We shouldn't get into this," Esme said. "Atty, you really don't have to talk about it."

"I gave a speech at parents' weekend. It was about casual cruelty. And I pulled the musket out of my STX field hockey bag. I wanted to make a point, like Flannery O'Connor, about how we'd all be better people if we lived our lives with a gun pointed at us, just on the verge of getting shot. It was kind of like a Chapel Talk if you think about it the right way."

"O'Connor was Catholic, right?" Liv asked.

"Yes and it's an Episcopal school," Atty said. "That hurt me in the end, I think."

"Did you fire it?" Liv asked again.

"They don't fire," Atty said. "I mean, they do. But they require gunpowder, scouring sticks, ramrods, and, like, lighting a match."

"So you researched how to pull the trigger," Liv said.

"Let's talk about something else!" Esme said.

"If I didn't, it would have been like not pulling the trigger during a production of a Chekhov play. I had to at least try. Once a gun's onstage, you've got to use it. Am I right?" The question was directed at Ru, in her role as writer.

"That's a writerly rule I've heard about guns," Ru said. "Ditto hugely pregnant women."

"What was the casual cruelty?" Liv asked.

"Garden variety," Atty said. "Some people quacked at me on the rope swing. Some invitations weren't extended to me, personally. Some rumors."

"I see," Ru said.

"I retain all rights to my own story," Atty said to Ru. Liv had warned Atty that Ru was a life stealer. She tweeted, *I retain all rights to my tweets.*

"What?" Ru said.

"Listen," Esme said. "We have no time to backpedal over the past. What are we going to do with the elephant in the dining room?"

"Actually, male elephants are solitary," Ru said. "They associate with other males a little but not much. The females form the family units with a matriarch and all. It's literally what she's called."

"Can we focus a little here?" Esme said. "We're talking about the *metaphorical* elephant."

"Right," Ru said, "I'm just saying it's a very apt metaphor . . . Never mind. Sorry."

"I think maybe we lost something as kids," Liv said. "Maybe we can go back and pick it up."

"Are you saying we should try to reclaim an entire lost father from our childhoods?" Esme asked.

"No," Liv said. "It's something else. It's how we got lost and that we're lost now. How do we get found?"

"Okay," Esme said, exasperated. "What in the hell are we going to *do* with him, though? I can't believe he did what he did. I had another life. A completely different life!"

"You've got a great life!" Ru said, hoping that Esme's regret wasn't hurting Atty. "It's hit a rough patch, but it's been good. Really good."

"You know he's killed people," Atty said. "Probably a lot of people. What he did to you is probably not even close to the worst thing he's done in his life."

"He's *a killer*," Liv said, as if testing it out. "My father is a killer." She'd made up so many outlandish things about her childhood, but never anything this remarkable and simple.

"We have to rely on each other now. Don't you see that?" Esme said. "Everything has changed, and we have to be rock-solid. Us. For the first time. Don't you know what I'm talking about?"

"I do," Ru said.

"You mean something profound has happened to us all," Liv said. "Something big that could alter our senses of self and our destinies. I'm really trying to be open to shit like this."

"I guess that's what I mean," Esme said.

"Did you ever like each other?" Atty asked. "Like when you were little?"

The sisters considered this, each staring at the fine cracks in the ceiling paint.

"Not really," Ru said.

"We wore each other's clothes," Liv said.

"No," Esme corrected. "You stole our clothes."

"We played Princess and the Pea," Ru said. "Remember that? We stacked the sofa cushions and hid a marble under them, and we'd have to guess where the pea was or if there was one at all."

"It was like we had a preternatural gift for it," Liv said. "When we had other friends over, they'd guess wrong, but we always got it right."

"We have *that* in common," Ru said.

Atty tweeted, *I come from a vast family of Princesses who hated peas.* "But it doesn't answer the question," Atty said. "Did you *like* each other?"

It was quiet.

"In rehab," Liv said, "other people's siblings showed up and people seemed happy to see them, more or less. I think the problem is that we've never done anything for each other."

"Well, that's because Mom always provided for us," Esme said. "She's overcompensated for a lack of a father. As a result, we never needed each other as sisters. I can call her and get an update on both of you. She's the center of the wheel. We're just spokes. It's her fault."

"She's going to die one day," Atty said.

"True," Liv said, and she remembered, viscerally, what it was like to stick her body half out of the apartment window at the Caledonia. That was a twisted moment, the rain-wet cement beneath her. "We're all mortal."

"Maybe we should do some things together, bond a little," Ru said, "and then maybe we'll learn to like each other."

"At this moment in our lives with our father downstairs, we've decided that we finally *need* each other," Liv said.

"Maybe that's the lesson," Esme said.

"Yes," Liv said. "But we should help our father on his path to wholeness too. I mean, he is completely indebted to us. In AA terms, he should make amends. And in practical terms, his moment of profound weakness should not be squandered. This is something you two have never fully comprehended. We're Buddhist lessons for each other, you know?"

"He should pay," Esme said.

"I already got a ton from him and had no idea, but I'm in it because *we* need this," Liv said. "I mean, look at our fucked-up lives!"

"My life isn't that fucked up," Ru said. It was. She knew it was. Her sisters knew it was without even knowing how exactly fucked up it was.

"I think the old man should stay here," Esme said. "He shouldn't be allowed to leave until we figure out what to do with him. Each of us. Not what *he* wants to do for us. And not what *Augusta* wants him to do. But *us*."

"Yes," Ru said. "Exactly."

"Don't you have to get back to Cliff?" Liv said to Ru.

"He's swamped right now," Ru said. "I don't have anywhere to go immediately. Esme, don't you have to get back to the . . ."

"Boarding school we were kicked out of?" Atty said. "I think that ship has sailed."

"What about you, Liv?" Esme asked. "Don't you have . . ."

"I'm between places, as they say."

Esme reached out and grabbed Liv's hand and then Ru's. "This has to be about us. Whatever happens."

"Agreed," Ru said.

"Maybe what we lost is each other," Liv said. "Maybe if we reclaim that, we won't be lost anymore."

"I don't have any sisters," Atty said.

"That's okay," Ru said. She reached out and grabbed hold of her niece's hand. "We'll be like your sisters. Right, Liv?"

"I've already taken Atty under my wing," Liv said, and she swung her arm wide and held on to Atty's hand too.

"No," Atty said, "I meant like *thank God I don't have any sisters*."

"Oh," Ru said.

Heads touching and holding hands, they stared up at the ceiling, marbled with water stains and fine fissures.

"But we loved each other," Liv whispered. "We didn't ever like each other, but we loved each other as kids."

CHAPTER *23*

"Olive Pedestro?" Augusta said. "You entrusted the safety of our family to *Olive Pedestro*."

Nick was rubbing the knotty bones of Ingmar's head with both hands. "Well, I had to—"

"And her *deranged* son. He's deranged, you know. He's been on house arrest before, with an ankle bracelet."

Nick fumbled in his pocket, pulled out a handkerchief, and wiped his nose. "He wasn't part of the deal."

"And she's *visited* you? In *Egg Harbor*? Where you have a *shih tzu*? And how dare you name a dog Tobias! How dare you!" It had been his first pick for a boy's name had they ever had a son.

He stretched his arms open, a supplication. His cheeks were so ruddy that she worried for a moment about his high blood pressure. How high was it?

But she couldn't let up either. "I bet you gave that dog your last name. Finally, a Flemming, a child of your own!"

"Dogs don't have last names."

She looked down at her knit hands. "Why did you interfere?"

"You knew I was there."

"I didn't."

"You've always known."

He was right. At certain events, she'd feel a surge and catch herself searching the audience before reining herself in. "I thought I was just trying to conjure you up," she said.

"Once, I sat just behind you so close I smelled your perfume."

"Orchestra?"

"Our third-chair clarinetist." He nodded. "It was never over, for me."

She hit him, the flat of her fist to his shoulder, not angry but not joking either.

"C'mon," he said, "do it. Hit me. Really do it. Like you used to."

"No," she said, as if denying him sex.

"I miss the way you used to really lay into me, beating my arms and my chest, sometimes in bed, you know, after."

"I had to."

"I should have gotten worried when you stopped getting angry at me."

Augusta knew the last time she'd hit him. She'd never forget it. He told her someone had been murdered—the oldest son of a colleague. It was Nick's greatest fear. He was trying to tell her that he'd made the right choice. "You'd have drowned me," she said. "I couldn't keep holding you up. We'd been through so much."

"I wish you'd just kept punishing me, but letting me back in. I needed you all so much, more than you ever needed me."

"You'll never know how much we needed you."

And then there was a cough.

They looked up.

There stood their granddaughter.

One knee cocked inward, her forearms crossed to hide her stomach that was a little pudgy, something she'd probably grow out of this summer. There was something undeniably raw and vulnerable about Atty. Augusta saw it for the first time, but it was so plain she was shocked she hadn't noticed it before.

Atty stared at them as if she weren't sure she knew them at all.

She and Nick had never been interrupted in the middle of an intimate moment by a child. The shame Augusta felt was familiar only because she'd felt it in her teen years—her mother walking out onto the porch and nearly catching her holding hands with her date.

"What is it, Atty?" Augusta said.

Atty looked at her dog, who was resting his chin on Nick's thigh, completely smitten. She felt jealous but also a little intimidated by her grandfather's magnetism. "I'm supposed to tell you that your daughters want him to stay until they've figured out what to do with him."

"What do they have in mind?" Nick said.

"I think they want you to make amends. I think there's going to be a process of some sort."

Nick looked at Augusta.

"They should have cleared this with me first," Augusta said.

"You're getting blamed up there too, if I can be frank with you," Atty said.

"Me? Are you kidding?"

"No, I'm not kidding," Atty told her. "But I've heard people say that mothers always get blamed for everything so you probably don't have to take it personally."

"Augusta?" Nick said. "What do you say to this?"

She drew a deep breath and looked at an ancient ancestor's portrait on the wall—a pale man with a bulbous nose and flowering white ascot. She didn't know what to say.

"I think this could help you take your grief for a walk around the block," Atty told her. "Remember? That's what you wanted, right?"

Augusta looked at the girl. "One day," she said, "you'll be a pair of eyes gazing at some new generation sitting in this very room. You'll be a portrait just hanging there, gazing away. This is how time marches on."

She didn't mean it as a threat but it might have come across that way because Atty looked at the paintings and gripped her own arms more tightly. "I think they want a yes or a no."

"Freud," she said, "I blame him on behalf of all mothers." She waved her hand over her head. "Fine! Fine! Like I ever had a choice."

CHAPTER *24*

By 10 P.M., Nick Flemming—father and husband—was lying on a cot in the large room on the third floor of the Victorian, under the row of windows where, once upon a time, Augusta had taught the girls to conduct a storm. He'd driven back to the retirement village, packed a bag, and returned. His shih tzu, Toby—after being thoroughly sniffed by Ingmar and given a little growl—was asleep at his side. The room was now used for storage, and he wondered if he was being stored there too. Was he some relic of the past, still obdurately drawing air, or was he really home, for the first time in his life?

On the second floor, Ru was sharing a double bed with Liv, who'd taken a sleeping pill. Liv was dreaming of Easter eggs, one of which was Technicolored, and she knew it held a demon rabbit. She was snoring lightly and wouldn't recall the dream in the morning. She never did when she took sleeping pills.

Ru got up, grabbed her phone, and walked down the hall to the bathroom. She locked the door. The bathroom felt large and echoey, and she didn't like how she still felt exposed. So she pulled back the curtain on the old clawfoot tub, stepped into it, and drew the curtain closed. This was better, more like a safe cubicle. She remembered for a moment loving the language lab in high school because it had little dividers between stations and headphones that made everyone else disappear.

She had to call Cliff.

Sitting down in the dry tub, she stared at her phone.

She was afraid he'd be angry at her, though he'd shown no signs in the letters he sent following the breakup. He'd never even really asked for more explanation, and he certainly didn't ask her to reconsider, which she had to respect.

She thought about what Esme had said, that whatever happened it had to be about them. They were reclaiming their sisterhood. Ru had felt it in the moment—a surge of love—but now she was uneasy. It was hypocritical of her to make that kind of promise without telling them the truth about her engagement. Why hadn't she already come clean? Jesus. Why was she holding back?

She thought about the writing tip of holding on to a secret—the power of the unspoken to charge a scene. She wondered if she was doing that, subconsciously, and if Liv was right. Had she invited Teddy just to play out some old story line or start a new one?

Maybe it was simpler than that. Maybe she thought that Cliff would convince her she was wrong. She'd seen him convince so many people of so many things as a producer. He was so winning, so vital. It was like other people just wanted to live in his het-up heartbeat and so they said yes, even when they knew they shouldn't. Maybe she thought she was wrong and it wasn't really over so why tell her sisters one thing when she'd just have to circle back?

She hit Cliff's name in her contacts. He was probably on Pacific Time so she wasn't worried about waking him up.

She hoped for voice mail. "Please, please, please."

But he answered. "Hello? Ru?"

"Hi."

"You're back safe and sound. Hold on, let me excuse myself."

She imagined him at a restaurant or a party. She heard him telling people he'd be right back. There was a hoot of laughter, some music.

In a few seconds, she heard a siren. She assumed he was outside now.

"Welcome back to the US," he said genially.

"Thanks."

"How are things?"

She was sitting in a bathtub in her childhood home and her father was with them; her family was, for once, all sleeping under one roof. Things were . . . reverting, upended, normalizing in a ridiculous way? "Good," she said. "How are you?"

"Pretty good. We got a first-look deal. Did you hear?"

She hadn't. She'd always wanted a first-look deal. "What studio?"

"Sony."

"How's Terry taking it?" Terry was his producing partner who'd had a Sony issue a few years back.

"Water under the bridge. He's happy."

"You sound really good."

The line went quiet. He was somewhere windy. She could hear the rippling fuzz. She wondered if he was choked up. "Just let me save face."

"Of course." He was asking her not to push him on how he was taking this.

"I'm in the city." He'd been born and raised in Manhattan. The city would always be New York City no matter how long he lived in L.A.

"I'll come in." What would that be like? Would there suddenly be passion? Would they end up having sex? What did people who used to be engaged feel for each other?

"Where are you?"

"At my mom's."

"Good. I'll come there."

This made her panic. "Why here? I mean, we're all here—my mom, my sisters, Atty . . ." She'd told him all about her father, but she couldn't mention him without opening up too much.

"I never got to see your people or where you came from. I want it to make sense."

"You want what to make sense? Me?"

"Why you gave up on us."

"I don't think it'll help," she said, tapping the shower liner and sticking her big toe up the faucet. She'd known her mother and sisters and this place she'd come from all her life, and it hadn't helped her make sense of anything.

"I feel like the negotiating power is tilted my way," he said. "My mother started smoking again. My father suggested suing you."

"On what grounds?"

"Whatever grounds. It's just where he goes, emotionally."

Ru wondered where Cliff had gone, emotionally. Did she really know him? She hadn't ever let him know her—not completely. She'd held back in tiny ways and then she'd broken up—in a letter from another country like a coward. "Okay. Come here. Do whatever you have to do."

"How about Saturday? I'll have to clear some things, but will you be around?"

Ru agreed and gave him her mother's address. They set a time midafternoon. But she thought of Amanda, Teddy Whistler's ex; Amanda should be allowed to stick with her plans, marry who she wanted—right or wrong. Teddy should disappear, let her go.

"See you then," Ru said.

"Remember when we used to make fun of married people?" Cliff asked.

"Yes."

"That seems like a long time ago now."

"It does."

"I refuse to miss you," he said and it was the most intimate thing he'd ever said to her. Then he hung up.

Ru slid down the tub's curved back and stared at the ceiling, spotted with mold. She thought of Teddy Whistler's face. It appeared in her mind in full color—the way he looked at her as she recited what he'd said on the plane.

Teddy was back. Her father was back. Cliff was coming. It was like an attack of men. What did it mean?

She didn't want to think of men. She wanted something soothing, something simple.

And suddenly she thought of the baby born in the longhouse where she'd spent the last nine months. The baby was a girl named Chau, and the family had let Ru hold her and walk her along the dirt road for long stretches every day. The baby had full cheeks, a slick of dark hair, and shiny eyes. Ru missed the baby's smell, her gummy smile, even her sharp cry. Ru understood why her mother had three babies with Nick Flemming. Her love for Nick must have been incredibly complicated, but the love you feel for a baby is pure and simple and visceral. Once you have one, you must just want another. The question wasn't why her mother had gone on to have three kids with someone she couldn't be with. Ru decided that maybe having three babies was an effort to counterbalance a complex, distant love with one that was primal, intimate, and close.

Atty and Esme were in the bedroom next door, the trundle pulled out from under Esme's canopy bed. Esme was wide awake and clear on one thing. Her bastard of a father would track down Darwin Webber, apologize, and retract any threats. She felt flushed with courage. She had sisters. It was their journey now.

But then again, it was her sisters—not just the idea of sisterhood—and she wasn't convinced that her sisters were trustworthy. Liv was a drug addict, for shit's sake, and Ru was a writer who, like a bottom feeder, relied on other people for characters. Liv ignored the facts of her addiction and only talked about her time in rehab like it was an extended spa stay, and Ru hadn't even invited her fiancé over to meet them. Was she embarrassed of Cliff or of them? Probably them.

(And of course Esme had looked up Rob Parks of Parks Cabinetry and there were no photos of him on the Internet. Who could avoid that these days—and still be an entrepreneur?)

Still, Esme was the one with an urgent need, and so she wanted Liv and Ru to get on board with the Darwin Webber mission. Would she bring Atty? Esme was worried about her. In telling her rendition of the musket incident, she hadn't made any connection to her father's abandonment. Esme wasn't sure how to approach the subject. She preferred not to talk about Doug herself.

"Atty," she whispered. "Are you awake?"

Esme wasn't sure what she'd say to her. Maybe she'd just ask her what she thought about the evening, help her process some of this. It could segue naturally to a discussion of Atty's father, couldn't it? "Atty?"

Atty was awake but she didn't say a word. She'd tweeted as many one-liners as she could.

Do synchronized swimmers sometimes practice out of water?
#someolympicsportsareBS

Being manipulative is different from being likable. #butbarely

If you're lucky, you'll wind up an oil portrait staring into a room
for eternity. #avoidpainters

She'd gotten a few retweets and favorites, but nothing from anyone at the boarding school who mattered, and certainly not Lionel Chang. He never retweeted or favorited. In fact, sometimes he went months without tweeting even a single peep.

She was turned away from her mother. She'd been crying, silently. She wasn't sure why, but it had to do with dying and being reduced to some portrait hung on a wall, doomed to stare out at the dining room; this is how she'd felt at boarding school all those years—a lonesome witness. She was lonesome.

There was also her ever-growing love–hate relationship with Nancy Drew and some unattainable version of self. Of course, Liv had told her to know how to cry on a dime but to never let anyone see her crying for real. Liv had told her many things—her guns, as they put it—but none of them seemed to help her in this situation: She didn't want to talk to her mother because she was trying to become someone else and her mother could never allow it.

Augusta was the only one who wasn't in bed. She was pacing her bedroom on the second floor, aware of her family, the house alive with them restlessly breathing all around her. She felt her parents' ghosts, batting around downstairs. Gulls—she remembered how, as a child with rheumatic fever, she'd hallucinated that their shrieking fights were gulls filling the house, all wings and noise.

"*Romantic* fever," she whispered. "Like I ever had a choice." She'd fallen in love and it was quick and deep and all-consuming. It overtook her body as the fever once had.

She could hear the snapping of the Rockwell flag out her open bedroom window. She dipped through the window—the air hot but gusty—and unhooked the flag from its post. She pulled it to her chest, ducked back in through the window, and stood there, holding the bundle like a baby.

At one point, before Ru was born, Nick wrote, "Let's at least try to live as husband and wife, let the kids have a father. I'm about to get three months of leave. We can rent a place. A lake house in Maine."

She said yes. They rented a house on Damariscotta Lake and he showed up thin and weak. Ulcers were eating him up. She quickly understood that he'd been sent on leave so he wouldn't bleed to death.

The summer was beautiful—canoes and an outdoor shower, a

fishing dock, a small island filled with blueberry bushes, distant campers singing songs that carried across the lake.

But as the three months slipped along, Esme and Liv got attached to him. Augusta had called him Daddy and Esme had picked it up.

"You could resign," she said. "You could get another job." But she knew it was too late. She saw the way he scanned the lake, everyone they passed on the street, in restaurants. She knew that he slept lightly, if at all. He was scared. That wouldn't end.

"I have to go back," he said. "I'll always feel hunted so I have to be allowed to hunt."

"I'm willing to take risks to be a family." She wasn't sure, though. She didn't know what she was trying to sign on for.

"Some people love a storm and some fear it," he said. "And some people love it because they fear it."

"What's that mean?"

"I can't let you all get swallowed by a storm."

Their cabin bedroom had two twin beds, with thick sheets and wool blankets. They made love in one of the beds, knowing that they'd failed, that he'd never really expected to succeed, and that this was the beginning of a long end.

Maybe Augusta was still in love. Maybe it was no longer possible. Maybe she wasn't ever a real wife.

But she would always be a mother.

# Part Five

*In which the family tries to reassemble.*

CHAPTER *25*

Over the next three days, Esme, Liv, Ru, and Atty worked hard at sisterhood.

Liv found an acupuncturist and they went in together and got individual sessions. Liv explained that this would help get their Zen straight and allow them to open up to life and all of its possibilities.

"Like your father orchestrating a big gift?" Esme said.

"Or like in the romance department?" Atty asked, earnestly.

Liv shrugged. "Just go with it." She missed Mrs. Kwok, though—in one swollen moment—and wanted to thank her for pulling her out of the window during the hurricane.

During her session, Atty tweeted, *Living pincushions. Is this really about love? #sisterhood* and *Feel like one of Nabokov's butterflies stuck to a corkboard. #sisterhood* and, finally, *F this sh\*t. I'm perforated. #sisterhoodnotworthit*

They played a few rounds of Spoons, but Liv and Esme grabbed a spoon simultaneously and even after a bit of wrestling, neither would let it go. They sat on chairs in the kitchen for forty-five minutes until Liv acquiesced. "This is stupid. You win. What's wrong with you anyway?"

"I win!" Esme said and then she restacked the deck of cards and put the spoons into the dishwasher.

Atty tweeted, *Watching grown women revert to middle school hierarchal structures. #uglysisterhood*

Early one morning, they pulled old bikes from the shed out back and worked on them for about an hour and a half before realizing that the tires were so rotted they'd never hold air. Sweaty but undeterred, they rented beach bikes and rode them on the boardwalk.

Atty tweeted, *I hate old lady exercise. #sisterhood* and *We're all wearing yoga pants and no one's doing yoga. #sisterhood* and, finally, *If my bike had a basket, I'd shove Toto into it. #sickofsisterhood*

They tried to teach Ingmar to climb the stairs with a series of treats and failed. Atty tweeted, *The collie clings to land, will never climb the ladder to success. #overratedanyway*

They hung out on the third floor, too. Ru found the old record player and put on some Sean Cassidy. Esme sorted through old photographs. Liv taped the best ones to the wall—for some reason, this was a comfort. Atty dug through old boxes, and inside one, wrapped in tissue, she found three wooden items she couldn't name. "What are these?" She held them like a strange three-stemmed bouquet.

"Conductor's batons," Ru said.

"You all took conducting lessons?" Atty asked.

Liv reached out and took one of the batons, lifting it in the air with a familiar ease. "We conducted storms," she said. "Augusta taught us."

Esme shook her head. "It was a strange childhood," she whispered.

"It's a strange adulthood too," Ru said.

And then a phone beeped.

"Gotta go check on the flan," Liv said.

"You're making flan?" Esme asked.

"It's a comfort food."

Over flan, the four of them took the time to devise a plan.

Esme already knew what she wanted from her father—to track down Darwin Webber and apologize—but they'd decided that they each needed to make a request.

"I'm just his granddaughter. Do I need to want something from him?" Atty asked.

"You can go either way," Esme said.

"I could use a hand looking for Nancy Drews," Atty said. "I'm missing six of them and I can't drive."

"Well, the old man can drive so there. You've got yours," Ru said.

Liv tried to beg off on the grounds that she'd gotten more than she'd expected from the man.

"That's just material stuff," Esme reminded her. "You can want something on an emotional level too, you know."

"I'm not really comfortable with wanting on an emotional level," Liv said.

"Well, we *all* have to ask for something," Ru said, inventing a rule.

"Otherwise, I'll get pegged as the needy one and that's not fair," Esme said.

"What do you want then, Ru?" Liv asked Ru.

"I'm not sure yet, but I know it'll come to me."

CHAPTER *26*

"I love you, Augusta Rockwell." The voice came out of the darkness. Augusta was in bed, wearing a nylon nightgown, just a thin
sheet over her. She knew the voice. She'd wanted to hear it, longed
to hear it—in this bedroom, coming out of the darkness—most of
her adult life.

"You're not allowed in my bedroom," Augusta said.

"I could back out and stand in the hallway, but it won't change
anything."

She sat up and pulled the string on her bedside lamp. "This is a
very difficult situation. The girls—" She could see him now. He
wore a T-shirt, a robe tied at his waist. He'd once been the man
running alongside the bus in the snowstorm on the eve of Kennedy's inauguration.

"I'm not talking about our daughters right now. I'm talking
about us."

"Well, we're in a difficult situation too," she said.

"Remember the hotel in Geneva with the Lilliputian elevator?
Remember the Montreal massage?"

They'd had sex in that Lilliputian elevator. She'd had a double
orgasm as a result of Nick's Montreal massage.

"I'm the only other person who holds it," Nick said.

"Who holds what?"

"Everything we ever were. And you're the only other person for me. You're my other person, Augusta. It's just the two of us."

She felt flushed. She nodded. "I know."

"Without you in my life, everything that happened between us is just a shadow. It's not real. You make the past real for me. Our past."

"Remember Maine," she whispered. "The wool blankets. The twin beds after the babies were asleep."

"We're still in love with each other."

"It never made any sense," Augusta said.

"No. It never did."

It was quiet a moment. Someone started singing out on the streets somewhere. Someone drunk.

"How long should I stand here?"

She stared at him then shook her head. "Not yet." And she lay back in bed, the down pillow puffing around her. "Not yet, Nick Flemming."

# CHAPTER 27

Ru ferreted through Esme's suitcase, put on her sister's sneakers and shorts, and announced that she was going for a run.

"You're wearing my clothes," Esme said.

"I know," Ru said. "We're in this together now."

Ru wasn't going for a run. She hated the idea of running. She thought it was something that someone should do either while playing field hockey, as she once had, where opponents wielded clubs, or if one was being chased.

She was actually meeting Teddy Whistler at an ice cream shop three blocks from the house. He'd texted her about his plans to crash Amanda's beach wedding. "What do you think? If I don't do it, will I regret it the rest of my life?"

She was going to talk him out of crashing the wedding but her reasons were suspect. The problem was that Teddy Whistler kept appearing in her mind—as she was trying to fall asleep, while washing her hair in the shower, even while talking to her sisters about their long-lost father. There were mini clips of him, running on loops.

Teddy Whistler on the airplane, saying, "No, I think it only matters who loves who last, but that also would have been me."

Teddy in his slicker at the reading, saying, "Sorry I'm late."

Teddy getting out of his rental car in front of their house. "Hi."

Teddy at the dinner table. "You're engaged?"

Teddy looking at her when she was saying goodbye to him at her front door. ". . . You are exactly the way I remember you, and you were only a kid, but you're still you."

Even when she wasn't thinking about him, she knew that the loops were playing in her subconscious, where she preferred them, but it was hard work not to think about Teddy Whistler. She tried to tell herself that she was thinking about him because he'd been the subject of her creative work. But she also was afraid of another possibility—one she didn't believe in philosophically or in reality: She was falling in love with him even though she didn't really know him and she couldn't really articulate why she was falling.

She jogged out of the house and down the first block just in case anyone was watching, then she slowed to a fast walk. By the time she got there, Teddy had ordered two scoops of lime and was eating the cone, one hand in his pocket, standing in front of the shop. His left eye was still swollen but also now tinged a dark blue.

"Hi," she said.

"Hi."

She ordered a scoop of mint chocolate chip, and they walked toward the beach.

"I want to confess something," Teddy said.

"What's that?"

"I've made families everywhere I've ever gone."

"How do you make a family?"

"I play the orphan hero and people take me in."

"Did your parents pass away?" Ru asked.

"No. I'm not an orphan or a hero. But my family never amounted to much by family standards. You nailed them in your book, to be honest. But your family is, by far, the most volatile and layered of any family I've ever seen."

"Thank you, I think."

"How's the fallout at the Rockwell home today?" he asked.

"We've decided that each of us needs to get what we need from our father, in some way."

"Like he has to pay off some debt?"

"I'm not sure."

"What do you want from him?"

"I'd like it to be something concrete. Nothing abstract, like love. That feels too open-ended to me."

"But the concrete thing would represent love, right?"

"I guess so."

"So why not just bypass the concrete thing and go for love?"

By the time they got to the beach, they'd eaten their cones. They sat in the sand and stared out.

"I'm trying to play this out in my head—finding Amanda before the wedding, somehow getting a moment alone," Teddy said. "I'm running out of time. Maybe I didn't tell you that, but some of the guests are on my side."

"I actually showed up to talk you out of this," she said.

"I thought you said I should go back to what I said about her on the plane."

"You crashed the engagement party. The groom punched you. I think she gets it. She's a grown woman and you have to trust her to know her own mind."

Teddy shook his head and smiled. "Sometimes people want to be saved from something. They want someone to swoop in and change their life." He pried off his loafers.

"Doesn't that sound sexist to you?"

Teddy took off his socks and cuffed his pant legs then stood up and walked toward the ocean. "No," he said. "Because it's what I want too. All those times I was playing the hero, I was a kid. I just wanted someone to save me. You know that, don't you?"

No. She hadn't known that. Was that the actual theme of her own work? "But you're a grown man now," Ru said, following him. "You don't need anyone to save you."

"Oh, really?" He reached out and took her hand, looking at the fat diamond ring. "Weddings are just dramatizations of two people saving each other. They may as well be set in shark tanks, not at altars."

She took a deep breath and held it, then said, "I'm not getting married. My family doesn't know. I called it off a while ago. Cliff is coming in a few days so I can give him the ring back."

"Really?"

"Really."

"And he's just letting you go?"

"Yes," Ru said. "That's actually the way it should be done." Why wasn't Cliff fighting for her?

Teddy thought about this for a minute or two. "I let Liv go," he said. "I mean, I didn't have a choice because I was in juvie and then that hospital, and when I got back she was at boarding school, and I gave up."

"You moved on. There's a difference."

"Tell me something, Ru."

"What?"

"Tell me a true story. Not something made up."

"Okay," Ru said. "Elephants can actually purr. It's more like a rumbling purr but it can carry for long distances. They use it to communicate, to bond, sometimes when they're trying to find a mate. That sort of thing. It's beautiful really."

"That's not exactly what I meant. Beautiful as that is. I was looking for something true about *you*."

"Oh." She thought of telling him about tracking her father down in Guadeloupe when she was just sixteen years old, and how he'd said that she was so like him. What did he mean by that? How did she interpret that then? Should she think about it now? "I don't deal in the truth," she said.

"Maybe you need an example. I once wrote I HEART AMANL on an overpass not too far from here when I was eighteen."

"Who's Amanl?"

"I had to run from the cops before I got to finish the *d* in Amanda. I'd only done the straight line, not the rounded part. Never got to the final *a*."

"Amanl. Very romantic."

"Now your turn. One thing. One true thing."

Ru thought of her mother's Personal Honesty Movement, the *Symphonie Fantastique* playing on the record player, the storm. "I don't like the truth."

"Why?"

"It never feels true enough." She'd tracked down her father in a bar in Guadeloupe. It hadn't seemed real—not while sitting there with him and certainly not as the image of him dissolved over the years, not even seeing him again now after all this time.

She pivoted.

"Whatever happened between you and Liv?"

"She doesn't believe in love and I do. Do you?"

Ru shrugged. "I believe it happens, but I'm not sure I believe it's sustainable."

"What if it's not sustainable, but it just keeps happening—to the same two people, over the course of a lifetime? Did you ever think about that?"

"No, I did not."

"No, you didn't," Teddy said. "But that would be worth fighting for, wouldn't it? Finding that person you keep falling in love with?"

"I guess so."

"You guess right."

And looking at Teddy Whistler, on the beach, barefoot and pants cuffed, she felt—for the briefest second—that everything else around them was gone and it was only the two of them. Alone. She felt like she could fall in love with him many times over.

CHAPTER *28*

As Liv got dressed that morning she thought about a sex addict named Glenn she'd met at the rehab facility. He'd told her how it all started way back for him with a girl named Pippa. He called her his point of entry. And Liv realized her own point of entry: In the summer of 1988, young Teddy Whistler was Liv's first cherry-pick. In fact, she'd found him in a newspaper.

Augusta had encouraged the girls to read the news every morning. She subscribed to *The New York Times* and *Washington Post*, as well as a few smaller local papers, which was where Teddy Whistler first appeared. The first story was of him saving an overweight woman from South Philly from drowning. Liv still remembered the woman's name, Tammy Fountaine. There'd been a picture of Tammy with her arm around Teddy's narrow shoulders, smiling broadly, thankful to be alive. In that picture, the front of Teddy's hair was a little sun-bleached and she decided she had to meet him.

Teddy Whistler needed to save people, and she needed to be saved. From what? Well, from the unbearable weight of the ordinary and a future that seemed to stretch before her with preordained ordinariness.

Now, as she brushed her teeth in the same mirror that she'd

stared into while brushing her teeth in the summer of 1988, she pictured Teddy as she first saw him—in the ticket booth on the boardwalk. (One of the newspapers had mentioned his summer job.) He stood there behind the glass—as if on display. He was tan and bored, pushing up his glasses and fiddling with the cash when no one was in line, as if perpetually on the brink of stealing it all.

She cased the joint, finding out she wasn't the first to be impressed by his heroism. One girl in particular had beaten her: Amanda Cross. She had long kinky hair, tightly permed and highly sprayed. She occasionally popped up with a bunch of other girls to tap on the glass of the booth and generally harass him. Twice, she stepped inside and Frenched him for about twenty seconds.

Liv thought, for the first time in her life, of a specific upside: *Good. He's the type to have a girlfriend,* and that this would play to her advantage. Of course, she thought she was prettier than the girl and that she could take him.

One night, Liv fixed her hair, swabbed her eyes with eyeliner, and paced in front of his booth, ignoring him. She paced until she felt his eyes on her, then she glanced at him. He nodded. She nodded back but then left.

She waited ten minutes and then returned. She paced some more and, looking a little teary, she walked up to the booth.

"What is it?" Teddy spoke to her like he knew her. "What's wrong?"

"Have you seen a guy, waiting here, an hour ago, maybe more?"

"I don't know. What'd he look like?"

"Dark hair and eyes. He's Lebanese."

"I don't know what Lebanese people look like really."

Liv covered her mouth and started to cry.

"Wait, wait. What happened?"

She walked a few feet away and stared at the passing crowed and beyond them, out at the ocean, as if this Lebanese boy might be lost at sea.

A father walked up to the booth, asking for a bunch of tickets for his rowdy kids. Teddy rang him up and then stepped out of the booth.

Another worker shouted, "Don't leave the booth unmanned!"

Teddy told him to shut up.

Liv was windblown. The night was warm.

He said, "Did this guy stand you up or something?"

Liv told Teddy how she and the Lebanese boy had met, how she'd snuck out after curfew, staying up with him until dawn. "He was leaving today to catch a plane to go back home. I was supposed to meet him here an hour ago, but I fell asleep. We'd been up all night. And I missed it. I didn't even get to say goodbye and now I'll never see him again."

"Jesus," Teddy said. "I'm sorry."

Liv started crying and he hugged her, saying, "It's okay. Don't cry. It's going to be okay."

Eventually, she touched the gold chain that sat flat and glinting on his collarbones. She touched it with just one finger. She looked up and he kissed her. That was all it took.

Over the summer, they got naked together. They told each other secrets, some true, some false. While his parents were out, Liv wandered through his house in her bra and panties. It was a crappy little house that smelled of mildew. His dad was especially hard on him, by Teddy's account. She told him that her mother had had sex with strangers and that her sisters were only half sisters, which she was pretty sure was true. But she never brought him home to meet her own family. She wanted to keep him to herself.

Augusta was no fan of Teddy Whistler. Liv came home drunk on peach schnapps more than once. When she missed her third curfew, Augusta told Liv she could no longer see Teddy and that she was grounded. All communication was severed. Liv explained this to Teddy on the phone while her mother stood beside her.

Teddy knew something was wrong. He knew she still liked him.

And there was only one line of communication still open between them. The newspaper. He saved a dog from a burning car, his way of telling Liv that he was waiting for her.

She knew that he'd done it for her the moment she saw the headline and his picture—him and the dog, Rusty, in front of the black hull of a VW Bug.

She snuck out after everyone had gone to bed. She went to his house, a ranch, and knocked on his bedroom window. They skinny-dipped in his neighbor's aboveground pool, in the dark, bobbing in the shallow end, drunk on peach schnapps.

And he told her that Tammy Fountaine faked drowning for twenty bucks—another five to call the paper. And Rusty was never in the car to begin with. Teddy talked a neighbor kid into the idea that he'd seen Teddy pull the dog out of the car. Why'd it catch fire to begin with? Well, that was what would put Teddy in juvie. Starting fires crossed a line.

She never told him the truth—that there was no Lebanese romance. Maybe she should have. But the truth was that she was falling in love with him and it scared her, especially now that she knew he was a fraud. He wasn't going to help her get out of Ocean City. He was doomed to live here forever, faking acts of desperate heroism.

She broke up with him, but she didn't tell her mother. No, she wanted her mother to think that she was going to run off with Teddy Whistler.

After the breakup, he faked his own escape from the neighbor's kinkajou. It was the third write-up in the paper. The headline read: "Local Hero Performs a Hat Trick." Another wrote: "Teen Hero Saves Himself." One other paper called them "A Trio of Miracles." Liv saw them all, but she'd started to read the engagement pages. She realized she could be saved by better.

Teddy tried to call to see if she'd seen the news, but Augusta hung up on him over and over.

Eventually, he showed up on the front lawn—drunk and

shouting—his glasses crooked on his face. "This time it was real, Liv!" he said. "I promise."

She felt like her heart was being ripped from her body. She wanted to run out of the house into his arms. She wanted him to lift her up and then, when her mother started screaming from the front door, they'd tear off down the street.

But she didn't because the emotion itself—love, pounding inside of her—was too terrifying. Instead, she fought with her mother.

But she could hear him, shouting, "Liv! Don't leave me alone like this! I love you!"

Liv walked to the window now and remembered that night, how he was shouting out his love and staggering around, and her mother ran to the kitchen phone to call the cops.

And eventually, Liv told the cops the truth—that he'd faked all those feats of heroism. She didn't have to. They hadn't even pressed her on it. She did it because she knew they'd probably take him away, and if he stayed here she'd give in to him; she knew she would.

It was an ending for Liv. From then on, she would pick more wisely—men who had something tangible to give, not this endless roaring emotion—something quantifiable.

(Not that it had always worked out. She'd dated two Olympians before realizing that it was sometimes hard to monetize the status. Senators were always failed experiments. Rock stars required too much nurturing. And while dating an NBA player, she'd found the wives and girlfriends to be the most viciously competitive women she'd ever met. The hierarchy was Byzantine; it was just untenable.)

And her father showing up was an ending too. Didn't his newfound honesty mean that he wasn't going to keep giving to her?

Liv thought back over her therapists. They'd wanted her to talk about her father, of course. She'd invented bankers and corporate stiffs—the type to work hard, drink too much, and remain emotionally aloof. One time, she talked about her father the spy but touted the old party line—there was no spy. Her mother had sex with strangers. The therapist, an overly preening young woman named Cheryl, liked this very much.

They all seemed to know that she needed that love from a father. How else could they explain her marriages to wealthy men, the longing to be taken care of?

She'd always countered that she wasn't longing. She was practical. Men and their various weaknesses, what could she do? It would have been like having a superpower and refusing to use it. Her looks, her cunning, these were her gifts, and they were profitable.

But now, how many marriages could she possibly still have in her? She was getting older, and the universe that she'd always relied on when she was in a tough spot turned out not to be the universe at all. It was her father and it was very likely that he was closing up shop.

Liv sat on the bed she'd slept in as a child. She thought of the nights she'd lie here, thinking of Teddy Whistler, the little punk. What if instead of shutting down when he cried out on the front lawn, something inside her had opened up, letting in all that love?

She'd be a different person.

But no, she was the kind of person to take her niece's iPad once again, which is exactly what she did, and she used it to look up Clifford Wells, once and for all.

This was simply a coping mechanism, she told herself. She was nervous and this was how she dealt with anxiety—well, in addition to pharmacology.

No one is perfect.

Except, perhaps, Clifford Wells.

She spent a couple of hours draining the Web of all information.

His *Estimated Assets and Income* were in the tens of millions, including *Family Money*, and a house in the Hamptons that had to be worth five million at least.

He had an incredibly high *Accessibility Rating*, as calculated by Liv herself. He went to openings, showed up at film festivals, had a family that popped up in society pages. It would be easy to orchestrate a chance encounter.

What was his *Desperation Quotient?* Well, considering the fact that he hadn't seen his fiancé in a year and might not have been invited to pick her up at the airport, she figured he was feeling some desperation—either to get back in or to get out altogether.

But there was one thing that made Clifford Wells easier to pick off than any person she'd ever come across before, and that was his *Apparent Attraction in Type of Woman.* Clifford Wells had proven that he was attracted to Rockwell girls, and Ru, to be frank, wasn't the looker in the family. Liv was.

This only left her catchall *Intangibles* category. If she were to go for Clifford Wells, would her sister's engagement—the mere fact of that emotional baggage—play against Liv or would her deep understanding of Ru—and all of her deep-seated weaknesses— somehow play in Liv's favor?

Was she going to cherry-pick her sister's fiancé? Was he really her fiancé anymore anyway? She was supposed to be relying on her sisters. They were in this together now, so why did she have to rebel against it?

"What if I am Gong Gong?" she whispered. "What if it's just who I am?"

She heard the front door shut and then saw the top of her father's head as he took his little dog, Toby, and Ingmar for a walk. Toby was barking and bouncing at the passing cars. Ingmar glanced nervously at the little dog while trying to exude a regal detachment about the great outdoors. Her father seemed focused on Toby, encouraging the dog to do his business. "Make peepee, Toby. Concentrate now. Go on and drop a lily."

Liv remembered that she was supposed to be figuring out what she wanted from the man. Good God, she didn't want to want love. She didn't want to talk to her sisters about wanting love. She didn't want to talk about love at all. Maybe all of her issues *were* his fault.

She leaned out the window. "Hey, old man."

He turned around and looked up, shading his eyes. "Liv?"

"You can't play favorites," she said.

"Favorites?"

"You've got to encourage Ingmar too. They both have aspirations, you know."

"Oh," he said, looking at the dogs. "Okay."

"Let's go out for lunch," Liv said.

"Lunch?"

"Yes. Just the two of us. Lunch." It was a simple enough thing to want. "Let's get this over with. Okay?"

"Get what over with?"

"Lunch."

Toby lifted his leg and peed.

"I promised Atty I'd drive her around to used-book stores to see if any more of those Nancy Drews came in," her father said.

Liv thought about this for a second. "Even better. Nancy Drew hunt with you, me, and Atty, then lunch." With Atty there, how much love-talk could they get into anyway? The kid could act as a buffer. Life needed more of them.

CHAPTER *29*

Augusta was trying to clear more space on the third floor. The house was packed. They needed more room to move about. Maybe she was feeling a little overwhelmed too—everyone was back. All of them! A family and she was the head of it.

She stacked some small boxes, making towers that allowed for a little floor space. She tried to clear off some of the long table in the center of the room. It was dusty, stuffy work so she went to one of the windows to let in more air.

But once she had one hand on the sill, she stalled.

She remembered going to the library after her bout of rheumatic fever was over. She looked up the workings of the heart. She wanted to know what might have gone wrong, the total damage.

She read the books in this very room, curled near the windows, and learned that the heart operates with electrical signals that cause it to contract. She felt electrical storms were the earth's way of getting pumped like a heart. The idea had terrified and delighted her. As a summer thunderstorm swept in, she pressed her face to the windows so she could see the ocean. She got so close she fogged the glass and had to wipe the glass clean.

And with every squall, she urged the ocean to rise up and swallow them all, whole. Love, she decided, was what weakened the heart most of all. She'd never fall for it. She stepped back from the window, let the glass clear, and decided to control the ocean. That was when she began conducting.

She looked out at the view now, the scuttle of tourists and cars, the distant dimpled glass of the Atlantic. She'd been wrong. Love was uncontrollable, but that didn't mean it was deadly. In fact, it was the only way to truly live.

The storm had come. She and Jessamine had weathered it, but she'd known then that it would churn things up, that change was coming. She hadn't expected to change, within herself. She hadn't seen that coming. She was old, yes, but she was changing. She could feel it—not unlike a fever.

CHAPTER 30

Atty had called ahead but when she asked about specific Nancy Drew titles, the woman who answered the phone got curt. "You'll have to come and paw through the stacks yourself." So now Atty was leading Nick and Liv through a used-book store's maze of stacks.

"That's her," Atty whispered, pointing to a white woman with a pale brown Afro reading a romance at her seat behind the counter. "I'm sure of it."

"Ask her where the mystery section is," Nick said.

"She's mean," Atty said.

"What's the worst she can do?" Liv said.

Atty walked up and said, "Excuse me, where are your mysteries?"

The woman lowered her book, glared at her, and then slowly lifted her book again. Atty reared back like she'd been bitten. She walked to Liv and Nick. "Vicious."

"Still, I've got a good feeling about this place," Nick said to Atty.

Atty nodded. "Me too." She headed off into the stacks.

"I hate used-book stores," Liv said loudly enough for the woman at the counter to hear. "It's where authors come to die, right? End of the road." Then it dawned on her that one of Ru's books might be in here. She turned a circle. As delicious as it would be to buy a copy in a place like this, Liv knew it was unlikely. Instead she muttered to her father, "Old books sometimes make me have to poop." They started wandering.

"I didn't know that," Nick said, more a comment on missing her childhood than anything else.

"It's a third-tier detail, really. Not a gem in my personality bracelet, if you know what I mean."

"But if we'd been pals, if I'd taken you to libraries and bookstores like this as a kid, I'd have known. Right?"

"But it's a stupid thing to know about me." She paused in the children's section, though it was only vaguely the children's section. The place was ridiculously disorganized. She saw a copy of *The Story About Ping,* the duck book that Ru had been talking about while the German artist had her body written on, for free, at the last party she and Ru had attended together. Liv picked the book up and flipped through its pages. "I don't even like books," she told her father. "So I would have had only sour memories of libraries and sad used-book stores like this."

"Where would you have wanted me to take you?"

Liv shrugged. "Who knows?"

"I found them!" Atty shouted from deep in the bowels of the place. "They've got a bunch!"

"Do they have the missing ones?" Nick asked as he walked toward Atty's voice, evidently invested in her search.

Liv stood there, speed-reading the book. It was about the owner of some fishing boat always beating the last duck to make it back onto the boat. And, this time, the last duck was also the littlest duck, Ping. He hid out, scared to get on the boat, but, in the end, he decided that it was worth the beating to be with the other ducks, his family.

"What a sucky lesson to teach young children," Liv said to herself. No wonder Ru was talking about it so vivaciously. Maybe it had haunted her, as she'd been the smallest duck in the family, as it were, or maybe she was agreeing with the message—family *is* worth taking a beating for, better than being alone.

Liv looked around. "Atty?" She thought of calling to her father but had no practice saying the word *Dad* so she didn't.

"They have number forty-eight!" Atty called out, popping back into sight at the end of an aisle, waving the book over her head.

And then Nick appeared at her side. "I'm so proud of you for tracking all these books down!" He looked at Liv. "It's fun, isn't it?" He turned back to Atty. "How many more to go?"

As Atty started talking numbers and titles, Liv froze. Holding A *Story About Ping,* she glazed over and thought only of those words *I'm so proud of you* . . . They were so simple and powerful. She realized that she wanted them from her father. She wanted stupid, inconsequential, deeply biased praise.

"Here," Nick said, "let me buy it for you." Atty gave him the book and as he passed Liv, she reached out and grabbed his sleeve, right at his elbow.

He turned. "You want me to get that book for you?"

"The boardwalk," she said. "I want to go to the boardwalk."

"We never go to the boardwalk," Atty said. "I've been wanting to go forever, but my mother says it's just commercialistic crap and a way to wring money out of people from South Philly."

"Exactly," Liv said.

"Let's haul ass," Nick said.


They rode the Scream Machine, the Sea Dragon, the Flitzer, and the Super Slide with its itchy burlap sacks. On the merry-go-round, Liv rode a zebra, Atty a dragon, and Nick a large sweet-looking bunny. When Nick won at the shooting gallery, Atty whispered to Liv, "Assassins have an unfair advantage."

Liv bested them at skee ball and Atty beat them at each video game they tried. "One develops a certain eye–hand coordination that's really specific to gaming," she explained. In truth, playing video games was how she'd first fallen for Lionel Chang, his hand guiding hers on the controller.

Eventually, the three of them were seated in a small cage, dangling at the top of the Ferris wheel. Liv felt exposed, vulnerable. She could hear the Ferris wheel's machinery, creaking around her.

"You can't give me gifts anymore, can you?" Liv said to her father.

"I have college costs," Atty said, "and am open to contributions."

"I'll be evening things out," Nick said.

"Why'd you give me the gifts?" Liv asked.

"I wasn't allowed to interfere with Ru's life and I thought Esme would be suspicious of anything that just showed up, a stroke of good luck like that. But I thought you'd accept it, without asking questions."

"Why am I like that, I wonder? Why didn't I question it?" Liv said.

"When I looked out at a crowd of kids to find you—at a performance or graduation or even just a crowd of kids getting off a field trip bus—you stood out because you wanted to stand out."

"Well, I didn't want to be ordinary."

"You seemed to want a charmed life. You looked around sometimes as if you were expecting someone to step in and grant you some special favor."

"True," Liv said. "I was kind of always expecting that."

Atty leaned to one side and said, "You can see the house on Asbury Avenue from here, just the top floor, the bank of windows. See?" She pointed.

Liv and Nick both leaned toward her, rocking the cage a little.

"To be honest, we had a good childhood," Liv said.

"Maybe it was better without me," Nick said.

"We'll never really know," Liv said.

"Do you want to have kids on your own?" Atty asked Liv.

"I don't care for the term *childbearing*."

"As in childbearing hips?" Atty asked.

"I especially don't like childbearing hips, but also, in general, I don't care for the term."

"You could adopt," Nick said.

"I don't like the term child *rearing* either."

"You could use different terms," Atty said.

Liv shook her head. "I don't really like children."

"But you like me," Atty said.

"I like you because you're no longer fully a child. You're outgrowing it."

"I hope I am," Atty said. "The in-between sucks, by the way."

Nick sat back and ran a hand over his gray hair. "What if you got that from me? I wasn't good at being a father. What if I could only do it from afar? What if I could only do it anonymously? I know what I *was* good at. I know what it's like to actually feel suited to something."

"Like killing people, right?" Atty said.

"There was a lot to my job. It was complex."

"Look," Liv said. "My sisters might not forgive you, but I do."

"You do?"

"I do."

"You do?" Atty said.

"You didn't want to be ordinary either," Liv said to her father. "And what's so wrong with that? I mean, look at all of that down there. All those people. All those lives. All of that regular daily living that people are doing so earnestly." The teacup ride, the boardwalk, the houses, the ocean—all of it seemed to teeter and swing beneath them. "Who could say yes to one teeny-tiny little piece of living when we all know there's a lot more?"

She tilted forward, making their cart rock. Instinctively, Nick reached out and grabbed her firmly but gently around the middle. "You okay?" he whispered.

She turned around so quickly that it startled him. "What?" he said.

"You," she said. "It was you on the subway platform." This was the old man who'd given her the Heimlich when she was choking on a menthol drop on the subway platform. She was sure of it. "Was it? Tell me."

"Yes," he said. "I told you I've been on the edges."

"You *saved* me."

"I tried to," he said, and she knew that he meant that he'd failed. He hadn't been able to keep her sober, to make her happy, to give her some kind of peace.

"It's okay," she said, and she meant she knew she'd have to do it herself.

CHAPTER *31*

That night, Augusta couldn't sleep. She padded down the stairs to the kitchen. She turned on the light and then saw a hunched figure sitting at the table.

She let out a small scream before realizing that it was Nick Flemming, his elbows on the table, eating buttered toast cut into triangles. Ingmar and Toby darted out from under the table, nosing Augusta. She shooed them away. "I'm fine. I'm fine," she assured them and then she asked Nick what he was doing awake.

"Can't sleep. Too much time to make up for. My brain keeps waking me up. Consciously and subconsciously, I don't want to miss any more. Not another minute, Augusta." His voice was almost angry.

She walked to the fridge, poured herself a glass of milk, and sat down next to him. "How was today with Atty and Liv?"

"It was perfect."

"Really? Perfect. With Atty and Liv." She laughed.

"It wasn't perfect in the traditional sense of the word. I mean, it was imperfect and flawed and I don't like riding those things. But it was perfect because it wasn't perfect. It just was, which is perfect."

"You never liked Norman Rockwell's kind of perfect anyway, I guess."

"Why aren't you asleep?" he asked.

"Too many people breathing in the house. It's so full of heart-beats."

"We made those heartbeats, you know?"

Augusta looked at him. "I imagine that your body is still full of scars, like a topographic map of old wounds."

"I got shot a lot and knifed too." He leaned forward and smiled. "You want to see it?" He motioned to his chest. "It's available for display."

She ignored him. "We were so close to telling them." There was a time when she gave an ultimatum and he'd agreed.

"But then we couldn't." A fellow agent's son went missing and then his body was found—in parts—in Miami.

"How is Gerard?" Augusta asked. She'd never met the man who'd lost his son, but she'd thought of him often over the years. "Do you ever hear from him?"

Nick shook his head. "My covers, the legends about who I was, where I came from. I wasn't Nick Flemming. I wasn't a husband or a father. It had to stay that way. It might have saved us."

"Who were you?" Augusta had never asked before.

Nick knew that only Ru had figured that out. For a while, he'd been Peter Wilderman. He'd grown up in White Plains, New York. His father had sold insurance. His mother taught violin lessons. He had no siblings. He'd played baseball decently in high school. He attended Penn State and got average grades. He joined the military. He didn't play the violin even though he'd been raised in a musical household.

None of this was true, but over time it reminded him of the truth.

"I can't tell you who I was," Nick said. "Sometimes it's still who I am." He rapped his knuckles on the table and said, "You know the real person. The kids will too. This is who I want to be." He reached out and slipped his hand over hers.

His hand was callused and warm.

"I missed you," she whispered.

"I missed you too."

This was said so softly that Liv, who also hadn't been able to sleep and was smoking on the patio, couldn't hear it. She'd heard all of it up until this point and now moved closer to the open window. The kitchen curtains were still. She was in the dark, unseen, and she stood there, watching her parents hold hands. She felt like she was seeing something rare and precious—a species that had been thought to be extinct. She'd heard that the passenger pigeon used to be one of the most common birds in the world, but the last one died in a zoo. Love—is that what this was? Rare and miraculously still alive.

CHAPTER *32*

Two days later, Esme found her father shaving in the third-floor bathroom; the door hung open, exposing him in the light of a single bulb. Wearing only a thin bathrobe that revealed a triangle of his gray-haired chest and black socks, he looked like an old man. He had jowls, leathery wrinkled skin, age spots, and liver spots—Esme didn't know how to distinguish the two—and small white spots where he seemed to have lost pigment altogether. He had to pull taut his loose neck skin to get a clean shave. His ankles were more delicate than she'd imagined a man's could be, much less someone who'd perhaps killed people, professionally. His little dog was sitting on the bath mat at his heels.

She'd planned on barging in and making demands. But he noticed her standing there and stopped shaving. He tapped his razor in the lip of the sudsy sink. Half his face foamed, he asked, "What can I do for you?" Because he owed her, was this how he'd have to address her from now on? He put his hands on his hips, his stance wide like a cop's, but then he slouched. He was tired.

Her mother had loved this man.

Maybe her mother still did.

Men are dangerous.

Who had they invited into this home?

"Nothing," she said. "I'll talk to you when you're dressed."

"I'm dressed enough," he said.

"That's okay," she said.

"Esme," he said. She hadn't ever really heard her father say her name. She cocked her head and tried to hold the sound of it in her mind. "I tried, kiddo. I really did."

"Tried what?"

"To be a father."

She shook her head. "I'll wait. This can wait. You should be dressed."

She walked down the hall to Liv and Ru's bedroom. She knocked on their door, glanced back at her father who stood there, framed in the bathroom doorway, then walked into the bedroom.

Liv was folding laundry, wearing a bra and matching lacy black panties.

"Someone actually buys that stuff?" Esme said.

"What stuff?"

"Uncomfortable frilly undergarments," Esme said.

"I think the term *undergarments* fell out of fashion in 1957."

Ru walked in, holding a cup of coffee. She instinctively turned her ring around on her left hand so that it faced inward. "What do we have here? A powwow?"

"She came in to discuss *undergarments*," Liv said. "And maybe Eisenhower and the new hula-hoop craze."

Then Atty called from down the hall, "Mom!"

"What?" Esme called back.

Atty popped her head into the room. "Augusta is making pancakes." She'd been calling her grandmother Augusta for as long as Esme could remember. "Are you all in?"

The three sisters froze.

"What's wrong?" Atty asked.

"Where's Jessamine?" Liv grabbed a pair of shorts and a tank top and started scrambling to get dressed.

"She's downstairs."

"Why is Augusta *cooking*?" Ru asked her sisters.

"This is what I came in to talk about!" Esme said. "I had this plan where we were all going to drive to Great Neck, and Nick was going to tell Darwin Webber he's sorry, but then, there he was, like an actual old man, shaving in an actual bathroom—my *father*. And I thought, what if my parents get back together? What if she's cooking in some weird attempt to woo Nick Flemming?"

"That's not how you woo a man," Liv said to Atty, yanking the tank top over her head. "And God, seriously, people stopped *wooing* each other around the time they stopped wearing *undergarments*."

Ru shook her head. "She's not wooing him. Not possible."

"Why not?" Atty asked, and there was a hopefulness that made Esme wonder if Atty hoped she and Doug would get back together.

Liv straightened up. "What if they did? Maybe they should." She hadn't told them about the night she eavesdropped on them in the kitchen, but she'd thought about them together ever since. Could it possibly work?

"I think they shouldn't. At all," Esme said. "He's a wolf in an old man's bathrobe."

"Regardless of what we think, they can't. It's been too long," Ru said. "Too much has happened. I mean, people can love each other and get knocked off-course by almost anything. You think their love can withstand all it's got to have been through?"

"Where's Cliff?" Liv said. She'd already properly medicated herself to face the day. Her meds made her a little more frank than usual. "You two really haven't seen each other in almost a year and he's still not showing up?"

"This isn't about me. Our mother is cooking. Food!"

"Have you and Cliff been kicked off-course?" Atty asked.

Ru shook her head. "He's fine." And he was fine. He had a deal with Sony. "Are we going to witness this historic cooking event or not?"

The four of them walked quickly down the hall, the stairs, and into the kitchen.

Augusta stood at the stove. Jessamine sat at the 1940s-style tin-top table, her pocketbook in her lap, her sunglasses still on.

"What's this?" Esme asked.

"She's cooking," Jessamine said.

"I'm cooking!" Augusta sang.

"What are you doing, Jessamine?"

"I'm waiting for a pancake." What Jessamine meant was that her life had changed forever. It was like watching one of her children grow up. She felt an itchy sense of impending freedom, tinged with nostalgia. Jessamine was bound for change as well.

"Who wants a pancake?" Augusta said.

"You don't cook," Ru said.

Liv sat down across from Jessamine. "I'll take one."

"Me too!" Atty said.

"With blueberries?" Augusta asked.

"I'll have one with blueberries," Esme said.

"I'm not sure if I should eat any at all," Ru said. "What does this mean? Why are you cooking?"

"I'm providing nourishment for my children," Augusta said.

Nick walked in, his dog padding along behind him. He was clean-shaven, wearing a short-sleeved buttondown and khaki shorts. He had bony knees. The kitchen's transistor radio was set to an old-ies station, playing "Ring My Bell," which suddenly seemed to Ru like a really dirty song. "Good morning," he said and he sat down, too.

"This isn't right," Esme said.

Ru wondered if this *was* right, but, because they had no experi-ence with it, it just seemed wrong.

"This is part of the gift of embracing the moment," Liv said. "We've got to just take hold."

Esme thought she knew what she meant and took this opportu-nity to announce the plans for the day. She had to take control. She had no choice. She wouldn't be able to scrabble on with her life without knowing the truth about Darwin Webber, without seeing him with her own eyes—and in so doing, seeing the life she didn't have. "We're going to Great Neck," she said. "So Nick Flemming can take the fatwa off Darwin Webber's head and apologize for fucking over our lives."

"It wasn't a fatwa," her father said. "Clearly, there was no fatwa involved."

"Do you do fatwas?" Atty asked.

Nick opened his mouth but Augusta jumped in first. "It'll be a family outing."

"We're all going?" Atty asked.

"Of course," Liv said to Atty. "This is about *us*. You included."

"Yes," Ru said, feeling loose in her joints. "I mean it's not like a picnic or going to the zoo or playing Frisbee in a park together, but it's *something*."

They all looked at Nick Flemming. He sat there and stared back. "I've jumped out of airplanes," he said, "swam away from an exploding boat once. I know torture—both ways. I've survived in the jungles of Zaire. I was shot at close range in the bathroom of the Vienna opera house. My body is peppered with shrapnel—some of it's been with me for decades. But you people," he said, sweeping the room with one crooked finger. "You people scare the hell out of me."

The radio was now playing Donna Summers singing "Love to love you baby . . ."—with its sexy backup moaning. The kitchen was filling with smoke. Augusta had lost track of the griddle.

"I think that's a yes," Ru said. "He's in."

"Yep," Liv said. "That was a yes."

"Okay." Esme took a deep breath. "We're going."

"Are we?" Atty asked.

"We are," Augusta said.

"The smoke detector is going to go off," Jessamine said.

And then it did.

CHAPTER *33*

Since the green station wagon was hit by the heavy limb in the summer storm of 1985, the limb that Ru had tried to keep aloft with the sheer force of her will, Augusta had replaced it with a second and then a third green station wagon. The six of them—Nick and Augusta, their three daughters and granddaughter—were standing around it, all of them unsure how the seating should play out.

"It's gotten weird with the green station wagons," Liv whispered to her sisters.

"It's like she can't get rid of the past," Esme whispered.

"I thought you'd have given up trying to psychoanalyze our mother," Liv said. "What with the sex-with-strangers and intimacy-issues theories going so very wrong."

"Who had sex with strangers?" Atty asked. They hadn't known she'd really been listening, but she was kind of always listening.

"What are you all talking about?" Nick asked.

"The alternative theory of our mother's life," Ru said.

"And what was that?" Nick asked.

"Nothing," Esme and Augusta said in unison.

"Maybe we should take a few cars," Liv said.

"We're a family," Esme said, and Ru and Liv had to believe that she was working from some grand plan—a vision.

"I'm driving," Augusta said, with preemptive defiance. "I'm the only one insured as a driver on the vehicle except for Jessamine."

Jessamine was inside, reassembling the smoke detector; Liv had had an adverse reaction to the high-pitched bleating and instead of airing it with a tea towel, as Augusta had suggested, she beat it with a broom handle.

"But do you actually drive?" Ru asked.

"I have a license."

"You know, it's okay if someone else drives your car once in a while," Nick said. "Insurance still kicks in."

"Don't explain the workings of the world to me," Augusta said. Ru wasn't sure if she preferred to be ignorant or she felt he was being condescending. Her parents together as a couple was foreign terrain.

"If the woman says she can drive, she can drive," Liv said. "But I call front seat because the backseat makes me carsick."

"Oh, this bullshit again," Esme said. "She threw up one time. One time! And has gotten to ride in the front forever after."

"She threw up *on Santa*, though," Augusta said. "It was scarring."

"For her or that poor fat Philly Santa?" Esme said.

"Both, probably," Augusta said.

"I wasn't sure I'd get presents," Liv said. "I'm not like you two. I *need* presents."

"I don't know what that means," Esme said to Ru. "Do you?"

"I associate the smell of barf and the holidays," Ru said, quietly.

"Atty," Esme said. "You get sick in the backseat. Don't you?"

"Only if I read."

"So don't read." Liv got in the front seat and slid to the middle. Nick moved to sit next to her. "I have long legs," he said.

"Not really," Ru said.

"You're actually pretty short. What are you, five foot eight?" Esme asked.

"I'm five foot ten," Nick said.

"What? In lifts?" Liv said.

"Oh, just let him have the front seat," Ru said.


Atty, holding on to a copy of Nancy Drew's *The Clue of the Broken Locket* and wearing her fanny pack over one hip, sat in the middle of the backseat between Esme and Ru.

"I wish I'd lost ten pounds before seeing Darwin," Esme said. "I bought a juicer but I don't like juice, turns out."

"Help Mom keep an eye on the road, okay?" Ru said to Liv.

"I'm fine," Augusta said. She drove two-footed—one on the gas, one on the brake.

"Tell a badass spy story like Jason Bourne," Atty said to her grandfather.

"Those movies are deeply flawed," Nick said.

"Then tell a love story," Liv said. "How did you two meet?"

Augusta shot Nick a look and then changed lanes. She was driving so slowly that traffic poured around them.

"We met on a bus in a snowstorm," he said.

"And when did you fall in love?" Ru asked, thinking of Teddy and wondering if the way he made her feel could turn into something real.

"On that bus," Augusta said.

"During the snowstorm," Nick added.

"Right then? Immediately like that?" Ru said.

"Yes," Nick said. "Right then. Immediately like that."

"Huh," Ru said.

"Why do you say that like you don't believe us?" Augusta said.

"The generations following yours have been led to believe that falling in love is something that only happens in movies," Atty said.

"It's like each generation is more super-jaded than the one before it."

"You're wise," Liv said to Atty. "Very wise."

"Thank you," Atty said, and then feeling emboldened she asked her grandparents, "Why did you have kids?"

"We had kids for the same reason most people do. We fell in love," Nick said.

"That's naïve. I mean, I don't think people have kids because they're in love," Liv said.

"Sometimes they just want kids and aren't in love with anyone," Ru said, thinking of the baby born in the longhouse. She'd been there for the birth—a wondrous slick head emerging then a tumble of body, her little face going taut with squalling.

"Are *they* the reason why you two couldn't hack it?" Atty asked, swooping her finger at her mother and two aunts. Again, Esme wished her daughter would talk about the pending divorce. Did she blame herself for it in some way?

"They're the reason why we tried so hard *to hack it*," Nick said.

"Did you try, though? Did you *really* try?" Esme asked.

Nick looked at Augusta. "Should I . . ."

"Tell her about Maine," Augusta said.

"After Esme and Liv were born, I had to go on leave for a while."

"He was dying," Augusta said.

"I had some ulcers. I didn't die so I wasn't dying."

"In Maine? You mean you went on leave with us?" Esme asked.

"Liv was still tiny and you were a few years old," Nick told Esme.

"It could never work," Augusta said.

"I was already in too deep."

"In Maine?" Esme said again. "Like on a lake in Maine? With a fishing dock?"

"There was a dock," Augusta said.

"Sure," Nick said. "Canoes and life jackets hung on pegs under this little wooden lean-to. And there was an island full of blueberry bushes."

"And fishing . . ." Esme said, her voice sounding distant and hollow.

"Esme?" Augusta asked. "What's wrong?"

"Shit," Esme whispered and then she rolled down the window and shoved her head out of the car.

"Esme!" Liv said. "You're letting hot air in!"

"Mom?" Atty said. "Mom, are you okay?"

Esme pulled herself back into the car. Her hair was blown back from her face, which was blank and pale.

"Esme?" Ru said. "Say something."

"Uncle Vic," Esme said and then she grabbed her father's headrest and pulled herself forward. "You're Uncle Vic!" Then she reached up and slapped the back of his head.

"Jesus!" her father said. "Who's Uncle Vic?"

Augusta sighed. "She'd started calling you Daddy. Remember? She couldn't go around talking about her daddy to people. That was the whole point of keeping us safe. There was no Daddy."

"And so you made up another man?" Nick asked.

"Yes. Yes, I did," Augusta said.

"You lied to me," Esme said. "You denied me the only childhood memory that I had of my father!"

"I don't have a memory of him at all," Liv said. She didn't want to share that her father had saved her life. He'd given her so many gifts that a lifesaving Heimlich would seem like piling on, especially in light of what he'd done to Esme's life; but at the same time, she didn't want to admit what she knew was the truth—he watched over her more closely because she needed him in a way her sisters hadn't and in a way they'd never understand. "I was just a baby in Maine," she said, knowing that her father understood that they now had a secret.

"I wasn't even born yet," Ru said and for the first time in a long time she was desperate for a Jolly-Lolly.

"He forced me to control the truth. I told you about him later. And you didn't believe me so what was I supposed to do?"

"Maybe we're all liars," Ru said. "None of us can be trusted."

"I just manipulate people. That's different," Liv said.

"You made all those men think you loved them, but you were using them," Esme said. "That's a *terrible* kind of lying."

"You didn't know your marriage was in trouble?" Liv said. "You didn't know your daughter was on the verge of some weird musket-stealing thing? Why? Because you lie to yourself. That's the worst kind of lying!"

"You went around telling us that your loves were these grand epics," Esme shouted, "so romantic we could never understand. But you're a gold digger. See?" She flipped out her palms. "That is what telling the truth looks like!"

Liv's face tightened.

"We can't turn on each other," Ru said, cautiously. "This is about us now. Together."

"And I suppose you're going to tell us, once again, that all is fine with Cliff the mysterious fiancé," Liv said, turning the anger onto Ru.

"I'm going to throw up," Atty said.

"There's a difference between being private and lying," Ru said. "Am I allowed a private life? Is that okay with you?"

"Seriously," Atty said. "I'm going to throw up!"

"But you weren't reading," Liv said.

Atty clamped her hand over her mouth.

"Pull over!" Ru said, rearing away from Atty.

Augusta put on the blinker and looked in her rearview mirror.

"Just pull over," Nick said.

"Don't tell me how to drive!"

"It's okay. It's going to be okay," Esme said, rubbing her daughter's back.

"We were just giving each other a hard time. It's what family does," Liv said. "We still love each other. Don't we?"

"Just hold on," Augusta said, very slowly edging onto the shoulder.

"If you don't hit the gas *with* the brakes at the same time," Nick said, "I think you'll find that the car goes faster."

"Being yelled at only makes me slow down!" Augusta shouted.

"Don't throw up," Liv told Atty. "Just keep telling yourself that. *Don't throw up. Don't throw up. Don't throw up.*"

"I thought you said lying to yourself is the worst kind of lying," Esme said to Liv.

"Okay, just throw up, Atty," Liv said, "if that's your inner truth."

Then Atty threw up.

CHAPTER *34*

Esme waited outside of the occupied mini mart bathroom with Atty, who was lightly doused in vomit. "You want me to go in with you?"

"No," Atty said.

"Good thing you were wearing flip-flops?"

"Don't upside this. Please." Atty had already cried a little. "I got some on my book."

"I told you not to read in the car."

"I wasn't!"

The bathroom door opened and a woman with a blond perm walked out. Atty rushed in and locked the door.

Esme didn't want to hover so she walked back to the aisles, where she found Liv and Ru idling in front of the bank of refrigerated drinks.

"How's she doing?" Ru asked.

"It's been years since she got carsick," Esme said.

"It's not carsickness," Liv said. "Don't shut down on this."

"We *all* should have shut down in the car," Esme said. "We said some awful things to each other."

"Do you think we're a family of liars?" Ru said.

"Who knows?" Esme said. "Maybe it's the human condition."

"Atty's freaked out," Liv said. "I think she might be depressed and anxious."

Esme opened one of the refrigerator doors and pulled out a ginger ale. "She just needs to settle her stomach."

"Esme," Ru said. "It sounds like she took the musket and fired it because she was being bullied. What was this quacking thing about anyway?"

"You can't imagine our year. That clusterfuckingphobic place. That place was crazy. I'm glad she told her French teacher to go poop in a hole. That woman is certifiable."

"Why did she tell her French teacher to poop in a hole?" Liv asked.

"Is that even an expression?" Ru asked.

"The headmaster brought me in and read the transcript. It was her first *ding*. He thought it was a sign that the time bomb was going to explode. That's how he saw us ever since Doug left, ticking away on his precious campus."

"What happened exactly?"

"I argued that Atty had actually said to the French teacher, *Why don't you go poop in a hole?* which felt a lot different than demanding that someone *Go poop in a hole.*"

"Well," Ru said. "That's one argument, I guess."

"She didn't want to do a project on Paris, and the teacher said something acknowledging that Paris, being the location of her father's indiscretion, must make the assignment difficult for her or some shit. And Atty merely . . ."

"Queried why this teacher didn't poop in a hole," Ru said.

"Exactly," Esme said.

"She wasn't accusing the woman of pooping in holes," Liv said. "Quite the opposite. She was wondering why she *didn't*."

"You all might think this is very funny. But I tell you Atty was the sane one in an insane world."

"Wow," Liv said. "She's right. You *are* proud of her for doing it."

"Of course I am. I should have done something but I was just being a stupid sheep, following the rules, going quietly so I didn't upset anyone." Esme turned to Liv. "Did she tell you I was proud of her?"

Liv nodded.

"Still," Ru said. "I think she might need to talk to someone. You know?"

"She needs family," Esme said. "Real family. The kind that doesn't walk out on her."

They walked to the counter and paid then looked through the plate-glass window at their parents. Augusta was pumping gas. Nick, who'd been put on cleanup duty, was holding a plastic bag of vomitous paper towels. He looked happy, leaning against the car, gazing at Augusta while she spoke. Wind kicked up wisps of her hair and she was gesturing wildly, not angrily, but passionately. And then he started laughing. She glanced at him and laughed too, covering her mouth almost girlishly.

"Jesus," Ru whispered.

"Those two are falling in love," Liv said.

"I can't believe that Uncle Vic was my father," Esme said.

And then Atty startled them. "Aunt Liv," she said, "you've got throw-up in your hair."

Liv reached around and patted her hair. "Shit!" She headed for the bathroom, but then stopped. "Come with me, Atty. I'll need help."

Atty sighed and followed her.


"Okay," Liv said, turning on the faucet and leaning over. "What's going on? Why did you barf?"

"I don't know."

"Get some foamy soap."

Atty pumped the canister attached to the wall, filling her hand with white fluff. "I feel these waves of awfulness like the world is going to end."

Liv held out her hand, and Atty passed the foam to her.

Someone knocked on the door.

"We're in here!" Liv shouted and then she said to Atty, "What's it feel like?"

"It's like being locked in a closet except it's more like I'm the closet. I'm trapped and I'm the trap."

Liv rubbed the suds into her hair. "Huh. Like people are stuck inside you?"

The knock came again.

"Seriously?" Liv shouted at the door. "People are in here. Do you not understand waiting in line?"

"No," Atty said. "I'm the person and the closet. Does that make sense?"

"And this feeling hits you like a wave how often?" Liv was rinsing now.

"Almost every day but this is the first time I barfed about it."

Liv put her head up to the hand blow-dryer and dipped under it. The bathroom filled with noise and hot air. Atty took a picture of her aunt drying her hair, Instagrammed and tweeted it with *#sad-yolo*. "How do you get all those rich men to marry you?" Atty asked. "Love must love you."

"Love loves me?" Liv laughed. "No, no. Love doesn't love me at all. It's scientific. I've invented a very precise system."

The dryer turned off automatically. The room was suddenly silent. Liv's ears started ringing. She felt raw and unclouded. Everything was clear and unmuffled like she'd just come up from underwater. She looked in the mirror. She remembered being naked in front of Teddy Whistler before she turned him in. When he told her the truth, she should have loved him more. "But maybe I've done everything wrong, Atty. How do I know?"

"I don't understand anything. I'm just the closet and the girl in the closet."

"No you aren't."

"You don't know what it was like when they *quacked* at me."

"Why did they quack at you? Did it have to do with the fanny pack somehow?"

"Why doesn't anyone in this family understand *irony*?" Atty patted her chest, her eyes widened and filled with tears. "One day we're going to just be oil paintings staring out at nothingness."

Liv grabbed both of Atty's upper arms and held on tight. "Why did you steal that fucking musket? Were you going to kill yourself?" And then she whispered, "If you were, you can tell me. I might be the only one in this fucked-up family who will understand."

Atty shook her head, refusing to comment.

"Tell me, Atty!" Liv said. "You'll die of an ulcer if you hold this stuff in and you'll never be able to heal because you can't be honest with yourself!"

"I can't tell anyone!" Atty said.

"Nothing is so awful that you can't say it to me," Liv said. "I'm an addict, for shit's sake!"

"I thought you were at the top of the drug addict hierarchy?"

"That was bullshit. Addicts are addicts. There's no hierarchy. Tell me! Tell me now! You wanted the musket to go off, didn't you? You thought it would? You wanted it to put an end to it all."

"I wanted it to go off! But I didn't want to kill myself!" Atty shouted and she ripped herself loose and threw her shoulder against the wall.

Liv watched her slide to the tiled floor. "I don't understand."

"I didn't want to kill myself," Atty said, staring at the tips of her fingers. "I stole the gun and wanted to get Brynn Morgan interested in it. I had this elaborate plan where I'd teach her how to clean it. I wanted it to go off in her face. Like an accident. This was before I really realized how time-consuming it is to fire a musket, of course."

"*Like* an accident?"

Atty kicked the large metal garbage can. "But I couldn't do it, could I?"

"Of course you couldn't," Liv said. Her heart was banging. She patted her chest and then scratched her arms and then she laughed. "You're not a killer, Atty. Is that what you think?"

"Brynn wasn't interested in the musket. Who wants to clean an antique? I wasn't thinking straight. You thought I was going to kill myself. You said all that stuff about the trigger and putting an end to it all," Atty said, staring up at Liv. "You said you'd be the only one who understood. You tried to kill yourself, didn't you?"

"It was a misunderstanding. There was a gun." She closed her eyes, but only lightly, as if she were remembering something peaceful. She'd gotten a pawnshop owner to assemble her ex-husband's pheasant-hunting gun. She'd taken it to her favorite restaurant on the Upper West Side. She ordered her favorite meal and then folded her napkin into the shape of a swan, propped it on the table, and went to the bathroom. She was going to do it, right there, where, she figured, it would be easy to wipe down the mess. "I couldn't do it either," she said.

"I need help," Atty said. She held out her hands, and they were shaking badly. "I walk around all the time feeling like I'm going to explode out of my body. I'm so anxious. I wouldn't kill myself because I already feel like I'm dying!"

"It's panic," Liv said. "You're going to be okay." She dug through her pocketbook. She pulled out a wallet with lots of zippers. She slipped her fingers inside one compartment and pulled out a ziplock bag with two pills in it. "This is a great gift I'm giving."

"What are they?"

"My last two Valiums." She shoved them into the front pocket of Atty's jean shorts.

"I can't take these!" Atty said.

"I find great comfort in just having them," Liv said. "But more comfort in actually taking them. Either way, it's not fair for you to feel this bad. Try them out. If they work, we'll talk to your mother about medicating you a little."

Atty stood up. "I probably shouldn't take drugs from a druggy."

"Realistically, they're usually the ones with the best shit." Liv rested her hands on Atty's shoulders. "This is how America survived the 1970s."

"Okay."

"Listen. Your shit is real. And this is a weapon in your arsenal. That's all."

"Thanks." Atty started to tweet something about having real shit going on in her life, but her aunt slapped her hand.

"What are you doing?"

"Tweeting."

"Well, stop. It's weird and dissociated or something. No one needs to know your business anyway. Be a little more mysterious, okay? Jesus." Liv unlocked the door, but before she opened it, she said, "I'm going to need another few minutes. Tell everybody I'm coming."

"Okay," Atty said.

Liv opened the door and found a middle-aged woman in purple yoga pants, glaring at them.

"I had throw-up in my hair," Liv said to the woman. "And we were having a tender moment."

"Like I care," the woman said.

Liv stiffened and stared at her. "Looking at people with that *face* on your *face* is making you prune up."

The woman was about to shoot something back but Liv raised her hand and gave her a look. "Why don't you go poop in a hole?"

Atty smiled at Liv then walked past the woman back into the store, tweeting, *Looking at people with a face on your face will prune you up.*

Liv shut the door again, locking it quickly, and as the woman in purple yoga pants started pounding, Liv lit up a joint, sat down on the toilet lid, and calmly smoked it.

# CHAPTER 35

They drove on in silence, each feeling battered.

Liv had moved to the backseat and Atty to the front. Nick stayed in the front with Augusta still behind the wheel. This put the three sisters side by side.

At one point, while stalled in traffic, Ru said, "Can you imagine all the things that had to happen in each of our lives—and the timing of all of it—that got us into this car at this exact moment. I mean, there's no other moment in our lives when this would have happened. Only now."

No one responded, not that it needed a response, but each of them thought of their current life situations—Herc Huckley's box of letters surfacing in Hurricane Sandy and getting delivered to the front door, a husband falling in love with a Parisian dentist, the ending of a stint in rehab, a trip to Vietnam in order to escape a doomed engagement, the firing of an antique musket at parents' weekend, a lonesome apartment in a retirement village . . . It was a miracle made of many intricate mechanisms, gears locking into gears and turning, seemingly, of their own accord.

Ru received a text from Teddy Whistler that invited her to crash a wedding with him. *There's always extra cake at those things.*

She texted back, asking if he planned to try one more win-back.

*Depends,* he texted. *Will Whistler be in a heroic mood like in days of yore? Or has he grown up at long last?*

After a minute he added, *Which would be better for your next book?*

"Shit," Ru said aloud.

"What?" Esme said but only out of knee-jerk politeness. She didn't care what was going on with Ru. She was about to meet Darwin Webber after all these years. She kept sucking in her stomach and pulling down her shirt, which she regretted wearing because it kept riding up.

"Nothing," Ru said. Maybe she wasn't a liar as much as she was a thief, robbing people of their best stories and then using them, for profit and, worse, to avoid living her own life.

Liv stared out the windshield thinking that today was the future, that her mother was driving them, physically, literally, and unalterably into each singular next moment. She was high.

After an hour or so, Atty held her hand up to the old plastic vents in the dashboard. "It's not blowing cold air anymore."

"Sometimes this happens," Augusta said.

Nick rolled down his window. "We'll have to air-condition the old-fashioned way."

Esme rolled down her window. "My face is going to melt. My hair is going to be an unmitigated disaster."

"What's the plan of approach here?" Nick asked.

"You're going to apologize to Darwin Webber," Esme said.

"He's probably going to be pretty scared," Liv said, and she laughed.

"What did you say to him anyway?" Ru asked her father.

"I don't remember," Nick said.

"Yes you do," Augusta said.

"I might have told him that I had certain connections that could make things unpleasant."

"You said you'd kill him, didn't you?" Atty said.

"I don't think it's good to surprise people in these kinds of situations," Nick said.

"Situations where you've already threatened their lives?" Esme asked.

Liv leaned back and said in a mock-deep voice and, for no apparent reason, a British accent, "I was shot at close range in a bathroom in the Vienna opera house . . ."

Nick looked over his shoulder at her, stunned. "Is that how this is going to go?"

"Parenthood is ultimately humbling," Esme said. "Didn't you know that?"

As they got closer to Great Neck, Esme pulled out her phone and directed Augusta off the highway and into the town itself. But then she handed the phone to Liv. "Here, you do it."

Liv handed it to Ru. "I can't read blipping dots like this."

Ru handed the phone to Atty. "Front seat navigates."

"She can't read or she'll get sick again," Esme said.

Atty handed the phone to Nick. "You've survived in the jungles of Zaire," she said in a British accent, "*you* do it."

Liv laughed.

"I guess I'll get used to it," Nick said.

"We'll just go in," Esme said softly. "Hopefully he's working, and if he's not, I don't know. But if he is . . ."

Nick put on a pair of bifocals. "Take the next right."

"We'll wait in the car," Ru said. "You don't need an entourage."

"It's about us," Esme reminded her.

"Everyone needs an entourage," Liv said.

"Seriously?" Atty said. "Six of us are going to walk into a cabinet store together? All at the same time? Descending like a plague?"

"A Plague of Rockwells," Liv said.

"We're clearly not a plague!" Esme said.

"You know there's a chance that you, Esme, are a hazy memory,"

Liv said. "I mean, isn't college hazy?" Esme was staring at her, obviously hurt, so Liv quickly added, "Not to be a bitch, I'm just stating a *possibility*."

"We were *in love*. He *disappeared*." Esme was pinching her thumb and index finger in Liv's face like she was about to do a charade clue for a bird's beak. "Do you understand?" She was over-enunciating.

Liv nodded then shook her head, which undermined the nod, and then shrugged a little, which further undermined the nod—it was an affirmation mudslide.

When they were a mere three blocks away from Parks Cabinetry, Atty spotted an antiques shop that had a special faded sign reading RARE BOOKS in faded gold lettering. "I'm still missing seventeen, twenty-four, twenty-five, twenty-six, and forty-nine," she announced, and they all knew, by now, she was talking Nancy Drews.

"It's okay if our childhood isn't completely replicated," Liv said.

"This has gotten personal," Atty said, and Liv wondered if it was some attempt to replicate her mother's childhood because Atty couldn't replicate her own.

"I could use a minute to freshen up," Esme said. "Mom, can you pull in?"

Augusta hit the aged blinker and cranked the wheel, clipping the curb.

"I'll be fast." Atty climbed out of the car and slammed the door. She jogged to the entrance then froze, one hand on the old-fashioned handle, peering into the shop with her other hand cupping her eyes.

"What's wrong with the kid?" Nick asked gently.

Esme held a hairbrush but simply pushed its rubber-topped needles into the palm of her other hand. "Doug's only Skyped with her seven times since he didn't come back. That's it. Seven."

"I can't understand it," Nick said. "If I could have, I'd have been there. Tell 'em, Augusta. I would have."

Augusta looked teary-eyed. She nodded. "He would have."


Atty opened the door and stepped inside. The shop was lightly air-conditioned by rumbly window units. Like most antiques shops, furniture was set up in small arrangements, framed paintings stacked against the walls, coats and stoles and hats hung on hat racks, and glass display cases jammed with bobbles. It stank of moth-bitten wool, dusty wood, varnish, and silver polish.

Atty walked to the counter where an old man sat in front of a heavy turquoise 1950s-style Eskimo-brand electric fan. He was sorting pennies, maybe looking for valuable ones.

"Do you have any Nancy Drews?"

He nodded. "Yep, far corner. Under the boxed squirrels."

"Squirrels?" Atty said.

He nodded again, holding a penny under a green accountant's light. "Under the boxed squirrels."

Atty had given up on finding the taxidermied tea-sipping squirrels that had been filled with water during the storm, but maybe she'd given up too soon. She moved quickly around settees and creepy prams with doll babies in them to the far corner.

And there she saw a stack of Nancy Drews hip-high, and on a shelf above them was a glass cabinet case of two squirrels—in a boxing ring, wearing little red boxing gloves and high-waisted silky boxing shorts.

Atty, feeling a little disoriented, knelt down, turned her head and started skimming the stack of books for the ones she was missing.

And there was number seventeen. She inched it forward, trying to stabilize the books on top of it, and finally yanked it free.

Atty held the book to her chest and pressed one hand to the squirrels' glass case—one squirrel was baring his small teeth. She thought about how they were once wild and free, now boxed up and boxing. It reminded her that she was a girl in the closet and she was the closet, too. She felt suddenly like she was locked in a glass box on display somewhere no one would ever see her. She looked at the squirrels' small fake beaded eyes—so dusty they no longer looked wet or real—and she imagined that, beneath the fur and padding, their little lungs still sipped air and their hearts pittered.

She Instagrammed and tweeted the squirrels but couldn't think of anything to say so she wrote, *No comment*. She felt dizzy again. She sat down in a pale blue wingback. Two measly blocks away from Parks Cabinetry now, she was keenly aware that she was about to be led into some alternate universe where her mother never met her father because she'd fallen in love with and married Darwin Webber and they lived here together in the shit-town of Great Neck with some other daughter or son or big fat brood of happy children being raised in a love-struck home.

She felt so sad that she was afraid she was going to barf again. Could sadness make you throw up?

She fit her hand in her front pocket and pulled out the ziplock bag. She popped it open and pulled out one of the Valiums.

She wished she had her ginger ale, but she didn't really need it. She glanced at the man behind the counter. He was consumed by the task of sorting pennies.

She put the pill on her tongue and swallowed it dry.

What if it was expired? What if her aunt had held on to it for so long that it was worthless? She decided to make sure it worked. She whispered, "Fuck it," and put the second pill in her mouth and swallowed it too.

Then she sat there, noting that she didn't like the way her thighs mushed against each other, and hoped that everything would change.

She sat there for a few minutes until she heard the door swing open. "Atty?" It was her mother.

"Can I help you?" the man behind the counter asked.

"No thanks. I'm fine." She heard her mother's voice—it sounded far, far away. "Atty?"

Atty told herself to stand up and she stood. She told herself to act the part—like the squirrels were acting the part of boxers. She shouted out as happily as she could, "Taxidermied squirrels!" she said. "Almost like the ones that were lost in the storm! They're here!"


The glass case of taxidermied squirrels wouldn't fit in the back of the station wagon. It had to be secured to the roof with bungees and twine. Atty was the only one overjoyed by the find, but they faked it—the unspoken, collective understanding that the kid was going through a rough time, let her enjoy the stuffed squirrels.

Augusta drove the final few blocks to Parks Cabinetry even more slowly to keep the squirrels safe. The car was quiet, almost prayerful.

Eventually, Augusta said, "This is it, right?" And everyone looked at the sign.

"Yes," Nick said.

She put on her blinker, slowed nearly to a complete stop, then inched into the parking area. When she finally parked the car, there was a collective sigh of relief and everyone quickly got out except for Atty.

Esme walked to the front-seat passenger's door. "Are you okay?" she asked her daughter.

Atty nodded, but she wasn't okay. "I feel weird," she said. "But weirdly good."

"Good," Esme said. "How many books until the collection is complete?"

Atty held up three fingers, but in a way she never had before— thumb, index, and middle fingers. It made her feel foreign, like she could become someone new.

Parks Cabinetry was a stand-alone store next to a small strip mall.

"What if Liv's right, and Darwin doesn't recognize me?" Esme said.

"Let's go," Ru said. "Come on."

"Atty!" Esme called.

Atty slowly crawled across the seat and out of the station wagon. She squinted at the Parks Cabinetry sign and said, "Personally, I don't like this."

They walked into a showroom with various cabinets on display. The ceiling had wood beams, the flooring was parquet. The showroom was empty except for a young man idling at the center kiosk.

Atty headed for the unisex bathroom. She hadn't yet felt much effect from the Valiums and decided to check her pupils under fluorescent lights.

Augusta had done so much remodeling from the flood, she was honestly drawn to some bookcases as if she'd come to shop.

Ru and Liv stuck together. They wanted to give Esme a wide berth, maybe even some emotional privacy. They flipped through flooring samples and Ru said, "Do you think that on some level, I wanted Nick Flemming to read my Teddy Wilmer book and be hurt by the lack of father figures in it? The lack of father figures really does a lot of damage to the main characters in the novel."

"I'm one of the main characters in the novel," Liv said. "And I didn't like being used so that you could play out some weird therapy session in front of the world. You've never apologized for it. Do you realize that?"

"Apologize for making art? Artists don't apologize for that!" Ru said.

"I will do this right here and right now," Liv said. "If that's what you want."

"Do *what*?" Ru said.

"You took my . . . You're like a cherry-picker of *lives* . . . and . . ."

"And what? This is what writers do."

Liv froze. Her arms went limp and her back stiffened.

"I'm going to check out the bamboo flooring," Ru said.

Nick hovered near the front door, the nearest exit.

Esme noted that there was a room in the back with a glass window to keep an eye on the store and a heavy door marked OFFICE. She assumed that if Darwin Webber was here, he'd be in that office, maybe ordering wood on a phone.

She walked up to the young man with shaggy hair and a white buttondown shirt sitting on a spinning chair at the kiosk.

"Welcome to Parks Cabinetry. I'm Matt. What can I do for you?"

"Is the owner in?" Esme asked, and then she looked around for her father. Spotting him near the door, she waved him toward her.

"Is there a problem?" Matt asked.

"No," Esme said. "It's just that my father has something he'd like to tell him."

"Is this about a renovation?" Matt asked.

"No. It's not about cabinets at all," Esme said. "Or wood."

Nick stood beside her, and Esme locked her arm around her father's. It was the closest she'd ever been to the man—he'd never walked her to a first day of school or down the aisle. It felt surreal to hold on to him now after all these years.

"I don't know what his schedule is like." Matt glanced toward the office window.

Now there was a man, standing on the other side of the glass, his back to them. He was wearing a light-blue buttondown and he seemed to be talking to someone else in the room, or maybe on speakerphone.

"Just tell the owner"—Esme leaned forward and lowered her voice—"we're looking for *Darwin Webber.*"

"No, no," Nick said, shaking his head. "Don't tell him that."

The young man recognized the name, which gave Esme a charge. Matt's hands disappeared under the counter for a moment, and Esme assumed he was going to pull out a big old intercom of some sort to page his boss. But instead he handed them an enormous catalog about kitchens. "Make yourselves comfortable while I go get him."

Esme looked at the office window again.

The man behind the glass turned quickly—as if he sensed she was there. As his eyes swept the showroom, Esme saw that it was Darwin. His hair was gray, close cut, and he was thicker and older. And then he seemed to fall to his knees, disappearing from sight.

Matt was walking quickly toward the office but veered at the last minute and took an exit that Esme hadn't noticed before, one that might lead to a warehouse.

"Where's he going?" Esme said.

"Our friend Matt tripped a silent alarm under the counter," Nick said and he called to the others. "Everyone out!" He spun around. "I'm going to get Atty. She went to the bathroom."

"What?" Esme was trying to piece together what the hell was going on.

Nick put his hand on his daughter's back and slid her to the far side of the kiosk. "Webber's probably been waiting all these years."

"For what?" Esme said.

"What's going on?" Liv said.

"Get out of the store!" Nick shouted. "Or at least crouch down!"

"Did he say *crouch*?" Augusta said. "I can't *crouch*."

And then Esme heard the office door bang open. She stiffened against the kiosk. "Has he told every stupid employee to ever work the floor to watch out for us? Does he show them photographs? Does he tell them to hit an alarm if anyone ever says the words *Darwin Webber*? What did you do to him?" she said to her father. "My God."


Atty tweeted, *My body has no bones in it. #valiumisgood*

Then she leaned over the sink, an inch from the mirror, and whispered to her reflection, "If you could see me now, Maeve

Brown, super-hateful Brynn Morgan and Lionel Chang and Myrtus *Ballbuster!*" Myrtus's actual last name was Ballister. "How'd you
like to invite me to one of your little petting parties now?" And for
the first time in as long as she could remember, she wasn't angry at
the kids in her boarding school. She wasn't even angry at her
mother and father for sucking at marriage or her father for leaving
them for a French dentist.

She wasn't even angry at herself.

She pulled away from the mirror and stared at her full face. She
ran one fingertip around her eyes like she was outlining an invisible
mask.

She noticed techno-sounding 1980s music being piped in, and
she danced just a little bit until the bathroom started to swim
around her.

Then she stopped and thought of all of the little orgies that
Brynn Morgan didn't invite her to because she'd failed the initiation. She'd kissed Lionel Chang with "duck lips," as he put it, and
talked dirty in a way that he found "hostile."

All she'd said was, "Do it to me before the uprising!" She was
thinking of an apocalyptic romance she'd read and he thought it
was racist because of his Chinese heritage.

That's when the quacking started and the mean looks and the
snickering behind her back. It wasn't Lionel Chang's girlfriend
who got it rolling. It was Lionel Chang's girlfriend's best friend,
Brynn Morgan—not that they all didn't kind of share one another
in sexually explicit ways that Atty couldn't understand and was
never educated on *because of* the failed initiation. Brynn Morgan
roamed the edges of the herd and her vulnerability made her particularly evil. Brynn even started making fun of the win-back in
*Trust Teddy Wilmer* because they knew it was written by her aunt.
*The dog dragged her in* became a favorite line whenever she walked
into a room, those effers.

Atty was sure her French teacher knew about the orgies.

Mrs. Brodsky lived on the same floor as Brynn who hosted them, and Brodsky wasn't deaf! She could hear an unrolled *r* murmured in a booth in the language lab. Why didn't she go shit in a hole?

"Why don't you all go shit in holes?" she said now into the mirror.

Then there was the day when Atty had actually walked into Little-Head Todd's house to change the litter box—she'd been cat-sitting while he was at a conference—and she stole the musket out of its unlocked glass case mounted on the wall. (She'd planned on returning it before he got back.) She took it to her dorm and, within hours, she had her plan.

But when she showed Brynn the antique weapon, Brynn didn't care. "You're so weird to steal that. You should put it back already."

Atty watched her walk out of the dorm and onto the lawn, where her parents had come to visit for parents' weekend. Brynn's parents held hands and were highly regarded doubles players. They were beautiful, but corroded. Brynn was beautiful too, but a horrible human being. Atty fitted the gun into her STX bag and swung it over her shoulder. She couldn't leave it behind in her room, and she wanted to feel the weight of it, something holding her down, a protection. That's all it was at first. The speech came along later. The speech—a blur to her now—was truly inspired.

And now she felt guilty. She'd fantasized about Brynn's face being blown open with musket fire. She just wanted them to feel threatened. To know what it was like. "Why don't we all shit in holes?" she said now, implicating herself, taking responsibility.

She wasn't thinking about her mother or her mother's college boyfriend or her long-lost grandfather, returned, or her aunt who had been suicidal and was still a druggy, or her other aunt, the writer who didn't seem to be writing at all, or her grandmother who looked at her with a slight palsy or was it a head-shaking disappointment?

She was thinking that she lacked the basic instinct for violence and that she'd have to find some other way to get back at people.

The best way she knew to get back at people was to make them jealous. And so, first of all, she would have to find her own greatness.

Her own greatness.

She wanted to tweet *My own greatness*, but she knew she didn't have the eye–hand coordination. The Valium had surely kicked in. She felt gelatinous.

She opened the bathroom door and, at first, saw no one.

The showroom floor was empty.

She could still hear the 1980s techno pop. She looked up, wondering where it was coming from and what it could possibly mean, symbolically. Just as she started to dance again—it was a timid slow dance that was only slightly lewd—she saw some movement out of the corner of her eye.

A rush of pale blue—like the sky coming at her. But the parasailor was then small, just man-sized. In fact, it was a man—his face bright and wide. And loosely attached to him, on one side of his body, a hand—with a gun in it.

The man grabbed her shoulders, pinning her arms to her body.

"No, thank you," she said, meaning that she didn't want to dance with him—on political grounds (she was pro gun control) but also on personal ones. He was much too old for her.

"What?" he said. "What did you say?"

"I said no thanks. To the dancing." But now she heard the echo of her words in her own head and she knew she was slurring.

"What's your name?"

"Atty," she said, "Atty Rockwell-Toomey."

"What?" He shook his head and then shouted at the nothingness of the cabinets and flooring. "I know what you're here for! You let me and this kid go. No one will get hurt."

Atty realized there had been some mistake. Her own greatness had been misunderstood. "I'm not an actress," she told the man though she'd always thought she'd be a really good one.

He wasn't listening. He was looking out at the showcase floor. Atty thought his face was so flushed it looked like a giant heart, pumping. There was a bright-blue vein on his temple. She wanted to touch it.

"It's okay. We're not here to hurt anyone." It was Nick Flemming.

"Are you armed?" the man holding her shouted back.

Atty saw her grandfather, his hands on his head. She wondered what she should call him. Grandpa? Pop Pop? Gramps?

"Jesus H. Christ!" Her mother's head and upper body popped up. "It's me, Darwin, and that's my daughter. Just let her go! My father's here to apologize. He's not armed, for shit's sake!" She wheeled around, facing her father. "Are you? Goddamn it! Are you packing?"

"He's always packing," Augusta said, stepping out from behind some floor-to-ceiling poster.

"I'm surprised to hear my family use the term *packing*." It was Liv, scooting out from behind a wardrobe.

Ru was standing next to her. "Something's wrong with Atty."

Atty was droopy but happy. She let the man hold her up now like her body was filled with flour. "My greatness!" she said.

"Is she having a seizure?" Augusta said.

"Gah," Liv said under her breath. "She's high." She squeezed her forehead. "This isn't good."

"Atty!" Esme shouted.

As she started to run to her daughter, Darwin Webber shouted, "Stop! Don't come at me!"

Afraid Esme was about to get shot, Nick leaped forward to tackle her.

And as he sprang, Darwin Webber, who'd been going to target practice for two decades, took aim, tightened his one-armed grip on the girl, whispered, "Hold steady. It's going to be all right," and then shot the old man exactly where he meant to—in the meat of his shoulder.

Nick hit the ground hard and rolled to his side, curling up.

Esme, Liv, and Ru screamed.

Atty smiled. "Noisy," she said. "In my ears." And her body remembered what it was like to lift the musket over her head at the penultimate moment of her speech and pull the trigger. The small jolt, the smell of a damp fireplace—the sadness of it all. This was what a gun should sound like, she thought abstractly, not really fully aware that one had just gone off.

Augusta didn't scream. She'd been waiting for this all her life—to see someone shoot her husband in front of her.

"You shot my father!" Esme said.

"He was here to shoot me!" Darwin said, still holding on to Atty. "I've got proof!" And then Darwin stomped his foot. "I didn't kill him."

"He didn't kill him!" Augusta said. "I can tell."

"He was going to say he was sorry and call the whole goddamn thing off!" Esme said to Darwin.

"Call it off? It! You mean the thing that altered the course of my life forever and that's defined every single day since? You mean *that* 'it'?" He gestured air quotes with the gun.

Nick was muttering some medical instructions about compresses and tourniquets. Augusta knelt at his side. "What's that?" she said. "Speak more clearly!"

"What's wrong with Atty?" Ru said again. "She's not right."

"Put the gun down!" Esme said to Darwin. "You shot him already."

Darwin lowered the gun but kept holding Atty because she was relying on him fully now.

Esme rushed to her daughter. "Atty," she said, holding her daughter's hands. "What's wrong?"

"Nothing at all," she said slowly.

Liv whispered to Ru, "Confession."

"What?"

"I gave Atty Valium and I think she took it."

"And you wonder why I've written about you?" Ru said, her eyes squinted, her head bobbing. "You make fascinating life choices, Liv. Truly."

"How about I just call an ambulance?" Augusta said to Nick.

He nodded.

Augusta stared down at him and he looked at her out of the corner of his eye.

"What?" he grunted.

"You'd have made a very good full-time father," she said. "You took a bullet for our girl and, maybe more important, you wear suffering well."

"Thank you."

Augusta called to Ru, "Honey, call nine-one-one, will you?"

"What did you do to my daughter?" Esme asked Darwin. "She's out of it!"

"What did I do? I don't even know this kid. You all came here with the intention of killing me—brutally murdering me. Slowly torturing me first, I might add." Esme realized he must be quoting from her father's initial threat.

Liv walked up and said, "Excuse me," to Esme. She cupped Atty's face. "Did you take a Valium?"

Atty held up two fingers. "Both!"

Liv patted Atty's cheek, took a step back, and said, "She's high. Very high."

"Valium?" Esme said. "Where did she get Valium?"

"Both!" Atty said.

"She suffers from anxiety, and she stole the musket to kill someone. Accidentally."

"See?" Darwin said. "This is a thing with your family, Esme. You're crazy, messy, violent people."

"I think we're messy people," Liv said. "I'll accept that. *Crazy* is sometimes a trigger word for some people. But then again, so is *trigger*."

"Set her down," Esme said.

Darwin eased Atty to the floor. She stared up at the drop ceiling.

Esme sat next to her and held her daughter's hand. "Liv," she said, "I don't have the capacity to blame you for this right now. But I will. Believe me, I will."

"Understandable," Liv said, but she still sat down on the other side of her niece and took her other hand. She whispered to Atty, "You're not the closet and you're not the girl in the closet. You hear me?"

Atty nodded.

After a few moments of awkward silence—and the distant threading of the siren through traffic—Liv pointed to the music playing overhead. "This is the Smiths, isn't it?"

"You look good, Esme," Darwin said, and he seemed to be seeing her for the first time. "I'm sorry I shot your father."

"It's okay," Esme said. "He deserved it."

Ru turned a small circle and then she said, "Not to elevate a moment or to state the obvious—if any of you are already on the same page—but I think this is exactly what we needed."

"What?" Nick whispered to Augusta. "What's she saying?"

"This could be really cathartic," Ru said.

The doors swung open. Paramedics ran into the showroom. There was a stretcher, equipment, heavy footfalls. Lights from the ambulance swirled around them.

One paramedic was asking Nick questions. Another turned to Augusta. "Are you his wife?"

Without a hitch in her voice, without a moment's hesitation, she said, "I am. Yes. I'm his wife."

The paramedics rolled Nick to his back. "She's my wife and these are my daughters and my granddaughter. My family."

"Except Ru," Augusta whispered under her breath so softly no one could hear her in all the noise. "She was actually conceived because I had sex with a stranger."

# CHAPTER 36

Four hours later, Nick Flemming was waking up in a hospital bed, surrounded by his family. Liv and Ru stood on one side of his bed, Atty and Esme on the other. Augusta was holding his hand. When she came into focus—her beautiful gaze—she smiled and stroked his hair.

"The girls," she said, "have decided what they really want from you."

He pursed his lips to ask what he could give them, but Augusta hushed him.

"We want to know you," Ru said. "And for you to know us."

"Before you die on us," Esme said.

"We probably need you," Liv said, "in a similar way to how you need us."

"In short," Atty said, "there's been a lot of bullshit in this family."

Nick nodded. "I'll try not to die. Not yet at least." And then the faces poised around him blurred to small bits of shimmering color. He blinked. Two quick tears streaked his temples. And then he fell back to sleep.

"All this time I thought you were the center of the wheel and we were all just spokes," Esme said. "But it's him now. It's him." She stared at her father while he slept.

"In the spirit of less bullshit," Liv said to Ru, "I've been thinking about cherry-picking your fiancé."

"He's not my fiancé. He's coming to pick up the ring tomorrow. It's over."

"Honey," Augusta said. "I'm so sorry."

"Why didn't you tell us?" Esme asked.

"We don't know how to really talk to each other, do we?" Ru said.

Atty was still a little woozy, but her brain function was back. She felt good, in fact. Better than she had in a long time and not just because of the drugs, but because things had felt strained for a long, long time and now they had finally broken. "You were really going to steal her fiancé?" Atty asked Liv.

"I was *thinking* about it."

"Are you still thinking about it?" Esme asked Liv.

"Well, it's no longer cherry-picking now," Liv said. "They're already broken up."

"I might be falling in love with Teddy Whistler," Ru said to Liv.

"It's because you absorbed all that love meant for me," Liv said, with a strange sense of peacefulness. "All that shouting when he was on our front lawn that summer."

"Remember conducting the storms in front of the third-floor windows?" Esme asked, wistfully.

The room was quiet except for the beeping of machinery, tracking Nick Flemming's vitals.

"I kept doing it, for years, storm after storm," Liv said softly, and then, inexplicably, she started to tear up. For the first time in as long as she could remember, she wasn't crying for the sake of manipulation. She was crying because she suddenly thought of herself as a girl then a teen, standing in front of the glass, with her pear-cork-handled conductor's baton. She was crying because she was recognizing this secret self, this vulnerable girl. She missed who she'd once been. More than her husbands and more than Teddy Whistler in a boardwalk booth or on the front lawn, she missed that girl in the window during a storm—most of all.

"About that," Augusta said to Esme. "You were right after all. I was afraid of daily intimacy, the kind you build a life on. I had trouble trusting."

"To be fair," Ru said, pointing at her father with both hands. "It was a tricky situation."

"I wanted a tricky situation, and I wanted a family." Augusta shook her head and said, "I didn't just want a family. I wanted *this* family."

"So I had it wrong," Esme said, "but also kind of right."

"Are you crying?" Atty asked Liv. "For real?"

Liv was too choked up to answer. She just gave a quick nod.

# CHAPTER 37

Esme, Liv, Ru, and Atty spent the night in a hotel in Great Neck while Augusta dozed in an armchair next to Nick's hospital bed. By midmorning, he was discharged. And in the hospital's pickup drive-way, they argued once again, though briefly, about the seating ar-rangements in the station wagon, the case of boxing squirrels strapped to the roof. Esme won the right to drive. Augusta was too tired to put up much of a fight. She and Nick sat in the front seat. Atty was bumped to the backseat with little discussion; there was unspoken agreement now that her barfing was anxiety-related, not carsickness.

As they headed back to Ocean City, they mostly listened to music and a few NPR spots. At first, they were each aware of the precarious balance of the boxed squirrels on the roof, but as time went on, they forgot about them and each fell into their own quiet thoughts.

They were a family. They were whole and new. Yet still, there were things that needed to be said, and, eventually, Liv said, "I'm sorry."

"For what?" Esme said. "I don't think you actually know."

"Well, I'm sorry I'm a drug addict, for one thing."

"That's not an apology. That's an excuse," Esme said.

"Yes, but I've never really said it out loud before."

"That's true," Atty said. "She's always hedging about it."

Liv sighed.

"So go on," Ru said, "what are you sorry about?"

Liv tapped the window with one knuckle and said, "I really just wanted to save somebody. I wanted to save Atty. I wanted to . . ."

"You gave her Valium," Esme said. "She's a minor!"

"I thought it might help. I thought she was in a bad way."

"She's not in a bad way!" Esme said. "She's rebounding from a difficult situation."

"Are you in a bad way?" Nick asked Atty.

"I'm kind of in a bad way," Atty said.

"We've all had times like that," Augusta said. "Haven't we?"

They all agreed.

The car was quiet. They passed through a toll, which they had to pay the old fashioned way because Augusta didn't have E-ZPass.

"I have an idea," Ru said. "Three Statements of Personal Honesty like we did at meetings of The Personal Honesty Movement."

"Oh, I don't know," Augusta said.

"What's The Personal Honesty Movement?" Atty asked.

"Your grandmother started a gazillion movements," Esme said. "It was a kind of coping mechanism, a bad habit, maybe even a weird nervous tic."

"How many followers did she have?" Atty said, knowing that she was approaching four thousand followers on Twitter, which was the most of any of her friends.

"I never got much momentum," Augusta said, as if merely being modest.

"I'd love to start a movement," Atty said quietly.

"I remember sitting in those meetings," Liv said. "One woman said that she didn't like her own dog. That was her Statement of Personal Honesty and we just had to sit there and not laugh at her."

"It ended badly, as I recall," Esme said.

"It did," Augusta said.

"Still, we could use it," Ru said. "I mean there was something to it."

"Thank you, Ru," Augusta said.

"This time," Esme said to her mother, "you have to actually say something specifically honest."

"Well, of course," Augusta said.

"You too," Ru said to her father.

"Me?"

"It'll be a good way for them to get to know you," Augusta said.

"Three statements each?" Liv said.

"Yes," Ru said.

"My drug addict thing counts as one of my statements," Liv said. "I should only have to do two."

"Fine," Ru said.

"You start," Esme said to Ru.

"Okay. All right." Ru scratched the back of her neck then rubbed her hands on her knees. "I stole things from my sister's life to make art and I should have at least asked first."

"Better late than never," Liv said.

"We're not supposed to comment after what's said," Augusta told Liv. "Remember?"

"I think that was a flaw in the Movement, by the way," Liv said.

"Regardless," Augusta said.

"Yes," Atty said, "I think it's way better if we just confess and no one says anything after we say what we want to. I mean, that would be a relief, wouldn't it?"

"I guess so," Esme said, a hint of worry in her voice.

"Go on, Ru," Atty prodded.

"My career is tanking because I can't write another book. And . . ." Ru wasn't sure what to say next. She searched her mind, but all she saw was the round face of the baby born in the long-house in Vietnam and so, although she'd never admitted it to her-self, she said, "I might want a baby. I mean, not one day, but soon."

"I didn't see that one coming!" Esme said.

"That'd be real nice," Nick said.

"Again, I think we're just supposed to listen and accept," Liv said.

"This is really good," Atty said. "You confess and no one can say anything. It's so not Episcopal or boarding school or family or anything. You, go," Atty said to her mom.

"Well." Esme rubbed her nose and glanced at the rearview and side mirrors and then finally said, "I got our father shot."

"No, no," Nick said. "I ran at him and I was the one who—"

Esme ignored him and talked louder. "I haven't really dealt with the fact that Doug left. And I haven't been the best mother to Atty because I'm scared."

"Scared of what?" Liv asked and then she quickly added, "That's a question, not a comment."

"I no longer trust my own judgment," Esme said. "I thought Doug was the safe choice."

Nick wagged his head. "I did too. I really did."

"Things change," Liv said. "People change."

"Do they?" Ru asked.

Atty thought of Lionel Chang. He was changing on her this very moment, day-to-day. He was becoming a memory, chunks of images, and what she imagined his days were now like—sailboats, pot smoking, the Vineyard.

"Now that I think about it," Liv told them, "saying I wanted to save someone, Atty in particular, was my second Statement of Personal Honesty so I only need one more."

"What is it?" Esme asked.

"I don't know."

"Okay," Atty said. "Here are my three. I did, in fact, want the musket to fire in Brynn Morgan's face, but I only wanted it to disfigure her. If she died, though, I'd have been okay with that." She paused. "Can that just be one because I have two more."

"Sure," Ru said.

"I want to see my father live and in person to tell him to fuck off. And sometimes if I don't tweet something, I'm not sure it ever really happened." She took a big breath, held it, and then said, "That's it! Oh, and I've tweeted almost everything from our whole time together as a family. And now you all just sit here and accept the statements."

And so they did, and Atty thought to herself—without tweeting it—Being honest sucks, but it's also very liberating. #startamovement

"Nick," Augusta said. "Your turn."

"I might need more time to think about this."

"It's an in-the-moment kind of thing," Liv said.

"Okay," he said, "I think it had to be this way or no way at all. I couldn't have been a father the way other men are fathers. I didn't have it in me. I did it the only way I knew how. And I'm not sure if this is one Statement of Personal Honesty or three or four, but the one good thing about our family is that I appreciate every second I get with all of you. Every single second."

"He's more of a speech type than a three-statement type," Augusta said.

"He's good at them. You're not the only wordsmith in the family," Liv said to Ru.

Ru glanced at Atty and smiled. "Nope, I'm certainly not the only wordsmith in the family." She was pretty sure Atty was the real writer. "I've just got a good memory."

And then Augusta said, "Correct, Ru. And I'm wondering if you remember the Statements of Personal Honesty that I made that day when you all were little and I taught you to conduct the storms."

Ru nodded. "I do remember. You said, *Your father is a spy. He can't be known. I love him, despite myself.* Any amendments?"

"Just one," Augusta said. "He *can* be known, as much as anyone on this earth can be known, that is."

# CHAPTER 38

They pulled up to the house on Asbury Avenue by midafternoon and found three men standing on the lawn.

One was Olive Pedestro's son. He was walking the two dogs—Ingmar and Toby—and smoking a hand-rolled cigarette.

"The dogs," Augusta said. "Why isn't Jessamine walking them?"

"Maybe she's taken the day off and got Virgil to cover for her," Ru said.

Jessamine never spontaneously took the day off.

"Clifford Wells," Liv said, recognizing the second man on the lawn from the engagement page.

"Go ahead and call dibs," Ru said. "Just please don't eat him alive."

"I'm in no condition, to be honest," Liv said.

Atty pointed to the third man. He had sandy windblown hair and wore khakis and a pale-pink polo shirt. He stood with his hands in his pockets, rocking up on the toes of his loafers.

"One of yours?" Esme asked Liv.

"Nope."

"And it's not Teddy Whistler," Atty said.

"Though he does have a history of stalking our front lawn," Liv said.

"Where is Teddy Whistler now anyway?" Liv said.

"Well, it's Saturday so . . ." Ru checked the time on her phone. "He's probably getting ready to crash a wedding."

"Oh, I know who that is," Augusta said. "It's Herc Huckley's son."

"Herc Huckley's son?" Nick said. "Why is he here?"

"He wants to ask you about the contents of a certain box," Augusta said.


Atty told Olive Pedestro's son that her grandmother would settle up with him later on.

"She's kind of busy," Atty said, watching her grandmother introduce her bandaged-up grandfather to the son of a man named Herc Huckley. "Her husband got shot yesterday so, you know . . ."

"Her husband?"

"Yeah," Atty said, taking the leashes from him.

Augusta and Nick started talking to the stranger and, together, they stepped into the house.

Meanwhile Ru said hello and Cliff said hello. They stood there a few minutes and then she started twisting the engagement ring off her finger. She handed it to him and said, "Do you want to come in for a drink?"

Cliff looked at Esme and Liv. "Your sisters, I take it?"

She nodded.

"And your mom is with . . . ?"

"My father, actually."

"Wow. That's big."

Ru nodded. "It's pretty huge."

"And your niece? Atty, right?" He pointed at Atty, who was now holding the leashes and staring straight up at the dark clouds overhead.

"Do you want to meet everyone?" Ru asked.

Liv and Esme stopped Virgil Pedestro as he was making his way back to his house and talked him into helping them unstrap the glass display case of taxidermied squirrels off the roof rack of the station wagon. He was rounding the car, sizing up the job.

"Are those squirrels?" Cliff asked.

"Yes, and they're boxing."

Cliff tilted his head. "I see that."

"I don't think they were caught in the wild that way."

"One would assume not," Cliff said.

"How's the Sony gig?" Ru asked. "Did I tell you how happy I am for you?"

"I think you did, but you're not."

"I'm trying to be."

He then stared at Ru, tilting his head in the same way he'd looked at the boxing squirrels. "You were in love with me at some point in time, right?"

"At many points in time," she said, though now she knew it wasn't true. She'd never felt what she felt for Teddy—something like being struck, to be honest, as in *lovestruck*. Sometimes words were so simple. She'd never thought of it as being struck like a bell and then walking around vibrating with love, the shock of it.

"I see," Cliff said.

"I'm so sorry about everything," Ru said.

He put the ring in his pocket and then started breathing heavily. He bent over and put his hands on his knees.

"Are you okay?"

"Uh, no. I'm not okay! Jesus! I can't even look at you. I can't . . ." He then straightened up, but he did it too fast. He reached out, and she tried to steady him with both of her hands, but he tipped backward then tried to right himself too quickly, driving his knees into the soft dirt of the lawn. "Jesus," he whispered. "I didn't believe it. I thought, all along, I thought once you saw me . . . I thought you'd realize . . ."

"Hey!" she shouted to her sisters. "I need a little help here!"

Esme and Liv walked over quickly, leaving Virgil Pedestro to wrestle bungee cords and rope.

"I think he's having a panic attack," Ru said.

"Let's bring him in," Esme whispered.

Liv and Esme steadied him, guiding him to the front door. Only Ru stayed in the yard. She watched them walk him to the door and disappear into the house. Then Liv immediately turned back, grayed behind the screen. She pushed it open and walked back down the steps and across the yard, passing Ru. She opened the car door, pulled out one of her oversized leather bags. She walked to Ru, reached into the bag, and handed her a picture book.

"Ping," Liv said softly. "You remember this book, I guess, because you remember everything."

Ru held the book. "This book scarred me as a child."

"Of course it did. You were the littlest duck."

Ru flipped through pages. "Why are you giving it to me?"

"I don't know," Liv said. "Except I don't think you're Ping, Ru. I'm Ping. I've been out in the wilds. I've been lost and almost eaten alive like Ping here and I've seen the birds who are slaves to men, and I'm glad I'm home."

"Thank you." Ru closed the book and held it to her chest. "I'm going after Teddy Whistler. I'm going to try to win him back before he wins Amanda back."

"And I might go and cherry-pick your ex-fiancé."

"That's okay with me."

"It's good to have sisters."

"I think so," Ru said. "I don't know who I'd be without you two. A lost star with no constellation."

"Right."

———

The note was taped to the front door.

*Augusta,*
  *Dogs taken care of. Casseroles in the fridge.*
  *Off to the beach for the day—to live a little.*
  *Live a little,*
  *Jessamine*

Augusta held the note so tightly that it fluttered in her hand. Jessamine was going to live a little and she suggested Augusta do the same. This was what living felt like, Augusta thought, and it was thrilling and surreal. She looked at Nick and there was no realism here. This man she'd known and not known all these years—a man she'd met by chance in a freak storm—was back in her life.

And this man, the son of Herc Huckley, who showed up as the result of another freak storm, was standing in her entranceway.

"I don't think we're up for this conversation now, Bill," Augusta told Herc Huckley's son.

"But you are Flemming," Bill said to Nick, "right?"

Nick nodded.

Esme and Atty walked into the house, escorting Ru's fiancé, who looked pale and slack-jawed. Esme said, "Excuse us! Just passing through!"

"You started The Amateur Assassins Club?"

"Long, long ago."

"And my father . . ." Bill said.

"He was a good man," Nick told him.

"Was he?" Bill asked. "I mean, he was always, I don't know, afraid."

"He was a better man than I was," Nick said. "He could hold steady. I couldn't. There's strength in holding steady in this world."

"Let's get you up to bed," Augusta said to Nick. "You need to rest."

"Yes, okay, sorry to intrude," Bill said. "I hope you're feeling better soon, and maybe we'll talk again."

Augusta and Nick slowly climbed the stairs.

This was where Liv found Bill Huckley. He was staring at the ground with his hands on his hips. "You look like you could use a drink."

"Are you offering?"

"Follow me."

Clifford Wells and Bill Huckley were given the good Scotch, kept in the back of the cabinet. They all sat down at the dining room table. Cliff's hand was shaking as he sipped. Bill tapped his glass on the table's edge.

Atty unleashed the dogs, who curled up under the table.

Huckley explained how he'd come to see Augusta Rockwell with the box of letters. "My father was in The Amateur Assassins Club with Nick Flemming."

"The Amateur *Assassins* Club?" Atty asked, with delight in her voice.

"Don't," Esme said. "Just please."

"I'm actually thinking of starting a movement," Atty said.

And Esme had a tiny pinprick of a memory — the desire to start a movement of her own — in defiance of her mother. Maybe that's what each generation had to do to define who they were. Now that she thought about it, she was sure that this had been the subject of her college entrance essay. She'd announced to the Ivy Leagues that she was going to start a movement. What kind? She couldn't recall. It was a total blank.

Bill looked at them searchingly, as if he might be able to recognize their faces somehow. "And you all are his girls, the ones he was always writing about. Let me guess." He rubbed his chin. "Your name starts with *L*," he said to Liv. "And yours with *E*," he said to Esme. "And you must be young A? Where's R?"

"She left me," Cliff whispered. It was the first coherent word he'd uttered since his collapse on the lawn. "Who's Flemming?"

"He's our father," Liv said.

"He's been shot," Esme added.

"It's like someone had to take some kind of blame," Atty said, "like we had to play it out somehow and this was how it went."

"Jesus," Cliff said. "This is a dangerous place."

Liv patted his arm. "You have no idea."

"I had a short-lived drug problem too," Atty said. "Very short-lived, but I learned some valuable lessons." She decided on the topic of her college entrance exam. She'd been mocked by her peers, kicked out of school and home, abandoned by her father. She'd been doped up on Valium and witnessed a shooting. But when you really looked at it, maybe all this meant was that she was a survivor.

"In the letters," Bill said, in a hushed voice, "it seemed like Nick Flemming was very, um, involved in your lives, but from afar. It's almost like he . . ."

"He rigged my life," Esme said, and then she sighed. "But I accepted the rigging. In fact, I'm probably my father's primary accomplice." Her eyes were glassy and distant.

Atty stood up and nodded at Cliff. "What do you think?" she said to Liv.

"I've got to work on my own personal Zen," Liv said. She was thinking about what Atty had said about how Liv had gotten wealthy men to marry her: *Love must love you.* She wanted love to love her. She wanted to believe in love. "You know, it's okay if you fire me and want to get out from under my wing. I get it."

"No, I like it," Atty said. "It's been really educational." She noticed Ingmar and Toby curled up together in the corner, which was sweet in a way she couldn't possibly feel jaded about. She announced to the rest of the room, "I'm going for a walk."

"It's going to rain," Esme said, but it felt like the last warning she'd ever give as the mother of a child; Atty was changing before her eyes. Telling her to put on rain boots and bring an umbrella— those days were over.

"Then I'll walk in the rain."

Atty marched out of the dining room through the living room, passing the many faces of dead Rockwells, and out the front door.

There, in the middle of the cramped front yard, was the glass case of boxing squirrels. Virgil Pedestro must have wrestled them loose from the hood of the station wagon and then abandoned them. The station wagon was gone now. Ru must have taken it. Atty assumed she was crashing a wedding or trying to stop the crashing of a wedding.

Atty unzipped her fanny pack to get her iPhone so she could Instagram the glass box of boxing squirrels in the front yard of her grandmother's old Victorian on Asbury Avenue, but then she stopped.

She zipped her fanny pack back up. She knelt down and tapped on the glass. "It's going to be okay, fellas," she said to the stiff squirrels.

She stood up and decided to keep this little moment for herself. She decided to live it and remember it.

Ru drove the station wagon to Fifty-Eighth Street and parked in a tow-away zone. She could see Teddy Whistler standing on the boardwalk. He had, in fact, dressed in a well-tailored blue suit, but his striped necktie was untied, flipping in the breeze—his back to the wedding itself.

She didn't want to tell him what had just happened to her father—and all of them. She wouldn't know where to start. And, about to break up a wedding, he wouldn't be interested in small talk.

Why was she here? To break up the breaking up of a wedding?

He looked earnest in his suit, determined, almost heroic. Ru wondered for a moment if, as a little girl looking down at the young, raging, brokenhearted Teddy Whistler, she'd actually really just wanted to save him. Maybe she'd been the young heroine after all.

When Ru got out of the car, Teddy saw her but didn't wave or say hello. She walked up next to him and looked out at the rows of chairs lined up in the sand, the red aisle, a large white canopy instead of an altar. Some guests had started to arrive.

"When does it start officially?"

"In about half an hour."

"Don't do it."

He looked at her, the wind rumpling his hair. "Why not?"

"I just think she deserves—"

"No," he said. "Why not? The truth this time."

"I don't know—"

"Do you believe in win-backs or don't you? Do you even remotely believe in what you do? Was it all just a jaded attempt to make money—your Teddy Wilmer win-back?"

Ru didn't like the way her heart felt—riotous. She didn't want to say a goddamn thing. She'd stopped believing in her work, and, once she made the money, she pretended that that had been her intent. It was easier than believing that she'd truly made an impact on people, that she'd given their hearts a shove, made some believe in love again. But she *had* believed; it was why she wrote it all in the first place. Personal honesty. A win-back. She felt like she was being thrust into living her own life. She said, "I don't want you to marry her because I think I'm in love with you."

He took a step toward her. "And?"

"And I don't have a window to punch, but I guess I was dragged in by the dog, if the dog in this scenario is my family." Could Teddy Whistler fall in love with her? Was he just trying to make a point?

"I love that metaphorical dog," Teddy said. "Go on."

"And Ru Rockwell isn't really Ru Rockwell, but maybe I'd like her to be. Maybe with you she could be."

His eyes were wet, but it could have been the wind. He let his eyes linger on her lips—waiting to hear what she might say next? Wondering if he should kiss her?

"But what about you, Teddy Whistler? Are you still trying to be a hero? Or will you be the one who's here, the one who stays?"

That's how the win-back in the movie ended. It was Teddy Wilmer's line and now it was a question. Ru stopped breathing. Her hands felt tingly.

"Come on," he said. "I want to show you something."

They took the station wagon and drove out onto the highway. She listened to Teddy's directions, but they were otherwise quiet. She felt like bursting.

Finally, he told her to pull over into a parking lot. "This is where you wanted to take me?" Ru asked.

"Look over there." He pointed out the windshield.

Ru saw an overpass. Traffic was a little busy but not jammed. "What am I supposed to—"

And then she saw it. I HEART RU spray-painted in big red letters on the side of the overpass. They got out of the car.

"Your name's shorter," Teddy said. "I had enough time."

"I'd assumed that the last time you'd actually drawn a heart, not written the word *heart*."

"In retrospect, that would have been considerably faster." He pulled her into his arms. She put her head on his chest. His heart was pounding away.

"I heart you too, Teddy Whistler."

"Good," he said.

"It's just the two of us," she said and it was. Everything else slid away—an entire universe.

And he leaned down and kissed her. She ran one hand up the back of his neck and through his hair. She felt breathless—like she was looking down at a drunk boy on a lawn from a very tall window, the wind rushing all around her.

It started to rain.


Augusta helped ease Nick onto the double bed in her bedroom.

"You sure you want me in here?" he asked.

"Easier to keep an eye on you," she said.

"We'll get to tell them everything now, Augusta," he whispered. "About the night we met in the driving snow and sitting next to you on the bus and the hotels opening their doors up to people on the streets."

"Who did you assassinate that night?"

"I just stood next to him at the urinal. That was it."

"But who was it?"

"Maybe a Polish diplomat."

"We'll tell them it was a Polish diplomat."

"And the motorcade," he said, "how it cut across the park in all that mad gusting whiteness. We'll tell them how we fell in love with each other that night."

"I'm not sure why people don't believe in that anymore, but it happens. Two people fall in love sometimes, and it's sudden."

"And it never stops," he said.

"Even when you'd like it to."

"I never wanted to split up," he said. "I understood what you meant when you told me you could have gone on but only if you loved me less, but it wasn't what I wanted. What with all the times I should have died, that was what nearly killed me. Do remember saying it?"

"Of course I do. It was the truth then."

"And now?"

"Everything's different."

"We can't do it all over again," he said.

"No, we can't."

"That's what I regret."

Rain beaded on the bedroom windows even though the sun was still bright, and Augusta sat on the bed and pushed off her shoes.

"I wasn't planning on taking the bus," he said. "And then I saw you through the window—your perfect profile—and I started walking fast so I could keep looking at you and then the bus lurched forward and I started running."

"I knew it was you before I knew you," she said, lying down beside him. "I felt something, saw your coat flapping out of the corner of my eye."

"We couldn't have had a little house and a little life."

"No, we couldn't have. This was all we could do."


Atty walked into the used-book store and wiped the rain from her face. She walked up to the counter. She was a regular here and the owner, a tan woman named Janice with stiff, shiny blond hair, knew what she wanted.

"We got a few new ones in for you. Bad condition. Real bad, but I didn't toss them because I thought you might want them anyway."

"Thanks for keeping me in mind," Atty said.

Janice reached down behind the counter and popped back up with a stack of about ten Nancy Drews—old and waterlogged, their puffed covers and warped pages made them hard to stack. "Might've gone through Sandy, by the looks of them."

Atty's eyes glided down the spines. The ones she needed were there—twenty-four, twenty-five, twenty-six, and forty-nine. "You got 'em!" she said. "They're all here!"

She lifted the top books off the stack and opened twenty-four.

"They're far from mint," Janice said. "You might want to keep looking."

Atty shook her head. "This isn't about the books. It's about the give and take of the universe itself, Janice."

"Well, these books were well read," Janice said. "Look at what some kids scribbled in them." She reached forward and opened the inside of the hardcover.

Atty read what was written there in pencil.

*E.R. 3 hours and 10 minutes*

*L.R. 2 hours and 45 minutes*

*R.R. 5 hours and 10 minutes, pretty much memorized*

These weren't just any copies of Nancy Drew mysteries. These were the Rockwell sisters' originals.

Atty flipped to the front of the other copies and found their initials, their times, and whether or not Ru had memorized the whole thing. Some of Liv's and her mother's marks looked like they'd been erased and then rewritten, perhaps a few times as if the times had been disputed. In those cases, Ru had read the fastest.

"This is it," Atty told Janice. "These are ours! They were lost, but now they're found!" The store was filled with light even though the rain was still ticking on the roof. Atty felt like this was a golden, hallowed moment.

She thought of Instagramming the books, but this wasn't about other people. This was personal. She hadn't even tweeted about The Amateur Assassins Club and she was pretty sure she wouldn't. She even decided, then and there, that she would go to Europe by herself to confront her father. If her mother didn't start shopping for plane tickets, she'd do it the way her aunt Ru had tracked down the old spy. Atty felt herself suddenly unhitching from the desire to snag the respect of Lionel Chang. The world was a bigger place. Screw you, she thought loudly in her head, as if those telepathic words could shuttle to the Vineyard and find Lionel getting high while lounging in someone's wicker furniture.

"You'll still have to pay for them."

"Of course I'll pay for them, but, Janice," Atty said, "it's the universe talking. Don't you hear it?"

"What's it saying exactly?"

"It's saying that it's all going to be okay."

"Because you found the books?"

"No," Atty said, looking at the dust motes spinning wildly in the air around them. "It means things are going to work out in the grand scheme. It means things that get taken apart can get put back together."

"Like what? Book collections?"

She thought, Like a dinged-up high school record, like a child-hood, like a family, like our entire lives, like the world, the universe.

And you.

And me.

All of us and everything.

# *Epilogue*

Ru Rockwell is living in Chicago with her fiancé, Teddy Whistler. She has recently turned in a memoir called *The Language of Elephants and Love* to her agent, Maska Gravatz—who loves it—and her editor, Hanby Popper, who's too nervous to discuss it just yet. Ru is expecting a baby in three months; no wedding date is in the offing. In fact, marriage itself doesn't seem all that important. Teddy Whistler and Ru Rockwell sometimes give each other a pre-emptive win-back, which feels more authentic to them than vows.

Liv Rockwell has opened up a mind–body–spirit dating service called Love Loves You in New Jersey, using a mix of quasi-Buddhism, yoga, and acupuncture—by master acupuncturist Sue Kwok—to prepare her clients for love. And because she tends to overspend, she brought on a more conservative business partner, Esme Rockwell.

Esme lives in Ocean City once again. An empty-nester, she finds having her own place is liberating. After dating Rob Parks (aka Dar-

win Webber) for a few months, she reconnected with her old friend
Todd Wentworth, aka Little-Head Todd, history teacher and antique gun collector. They've been dating, long-distance, for about
six months. Esme and her father frequent a dog park together with
Ingmar and Toby in tow. Sometimes they talk about important
things.

Atty Rockwell wrote a brilliant college essay and now attends a
major public university on the East Coast where she studies social
media and, as a freshman, has founded three on-campus movements, one of which—Take Time to Tune Out—is extremely successful with three budding chapters on other campuses.

Doug Toomey, Atty Rockwell's estranged father, was insinuated
into a threesome by the French dentist who'd fallen in love with
Arnaud, a Parisian photographer of some renown. Doug couldn't
sustain the intimacy of the threesome and begged out of the relationship. He now works in a private Episcopal school in Indiana.
He is trying to regain the trust of his daughter.

Virgil Pedestro has moved out of his childhood bedroom, having
converted the third floor of his mother's home into his bachelor's
pad.

Mrs. Pedestro remains virtually unchanged.

Clifford Wells and his producing partner have recently had a film
project—about a televangelist who turns to drug smuggling—
greenlit, but not with Sony.

Bill Huckley took over the care of his father, Herc Huckley—feeding him, bathing him, singing to him—and he was present when, in the middle of the night one month ago, Herc peacefully passed away in his sleep.

Jessamine is in semi-retirement and only comes to work at the Rockwells' house three days a week. Augusta Rockwell, whom she refers to now by her first name, is her closest friend.

Nick Flemming and Augusta Rockwell live together in the house on Asbury Avenue. They are still not married.

# A Conversation with Bridget Asher

**At the risk of asking what Ru would consider a "stupid question," would you shed some light on where you got the inspiration for this novel? Do you agree with Ru that we should stop asking this question as a society?**

Ru and I have a lot in common. We both have two older sisters, both write, both brood in similar ways. But, no, I don't think we should stop asking this question. Honestly, some writers are struck by moments of brilliant illumination — their skulls suddenly lit up with story. Each of my novels contains a million tiny flares, many of which happen while I'm living my life and scribbling notes and many of which happen while writing. But, also, it's worth noting that some of the flares that made this novel have been around for a while. I once wrote a love letter for a stranger on a plane, a kind of win-back. (The essay appeared in Real Simple.) Liv, the cherry picker, has been a character I've wanted to write for a long time. I could never find the right place for her to land. And I've also written a little about the snowstorm that hit DC the night before Kennedy's inauguration, using my father's memories of that night, but I finally found the larger love story within it.

Society should keep asking, but, from me, one can expect a longer, more intricate answer.

**How is your authorial approach and perspective similar to or different from Ru's? Was it surreal to bring another writer to life in this character?**

It's a relief to write about a writer. So much of our lives we can't quite shove into the lives of characters with other professions, so there's a feeling of ease in writing about a writer and a lot of opportunity to be comedic. Ru's disastrous reading at the public library, well, let's just say I didn't have to rely wholly on imagination.

**You've written more than twenty books, but said *All of Us and Everything* is your favorite one to date. Why is that? How is this book different from your others and what was the experience of writing it like?**

I've written as Asher, but also under Julianna Baggott and N.E. Bode, and people ask me all the time which of my own books is my favorite. The intent is often to find out which of my books they should pick up. I usually ask them what they like to read, rearranging the question so I'm not forced to answer. But *All of Us and Everything* is the novel that I want my really good friends and family to read, the people who know me very well and who've known me for a long time. In writing this novel, I had the opportunity to write out a kind of spirited take on sisterhood and motherhood that I've never allowed myself to do before.

**You paint Nick's background as a spy with such finely rendered detail. How did you go about investigating that aspect of the novel?**

I had the opportunity to interview someone who worked in intelligence for his entire career. Twenty years retired, he was able to answer questions; what I really wanted to know wasn't about his assignments, but rather about the culture of the work, how love, marriages, and families operated within that culture. I asked him if he was nervous about divulging things. He said that he lived his life assuming that anything he said might be on the record. That was very telling.

**This book features a predominantly female cast. Did you find it different/exciting/challenging to focus pointedly on this singular matriarchal family while the men are so behind-the-scenes? Did you arrive at any new revelations about the relationships between mothers/daughters and sisters by zeroing in on the Rockwell women? Which aspects of their family dynamic do you think makes them universal?**

I come from matriarchal family lines. My father was raised with his two sisters by a single mother and her sister. My mother's mother was the clear matriarch of our family for most of my life. I would say that my own mother has taken her place in that role. I have a brother and two older sisters, and I have two daughters and two sons. This novel allowed me to really dig into the ways I've seen sisters operate: old scores, unwanted nicknames, family jokes and secrets, petty turf battles—that don't feel petty at all, some thievery, long memories, as well as incredible tenderness and love, the ties that bind sisters. This goes for friendships as well, people who've known you for what seems like forever. There is something about being known by others for an entire lifetime. When it comes down to it, these sisters are truly there for one another. Just the way in which these sisters—and Atty too—orchestrate a guy showing up for dinner is, I hope, familiar to a lot of people. I think that these kinds of politics, as well as clumsily expressed love, exist in many families.

**Did you relate to, sympathize with, or want to spend time with any of the Rockwells in particular? Which of them was the most fun to write?**

I relate to Ru, absolutely, as the precocious youngest of three daughters, and as a writer. But Liv was the most fun to write. I love her edginess, her self-delusions, her strange acts of kindness and generosity. I miss her the most, though Atty is a very, very close second. She would always surprise me, offering up my favorite lines.

**Channeling the spirit of Augusta and Atty, if you could lead a personal movement of your own, what would it be?**

Tolerance. If we could allow others to live as they choose, to be who they are, to honor and celebrate our rich diversity, and not perceive others as a threat, I believe the world would be a safer place.

**Atty's observations on life and her family lend such comic relief to the narrative. Did she spring from a conscious effort to explore the ways we interact with social media today, or is she just a product of her time?**

One of my husband's first jobs was at a boarding school in Delaware, and that school and certainly the spirit of being a faculty brat living on campus is something I've always wanted to write. I didn't set out to make a statement on social media. Atty arrived pretty whole, live-tweeting from the get-go.

**You've written some epic win-backs in this novel. Have you ever had to script one in real life?**

Well, in addition to the win-back that I wrote for the stranger on the plane, I do write win-backs in various ways. I still believe that words are powerful and change someone's way of thinking, change their mind, as well as possibly win their heart. When my mother hands you a letter, you know that she has something to tell you that she can't tell you without crying. The tradition began there, perhaps. The truth is win-backs don't always work. My oldest sister, actually, is the one who's tried to tell me that I always think I can fix things with words. Sometimes words fail. But when they win, it's a beautiful thing.

**What is the most important message you'd like readers to take away from this story?**

I want people to see pieces of themselves, their sisters, their mothers, their best friends, the loves of their lives. I want people to find lines that nail some emotion or thought or family dynamic so hard that they have to share them with someone else. After my father read the book—he was one of the first—we had an immediate set of catchphrases, a secret language of inside jokes. I want this book to do that for people.

**Are you a Nancy Drew fan yourself? What shaped your own reading tastes as a child? What sorts of books do you gravitate toward now?**

I liked stranger, more magical stories. My love of Roald Dahl quickly turned into a love of Gabriel Garcia Marquez, then Lee Smith and, for family dynamics, Anne Tyler and John Irving. I also saw a lot of theater as a kid and that may have been even more influential than what I was reading in terms of developing my ear. What's in the works next for you?

I want to write a Paris novel. I loved writing *The Provence Cure for the Brokenhearted* and, of course, doing the research it required. I'd love to find an excuse to go to Paris for a little while. Who wouldn't?